A
Reasonably
Viable Marriage

Skip Yetter

A Reasonably Viable Marriage

DEDICATION

For my friend Nguyen Thua Nghiep, who inspired this story.
(See full dedication at conclusion.)

Cover design by Sue Timpson
Photograph by Pete Lawson

A Reasonably Viable Marriage

A Reasonably Viable Marriage

ACKNOWLEDGMENTS

Many thanks for the comments and advice generously offered by beta readers Perry Colmore, Victoria Wallack, Sheila Consaul, Joyce Bartlett, Pete Lawson and Tim Lundergan, who also proof-read my final draft and held me accountable to his keen eye for detail and practical counsel. As with anything I write, I am deeply indebted to my wife Gabi for her patience, wisdom and advice as she tolerated and commented on draft after draft.

1

A day unlike the others

A small island of red emerged on the fabric of Ben's tan trousers, doubling in size as blood seeped from the gash on his knee into the crisp, ironed pleat. Ben pushed himself into a sitting position on the slick concrete steps, assessing the tear in his trousers and the bloody patch with detached fascination.

He swept away raindrops that had gathered in his eyes and scanned in a quick half circle, checking to see whether anyone had seen him fall. He flexed his elbows, rotated his shoulders, and then toggled his knees back and forth, one after the other. He'd be sore the next morning, and the cut would need tending to, but he was otherwise unscathed.

"He's safe!" he exclaimed with a leathery grin, using a favorite saying that combined his love of baseball with Washington Irving's ominous short story. "Ichabod Crane slides safely into third!"

Humor was one of Ben's favorite antidotes for troubles, and he had grown accustomed to entertaining himself with his quips. This morning's mishap provided the perfect opportunity.

He tugged the raincoat around him to offer protection from the light drizzle and morning chill, covering his knee in the process.

He chuckled, relieved that there would be no public fuss.

"Like good deeds, sausage making and murders," he muttered, "stumbles like that are best conducted out of public view.

"Out of sight, out of....."

He choked back the rest of the saying, noting that the unspoken words carried more weight than he cared to acknowledge. He allowed his gaze to sweep down the hill to the town still waking to the drizzly morning, faint in the distance, silent, unaware.

Ben took deep breaths to calm his pulse, sighing heavy morning air into his lungs.

He sat on the concrete for several moments, steel railing grasped in his right hand, his left anchored to the step. He tugged the raincoat aside for a closer look at the damage, poking through the fabric to examine the gash on his right knee.

"I must be quite a sight."

Ben huddled against the pattering of the rain on his back as he rested on the steps: a gaunt, 83-year-old man in a wet rain coat and torn trousers, alone and talking to himself as he celebrated having avoided a potential disaster that would have kept him from his daily routine.

He brushed specks of dirt from his trousers, then retrieved a wrinkled handkerchief from his pocket and dabbed at the blood stain. He spit on the handkerchief and scrubbed the stain. It gradually yielded as he repeated the effort until the tear was more noticeable than the blood.

"There. This is nothing. As if she'd notice, anyways."

Even on leisurely days, anticipation and dread left Ben anxious as he approached Stonybrook Acres. On occasions like this - when he was making up for lost time - he arrived out of breath, with clammy skin and brow dotted with perspiration. Today's incident – coupled with the combined loss, sadness and isolation that consumed his days - left him short of breath and sick to his stomach.

Hurrying to adhere to a rigid, self-imposed timetable, he had tripped on the second to the top step to the facility's entrance. His umbrella clattered to the ground as his right knee crashed into the unforgiving concrete. His baseball cap fell from his head, tumbling into the weeds that crowded the side of the stoop.

He rested for another moment, his breath spearing the frigid morning air with plumes of condensation that slowly dissipated, as did the pain in his knee. He used the hook on his umbrella to retrieve his baseball cap, grinning when he was successful on the first try. He neatly folded the brim into the hat and tucked it into his coat pocket.

"Cherish the small graces," he mused.

Ben groaned to his feet, pulled open the door and entered the sterile corridor bathed in bright lights, into familiar surroundings that reeked of institutional food, cleaning solvents, and body fluids.

He scowled: "Smells like death, just as always."

Walking the same 118 steps he took every day, he ambled past numbered rooms with white-headed, immobile inhabitants vaguely present in the institutional fluorescent buzz, and then turned left to a spacious corner room with a view of the sloping lawn and valley below.

He paused in the doorway. Soft, warm lights glowed in each corner from lamps he had placed there to offset the facility's sterile glare, and to give Brenda's room a feeling of home.

Ben squared his shoulders and gave his clothing one more evaluative scan.

"It's show time," he said aloud, and strode through the door to say good morning to his wife.

2

Hours earlier: daylight

Ben scanned the horizon, pressing his face close to the kitchen window. He squinted in the dim light, searching for movement on the hillside that stretched into the dawn behind the condominium complex.

"Ah, there you are," he said, face breaking into a grin as the mother coyote appeared on the ridge, silhouetted, silent. "Good morning to you! And where might your little ones be?"

The coyote stood on an outcrop of rock that overlooked the valley and the town below. Soon three coyote pups joined her, tumbling over one another as they scampered to join their mother.

"Look, love," he said loud enough for his voice to carry throughout the apartment."There she is! And the pups, too! Come see..."

He turned to the empty room, and to the silence. His smile fell away as the stillness swallowed his words.

"Nothing like a mother and her kits. Kits? Or Cubs? Pups? I forget. Which is it?" he mused, a tightness in his throat choking the words as he watched the family cavort. His voice absorbed by the emptiness of his four-room condominium, again. "A mother's love....what a sight to behold...."

He snapped off the light that he left burning over the kitchen sink each night - a beacon of hope he maintained in case Brenda should see it and take consolation in its presence. In defiance of his frugal nature, Ben diligently lit the light each night, wishing for the morning when she might comment on the light and what it meant.

"Even the tiniest of lights can penetrate the darkest of the dark nights," Ben believed with stubborn optimism.

"G'morning, my love," he said as much to his wife's memory as to the empty room. "I'll be on my way soon."

He shifted his attention to the sky.

Rain was imminent, born of clouds the color of galvanized steel that hung over the mountain range. It had begun already in the distance, and the clouds cast a soft mist as the rain crawled down the rock-strewn slopes higher in the mountains toward the quiet brown valley below. It was less than half an hour away, he reasoned. He'd get wet on today's walk, no doubt about it.

"A day for the Macintosh *and* an umbrella," he mused, acknowledging fact without judgment; a sterile, measured response to circumstances, as was his wont. Rain would not deter him; he simply needed to prepare.

Problem solving was deeply within his DNA.

Circumstance.

Conditions.

Options.

Response.

Problem solved.

Rain meant nourishment for the parched earth, bringing a palette of life to a land painted in dull colors. In the days following the storm, a bit of green would emerge across the landscape of muted earth tones, bringing visual relief to an expanse of arid New Mexico desert that Ben likened to the surface of the moon. This land was dry most of the year, so locals celebrated when rain arrived in July. Precipitation meant respite, relief and life; a break from the monotony of sand, dust, rock and the arid southwest terrain.

Rain meant hardship, too, for people like Ben - retirees who were mobile yet mostly made their way on foot. Much of the world sped by in steely enclosures - cars, buses, taxis and trains – their inhabitants warm and dry, protected from wind, sun and harsh weather. Ben and his ilk – resilient, independent to a flaw - scowled at the inclement weather and donned raincoats and sturdy rubber boots. They opened umbrellas to face the elements on foot, trudging with cautious, stubborn determination through water that this time of the year often streamed from the mountains into the town's streets, sidewalks and gutters.

Walking fights off the stiffness one feels at 83 years of age, Ben reasoned; *keeps you fit and flexible; gets the blood moving. It's one of the small graces we retain as we grow old. Besides, our feet remain the most efficient and cost effective mode of transportation there is.*

He returned to his seat at the kitchen table to gaze across the hillside into the mountains, searching for a sign of the wild horses that sometimes came to graze on what weeds and grass took root on the rocky slope. Not today. The horses sensed the rain – and, likely, the coyote family - and remained out of sight. So did the birds whose calls typically woke Ben and coaxed him from beneath the warm covers into his chilly, pre-dawn routine. Even the morning walkers were absent from the sidewalks, their exercise on hold until the foul weather passed.

He shook his head. The rain would make his joints ache, his muscles strain, and his half-hour journey all the more challenging. A gust of wind rattled the kitchen window. He glared through it as if to impose silence and will away the breeze.

"Wind makes a short walk treacherous for an old man," he said to the room. Despair rarely visited Ben, but it was creeping around the edges of his world on this gray morning.

"Oh, stop whining and shut up, you old fool," he berated himself. "Get on with it."

Ben spied a scattering of toast crumbs on the kitchen table and swept them into his palm. He discarded the crumbs in the kitchen sink, surveyed the kitchen to ensure order, and entered the bathroom to get ready for the day.

Ben regarded himself in the mirror. After eight decades, he was slightly stooped but otherwise in decent condition. Not rotund like some of his friends, nor crippled or stooped at the waist like others. He was tall, strong, resilient; a pillar of quiet competence. And to Brenda and those who knew him and his unshakeable constitution, defiant in the face of extreme adversity.

"Still skinny enough to blow away in a stiff breeze like today," he sniggered.

He stepped closer to the mirror for a closer look.

Black circles settled into the sagging skin beneath his eyes, giving him a sad, clown-like appearance that from a distance was frightening, or at least off-putting. A glimpse into the depths of his eyes – on the surface rich with kindness and intelligence – revealed something different, complicated. A deep sadness quietly rested there, evident to those who took the time to acknowledge the deep yearning that haunted him yet inspired him to continue.

Ben had an active mind and sharp intellect matched with a kind heart and amiable disposition that created one of the valley's most respected retired gentlemen. He was a man with deep secrets, and the mystery he created by his

6

passive, dutiful life made him the subject of many speculative conversations, often at great length among the valley's hopeful widows.

Ben saw something else in his own eyes: a penetrating, spiritless void. Where most saw strength, he saw weakness. What appeared to others as confidence to him revealed acquiescence, capitulation. Had he not committed to a life of aloof solitude, he could have had the valley's most active social calendar.

But he had given up on all of it. All of it except for Brenda.

He shook his head to shift attention from what was not to what was, and stepped back to survey his clothing.

"Wouldn't do to show up with egg stains on my sweater," he warned himself as he stared into the floor-length mirror, searching his trousers and chest for signs of breakfast. Seeing none, he approved with a nod, smoothed the front of his sweater and moved to the hallway.

He sat on the rickety chair next to the shelf where he kept his keys and umbrellas. A small stack of mail lay by the seat, mostly supermarket flyers and "Important Shareholder Information" notices from his financial adviser. He removed his slippers and reached for a pair of blue Nike trainers, easing one foot then the other into the shoes and tugging the Velcro clasps. Placing a hand on either knee, he pushed with a loud grunt and rose to his feet.

Ben eased into his calf-length raincoat and chose a faded blue Cleveland Indians World Series 2016 baseball cap from his collection near the door. He held the cap to his face, mirroring the grin stitched into the face of Chief Wahoo on the front of the cap.

He retrieved an umbrella and his house keys from the shelf and then turned once more to survey the apartment: clean and ship-shape, lights off, heating on low, good to go. He tucked the umbrella under his left armpit and fumbled with the keys as he exited the apartment. A slight tremor caused the keys to jangle against one another; faint, lyrical chimes that shattered the silence and reminded him of his increasing instability and frailty.

He steadied his hand with the other and locked the door behind him.

Once outside the apartment building – a ground-floor retirement condominium he and Brenda had purchased when her health began to decline and mobility had become a growing issue – he checked to be sure the door was locked. Thieves often targeted the elderly, even in a place like Hillside Gardens; gated, patrolled, safe.

Can't be too careful. Brenda would fret if I had a break-in.

Satisfied his home was as safe as he could guarantee, Ben filled his lungs with chilly morning air heavy with the promise of rain. It would begin soon. He would need to hurry.

Using the umbrella as a walking stick, he marched the length of the flagstone walk from the apartment complex to the broad sidewalk. He swung the umbrella in a broad forward arc, snapping the tip to the walk to match the crunch of his right foot on pavement. Turning right at the end, he picked up his pace, battling to replace the slight grimace that defined his countenance these days with a crooked grin that sometimes brought a smile to Brenda's face.

Old age's small pains merged with solitude to leave Ben with something resembling a scowl. When he squinted to think, or to read signs in the distance, acquaintances said he looked like a slightly less handsome version of Clint Eastwood.

"You're just like him," his friend Jim jokingly opined, "stubborn, irascible; all the crankiness, only not so talented, or Republican."

He looked at his watch: 7:50.

"Late," he complained, and accelerated his pace. If it was a good day today Brenda would be expecting him in time for breakfast. She might be anxious. "Can't have that," he chided himself.

Ben had carefully built routine into his life. He rarely deviated from his schedule.

Each day started with an early breakfast, then a brisk walk to Stonybrook, where he spent the day with Brenda. Hours dragged on as he sat with his wife, hoping for a glimmer of recognition behind her vacant eyes. He lived in patient hope for a brief encounter with their history together, and a moment of respite for an old man desperately longing for his wife to escape the relentless, cruel grip of Alzheimer's disease.

After a full day at Stonybrook, he would putter around his condominium, then eat a late dinner at the tiny kitchen table, kept company by National Public Radio. Two hours of television would follow – mostly news and an occasional game show – then a few pages of a crime thriller and 6.5 hours of sleep. On Fridays a day off from the walk to Stonybrook for the weekly Senior Shopping Bus trip to the market to re-stock the meager larder. Now and then an evening cribbage game with Jim at the kitchen table, pacing himself through a glass of Coors Light beer and a bowl of Bugles, the sour cream and onion flavor that Brenda always liked so much.

His was a measured, conservative life of singular purpose.

When he wasn't by Brenda's side, he spent most of his life alone. His thoughts, memories, worries and fears were his only companion, and he was perpetually overwhelmed by a deep, awful sense of loss and separation.

He loved to watch the wildlife on the hillock behind the development, and had taken particular delight in the development of the coyote family. The mother and her young reminded him of his early years with Brenda, and the memories of those promising days sustained him through the silence.

Ben reclaimed a small taste of his former life when he made his daily pilgrimage. The trips up the hill to Brenda's side nourished him; motivated him. The energy, time and commitment required so he could spend his days with his wife kept his feet moving, his lungs breathing, and his heart beating.

Now, turning a corner as the sidewalk rose once again, he caught a glimpse of his destination: a low v-shaped institutional white structure, south facing to capture sunlight with its windowless back against the hillock that rose to the west. The building clung to the hillside's shoulder like a vinyl-sided epaulet; two single-story wings conjoined by a common area and administration office. A red terra cotta roof allowed the building to visually merge with the rocky edges of the mountains that rose behind.

Ben fought to keep the faint smile in place while he pressed on, achy knees protesting as the sidewalk rose to the building's entrance. He was working hard to reduce the usual 30-minute walk so he could arrive as close as possible to his target of 8 a.m. A white sign with black lettering told him he was nearly there: "Stonybrook Acres" it read, and below, "A quality care retirement and nursing facility."

He wound his way up the hill along the narrow path that led like an artery to the heart of the building, a double-door portico designed to keep residents from wandering and visitors in check.

"As if anyone would come to this place without cause or need," Ben often mused.

Stopping before the steps that led to the building, he glanced again at his watch.

"8:09! This won't do!" he exclaimed aloud, and hurried up the steps.

3

Brenda was always careful with her hair, meticulously keeping it neat and presentable, though never ostentatiously so. As the years turned her thick chestnut curls to wispy gray, she carefully managed the strands, keeping it fashionably short for easy maintenance.

"Women who visit the hairdresser more than once a month have too much money and time on their hands, not to mention an overabundance of vanity," she groused.

Even now, though the time had long past when she was capable of tending to her own appearance, her hair remained perfectly coiffed by Stonybrook's staff. It was a statement of order and propriety that defied the reality of Brenda's physical and mental state, put in place by stern reminders from Ben on the few occasions he arrived to find Brenda's hair or clothing in disarray.

Her head was slightly tilted to the right, unmoving atop rounded shoulders that slumped beneath a lavender velour house coat. Her cheekbones had been lightly dusted with rouge by the thoughtful caregiver who had combed her hair into order and was just now completing her task, eager to bring a bit of color to Brenda's pallid countenance before helping her to dress. Any more makeup would have given her a clown face; any less would have left her with the gray-beige skin color of the terminally ill.

Ben regarded his wife through red-rimmed eyes that shone with hope, and love. Brenda's appearance meant all the world to him, as though the veneer of wife's physical being might in any way compensate for her mental absence.

But this was a start, Ben reasoned, and he tended the superficial aspects of Brenda's world in a frenzied commitment to retain as much familiarity as possible.

She looked particularly beautiful today. Considerable effort had been made.

Ben reached into his pocket and produced a chocolate wrapped in gold foil.

He offered it to the aide: "For you. A gift for a giver."

The nurse's aide smiled at Ben, nodded her thanks, and gently passed her palm over Ben's hand in appreciation and understanding. She rose from Brenda's side.

"I'll finish dressing her later. You two say good morning," she said, leaving the room. "Take your time. I'll be close by."

Ben stood feet from his wife, studying her, looking for a sign that the woman to whom he owed so much would be present. Perhaps she would recognize him, maybe address him by name. Or perhaps she would regard him as an inanimate object, from a cold, impersonal distance.

How to repay an incalculable debt? Ben lamented. By doing as I do. This. Always this, and whatever more is asked of me, to keep her safe, and warm and comfortable. To be close by for those moments when she emerges the fog and joins me in remembering. And to remind her how much she means to me.

His mantra: My job is to provide, protect, be present, and at the ready. Today might be a good day. Anything is possible.

Brenda sat unmoving, as though transfixed by activities only she could see outside the window that faced the manicured lawn and into the valley below where mist had begun to fall in soft sheets.

She was a picture of aging frailty. Hands gently clasped, held loosely in her lap, their backs mottled with age spots, veins visible through translucent skin. Her lower back was erect below her rounded, defeated shoulders, the only telltale sign that Brenda was anything but healthy. She had lost weight, noticeable even beneath the bulky polyester robe that wrapped her in synthetic warmth.

She turned from the window to face him with vacant eyes devoid of recognition or interest: Lost, and long, long gone.

Ben approached Brenda as he did each day: softly, fearfully, hopefully, with dreaded expectation that he was about to be disappointed yet again, yet every day hopeful that he might be gifted a welcomed surprise. He was a man in search of a lost love he could imagine and remember, but that was forever out of reach, thanks to a disease discovered by an obscure German neurologist who in 1906 gave his name to one of life's most dreaded fates.

Alzheimer's disease – an advanced form of it – had gradually claimed Brenda in an agonizingly slow crawl that Ben relived in awful detail every day. This – the daily pilgrimage to his wife's side – was the penultimate gesture of love in a marriage that had spanned six decades.

Where once lived laughter, and love, and fear and suspicion, and pain and joy, and sometimes lust – all the elements of a typical marriage - was now mired in simple co-existence. This was life's final waiting game - the final test for the couple; inexorably connected yet separate, physically and mentally.

One of them bore the duty to find peace within the unthinkable truth of isolation. They lived in parallel worlds, he and Brenda: she in the safe, predictable environment of institutional living; he in the condo they had bought together that rested within eyesight of the "home on the hill," as the locals called Stonybrook. As the months passed and Brenda's condition had worsened, they cautiously diverted their eyes from the building as one would a funeral home, or a prison, as if acknowledging Stonybrook's presence would foretell their own residence within its walls one day.

Now Ben tossed his coat on the bed and crossed the room to the window where she sat. This was her retreat, her bubble; her view into the world. Once an effervescent, willowy maelstrom of activity, Brenda's movements now were limited and almost entirely guided by Ben or one of the caregivers.

Rise at 7:30.

Bed to bathroom.

Bathroom to seat by the window for grooming, and then dressing.

Bedroom to dining room.

Dining room to bathroom.

Bathroom to seat by the window, or on bad days, back to bed.

Then, come next mealtime, repeat the migratory pattern again.

Day in. And out. Over and over, in wordless, expressionless flow along a river rippling toward the end that Ben dreaded but of which Brenda was unaware, as she was with all other aspects of Ben's world.

Most days she would gently smile at him, accepting him with the benign appreciation one offers a beautiful flower, or a child playing in a sandbox. A non-committal look, vaguely approving, yet unfamiliar, distanced. Not a look one would give a son or daughter, or a friend, or a lover and lifelong companion who dedicated his own life to bring what comfort he could to his slowly dying partner.

Most days she was unresponsive, expressionless.

And there were other days – though mercifully few – when she was agitated, angry; incongruously obscene, with hateful rhetoric and judgments as unlikely in her behavior as would be an premeditated act of violence, or an intentional unkindness. On the worst of days, the hatred intensified as she assumed the identity of another loved one long gone from their lives:

"Belinda, goddamn you," she would shout at a nurse's aide, swapping her identity with the name of their long lost daughter. "You stupid, ignorant bitch. My name is Belinda, if you could at long last get that through your inadequate fucking brain."

Twice Ben witnessed these outbursts, and the shock of hearing his daughter's name spoken by her mother with such venom cut to his soul's core. Worse was the knowledge that he alone carried memories of what had happened to Belinda so many years ago. The lowest point of their marriage was left for Ben to manage, avoid, and endure, when such memories came calling, alone and without help, consolation, or hope.

Such language and anger were anathema to Brenda, whose upbringing demanded propriety and civility.

Then there were rare days of lucidity, and she would hold Ben's hand, reminisce and recall with perfect acuity, tiny islands of intimacy in a vast ocean of absence. In these moments she would echo the joys, highs, successes and beautiful experiences that come with decades of marriage, charitably relegating the challenges in their relationship to the shadows. In these diminished moments reliving their past, she gifted her teary-eyed husband with memories he would cherish long after the interlude passed and Brenda once again retreated into herself. Ben would take these moments home with him, and he would replay them over and over in a gratifying yet frustrating loop that kept him awake at night with the hope the next day would give him just one more taste.

Mostly, though, Brenda sat in a private silent bubble, with a slanted grin on her face and a look that implied she had a secret, perhaps the answer to a central question on life that the rest of the world would never comprehend.

Like all marriages, Ben and Brenda's had had challenges. There were passing discomforts and lingering periods of angst, some of them crushing, character-testing marathons that left deep scars on the skin of their union. Ben had neither the space nor time for the photos, videos and memories most couples retained as their time together grew short. His was a determined quest to restore trust, to reclaim love, to beg for and receive forgiveness.

So he was buoyed by the happy moments when Brenda was lucid and present. Alzheimer's may have taken the essence of what constituted Ben's wife, but in the moments she was present, Brenda was happy, and her smile wrinkles often puddled with tears of joy as the memories spilled forth.

Ben filled the hours with one-way chatter, asking and answering questions, recounting the stories of their life together in slow, anguished detail. He sang songs, played music, read the newspaper aloud, always hoping his acts would trigger her into the present. Now and again, she would respond, and perhaps interact, though these seconds had become rarer, more fleeting.

Cherish the gifts of small graces, Ben would remind himself in those moments when she showered him with happy memories and they relished time together sharing what was. This is what allowed him to continue, day after day; the hope and promise of one more moment just like this.

The slow, horrible erosion of her mind had gradually stolen most memories and robbed her of familiar names, faces and places where she and Ben had visited. But on those days when it came back, when she was able to connect the face and name of the person who stood before her – exclusively Ben, her sole visitor for months on end; who else was there to come? – it brought both of them pure, honest joy.

Today would not be one of those days. Ben sighed and settled in to wait for the hours to crawl by.

"Have you eaten your breakfast, my love?" he said, stepping in front of her and smoothing the hair from her eyes so he could look deeply within.

What greeted him? An unrecognizing stare, eyes emotionless and rheumy on the surface. Ben preferred to look deeper. He probed into the deep rich brown of her irises, the soft smile wrinkles that fled from the corners of her eyes to her temples, and he followed the curve of her face to her gentle, sloping lips, now cracked and dry.

15

He retrieved a tube of lip moisturizer from his trouser pocket and applied a liberal dose to her lips.

She smiled.

"Mmmmmm...."

Ben paused. Stared, and hoped for more.

The smile evaporated. The light in her eyes dissipated. The smile wrinkles disappeared.

She turned back to face the window, and to the irrelevant world outside her room.

Brenda had had been thus for one year, four months and 15 days, since heartbroken Ben and the kindly neurologist had at long last agreed that Brenda would be safer and better cared for in an institution prepared to deal with the horror of advancing Alzheimer's. Their condominium had become a dungeon of risk, a gauntlet of threats and dangers that grew with each day and challenged Ben to anticipate his wife's movements and needs, and keep her safe.

One day he entered the kitchen and found her at the stove, all four gas burners blazing as she stood with her back to the surface, confused, her light blue housecoat draping dangerously close to the flames. Days later, he awoke before dawn to the shock of an empty other half of their queen-sized bed. He felt the mattress. Still warm. He scrambled into his dressing gown and out the front door, catching Brenda by the elbow and gently turning her back to their home as she walked along the sidewalk not far from their home, barefoot, clad only in a thin nightgown.

A few weeks later she fell as she made her way into the living room. Though she suffered no broken bones, the accident limited her mobility as her joints and back muscles took time to recover. She became a prisoner of her home, and Ben, her warden.

And as the scope of her world shrank, her mental state diminished with alarming speed.

She was confused, lost, and the reality of Alzheimer's Disease pulled Ben into the abyss of despair with her.

"Brenda: lunch is ready. Would you like it in the living room, or in the kitchen?"

Nothing.

"Sweetheart. Lunch. There, or here."

Nothing, again.

He went to look.

Brenda sat half naked in her chair, clothing strewn about her feet.

"I'm getting ready for bed. The TV is broken."

The neurologist, who had become a friend during the course of Brenda's increasing visits to his office, ultimately made the recommendation: Stonybrook was not just a convenient change of address for Brenda, but a necessity.

Alzheimer's, he explained to a grim-faced Ben – particularly Brenda's version, Creutzfeldt-Jakob disease - was one of the worst forms of dementia possible, a one-way journey that would slowly rob her of all her memories, leave her a shell of what she once was, and ultimately take her life. Creutzfeldt-Jakob was a death sentence with no possibility of appeal or parole, a fatal form of a cruel disease that affect a small portion of the 5.5 million Americans afflicted with Alzheimer's.

The doctor offered hope, not for Brenda's recovery, but for her safety.

How fortunate that Stonybrook was nearby, and that a vacancy emerged, as always happens in long-term care facilities: by a death. In this case, it was a woman who, like Brenda, had entered the facility with some of her faculties intact but had gradually slipped away. Death, when it came, was a mercy, a tender, final gift that the woman's family accepted with quiet gratitude that the battle was at last over. Now the survivors could begin to reclaim their tattered lives.

Ben packed Brenda's clothes, and with the help of his friend Jim, moved his wife from his side to the long-term care facility that rested less than a mile from his home. He settled her into the room that had been scrubbed, sprayed and cleared of her predecessor's presence as the nursing home's staff prepared for the next temporary inhabitant.

As was his wont, Ben softened the change with positive reminders to make the best of the horrid situation.

"How lucky we are to have the corner room, my love. With all these windows, and a clear view of the valley. And you can even see our kitchen window from here. I'll leave a light on every night so you know just where I am any time of the night."

Most days since, he had made the pilgrimage to his wife's side, rising early, as had been his life-long custom, and briskly tending to his personal needs at home before joining her. Ben spent his time working to remind Brenda of what once was, exclusively focused on her well-being.

"Did you see the light I left on, above the kitchen sink, my love? It's there to remind you that I am close by. Always close at hand…"

He would sing to her, soft, breezy songs from their youth offered as calming, restorative reminders of happier days.

At lunchtime, he would guide her to the communal dining room to a small table for four in the corner where they sat by themselves. This was an accommodation the Stonybrook staff had made for him when they saw the deep, sad wounds behind his eyes, and the desperate longing for just one more moment of intimacy as husband and wife: talking, laughing, being. Ben had no capacity for small talk with strangers, so Stonybrook staff overlooked the requirement that all residents must share dining tables. Ben had earned the right to dine in peace with Brenda.

He would carry the conversation as she nibbled her way through tiny sculpted mountains of fruited Jell-o and picked at ashen, bland chicken. He heaped compliments on the chef and made observations as each course came and went, partially eaten in spiritless acts that Ben did his best to embellish.

"This stuffing is delicious, my love. Not as good as yours, of course, but with the tiny bits of celery, and seasoned just the way we like it…"

Or, "Oh, that poor, poor woman across the room who always cries during lunch…how fortunate we are to have one another, and that one of us is not alone, as she is…"

Or, "Today's server is simply lovely. So kind, and such a brilliant, warm attitude and smile. Wouldn't you agree, Brenda?"

He would offer these bromides not to calm her or assuage her angst, but in flimsy attempts to stimulate a reaction. Any reaction at all to pry her from the silence. Now and then she would nod, or turn to him and smile, and there would be a moment of normalcy, of connection between husband and wife.

18

But such moments had become increasingly rare, and each day Ben took Brenda back to her room after lunch, help her use the toilet – always averting his eyes to ensure her privacy - and then into the single bed. He would ease her shoes from her feet and cover her with the polyester afghan she had knitted decades earlier. He would watch her nap, perhaps doze himself for a bit, and then help her rise an hour later and return to the seat by the window.

They would sit side by side, silent and unmoving; two bookend sphinxes bound by the years and by a marriage once vibrant but now wed to silence.

Sometimes he would read to her, a romance novel or biography of one of their generation's heroes. Music, too, was an important part of their rituals, and Ben expertly twirled the clock radio's dial to find the local classical music station.

"Mahler, today, my love, I'm sorry to say. So dour…."

Around 5, he would concede defeat, peck her on the cheek with a *"Until tomorrow, my love,"* and make the slow walk to his quiet, dark condominium to listlessly complete another day in the shadows of his life.

Now, as he bent to kiss her goodbye, he was stunned when Brenda took him by the hands. She turned to him and stared deeply into his eyes with a gentle recognition that caused his breath to catch in his chest.

"Trust…honesty..fidelity…openness…acceptance…partnership…commonality of purpose and values…and love," she spoke in a soft, warm whisper. The words danced across the space between them.

"I remember."

4

Theirs was an unlikely, awkward relationship from the outset; two intelligent youths with enormous potential and similar values joined by common history and interests yet separated by class in a rigidly judgmental Midwestern town. They would have eased into one another's permanent company had it not been for Brenda's father's heavy-handed insistence that Ben simply was not worthy of his daughter. He was below her family's social rank - working class, common.

"My daughter with that boy is like a prize setter with a mongrel," her father sniffed, deploying an elitist analogy that elicited no reaction from his compliant wife but disgusted his daughter as he spoke about her in the third person, as though she weren't present. "Why one should think I would allow my bloodline to be sullied so is quite beyond me."

Ben had been raised in a loving yet unremarkable lower-middle class family in the small Ohio city where Brenda's father lorded with superiority as the town's premier lawyer, business icon, and mayor. Ben developed a reputation by achieving excellent grades, a quiet, calm demeanor, and by working harder than anyone else his age.

Ben was tall for his age, dark and angular; average in physicality other than for his height, but with a sharp intellect and a comfortable, welcoming spirit and quick, easy smile that was commonly held in high regard. He was the smart, good guy with potential, whom many mothers in town imagined as an ideal match for their daughters. Hawkish and bookish, he was the sort of boy easily overlooked by girls of his age, unless one took the time to notice his sharp, piercing eyes or respond to his warm smile.

Ben's parents poured time, energy and love into their son. Theirs was a conscious effort to build the foundation of a quality human being, as though erecting a brick building block by block that would comfortably withstand the storms of life. They imbued him with solid middle class values: honesty, integrity and commitment, and vigorously taught him the crucial relationship between hard work and success.

More instinctive gift than premeditated plan, their parenting style taught Ben how to be a good man.

"You'll be judged not by what you say but what you do," Ben's father taught him. "If you show up, do the work, keep your mind and ears open and your mouth closed until it's time to speak, you'll do well. Be generous in spirit and action, reserved and conservative in speech."

Ben listened, learned and did as his parents advised. His efforts gave them enormous pleasure, and they perfected the art of ensuring further positive outcomes by lavishing praise on their eager, over-achieving son.

Love and laughter formed the pillars of Ben's childhood. His parents' efforts proved fruitful, and Ben grew taller, more confident and competent, and soon earned a reputation in school and throughout the working community as a young man of substance and unlimited potential. He was captain of the debate and math teams, ranked second in his class academically (close behind a gifted young woman who would go on to become a federal court judge), and was a leading voice in the Young Men's Business Club. Ben's life's trajectory was propelled by his determined pragmatism and quiet dedication to each task, no matter how small. He was an understated star in the making, though not by any measure in the cloistered confines of Bedford Heights' class-centric elitists - most notably the mayor.

Brenda eased into adolescence branded by the highest social rank in the tattered city, entitled by default, and blessed by all the accompanying benefits of the city's upper class.

Her upbringing presented her as an attractive bauble for a worthy husband while horribly understating her own potential. Her parents' stubbornly conservative values were laced with old-fashioned notions about a woman's worth, and they prepared Brenda for a life of marital service that to Brenda sounded like indentured servitude.

"Your job is to look the part of a successful man's wife," her father lectured.

"That's the wrong spoon, my dear," her mother corrected, disapprovingly clucking her tongue.

Together, her parents painted her childhood with bold, broad strokes designed to increase her superficial appeal. They clothed her in expensive dresses and paid handsomely to have her hair coiffed with the latest styles. She learned table manners, the importance of listening attentively and speaking rarely and softly, and was force-fed skills to make her a properly capitulating wife.

"She will be defined by who she marries and what her husband achieves," her narrow-minded father lectured to her subservient mother, who was too awestruck and intimidated by her windbag of a husband to see the depths of his insulting beliefs and how they had restricted her own potential as well as her daughter's. Both parents failed to see the intelligence, independence and fire that burned deep within Brenda.

Brenda viewed her mother as a simpering, dependent fool who was missing the point of living. As a teenager, she assessed her mother's predicament ("She's a prisoner in her marriage. She doesn't know where to go, what to do…") and quietly made up her mind to pursue a dramatically different path. She was sympathetic to her mother's plight and wise enough even in her younger years to prevent her life from meandering into a similar result: trapped, voiceless, powerless.

She had other ideas for her future.

Genetics had somehow gifted Brenda with a keen mind and a diabolically practical spirit, and she crafted a shrewd strategy to live in two worlds. She maintained peace at home by dutifully following her parents' agenda while privately preparing for a life of independence, ceding the front line of her training to her parents while she surreptitiously looked after the development of her mind and soul. Working in the shadows cast by her overbearing mother and father, Brenda developed strong opinions and beliefs that she strictly kept to herself.

She would bite her tongue and nod when her father railed about the "women's liberation movement that was undermining the hard work and progress created by the men of this country," and smile softly when her mother would lecture her on "the value of keeping good help to make sure a woman's home is acceptable for her husband.

"You are beautiful, quiet and intelligent," her mother cooed. "You'll make someone a lovely wife. A silent beauty: that's what most men want."

Brenda was chestnut-haired, lissome and soft spoken, not extraordinarily beautiful, but striking in a way some of her friends likened to Jane Wyatt. Her soft curls framed a slightly rounded face and dark brown eyes that to some appeared harsh and unforgiving, but to Ben revealed intelligence, wit, and strength. Brenda was protective of her secret agenda to outstrip her parents' goals for her, revealing her innermost opinions, wishes and dreams to a select few – most notably Ben. Hers was a guarded, calculated existence with two objectives: to achieve more than her parents envisioned, and to get out of Bedford Heights.

Ben and Brenda cast awkward glances at one another in junior high school, and months later they finally spoke to one another at a school dance. They fox trotted and waltzed at the ninth-grade prom, gangly Ben all arms and uncontrollable feet, Brenda a cautious whirl of yellow taffeta tolerating the unpredictability of Ben's gyrations while deftly avoiding his oversized feet. After several dances, many furtive glances and awkward moments over trips to the punch bowl, they officially became a couple with a terse query from him and an even shorter reply.

"Wanna go out?"

"Sure."

Ben cemented the relationship when he handed her his Boy Scout tie tack as a symbol of commitment. She accepted it with a shy smile and, returning home later that evening, placed the treasure in the tiny wooden box that held her scant jewelry and few personal possessions. She carefully tucked the box into the bottom of the top drawer in her bedroom bureau, her treasure trove of secrets hidden from the prying eyes of her nosy, untrusting mother and stern, demanding father.

She fell asleep thinking of the tall, thin boy who grinned sheepishly as he did his best to keep his polished brogues under control as they twirled around the dance floor.

He lay awake for hours, thinking of Brenda's eyes.

Brenda's eyes were portals to her soul and guardians of her truths, and she protected these hallowed grounds with fierce determination from her parents. She practiced the art of diverting her gaze to hide her strength from public view, lest someone see past the façade and into her private thoughts.

Ben was one of the lucky ones who increasingly gained full access into Brenda's complex, powerful psyche.

As they spent more time with one another, he saw through her exterior and fell in love with her potential. He loved the fire, and intelligence, and depth behind her eyes, and he foresaw in her a force with power equal to his own. Where he was the draft horse, shouldering more than his fair share while straining at the harness in his quest for advancement, she was the skillful chariot driver, anticipating the uncertain paths ahead and deftly avoid trouble while plotting the best course at full speed.

She would be in the driver's seat, a vantage Ben willingly ceded with the knowledge that he would be a principal beneficiary of Brenda's power, wisdom and dedication.

Ben alone fully appreciated Brenda's unlimited strength.

How her eye lashes fluttered and lids slightly narrowed when he said something awkward, an indication of her innate ability to quickly form independent opinions based on intelligence, instinct and insight. How she would dip her head slightly and then grace him with a slight smile to receive a compliment, yet seek to confirm its authenticity with the same narrow, unblinking look when she met his gaze. Ben came to rely on her ability to assess problematic situations ("Oh, for God's sake, Ben…study for your math test first. Chemistry finals aren't for two weeks, and you always ace chemistry, anyway…") and avoid conflict ("We'll celebrate Christmas together either before or after. It won't do to try to get away from my parents, and they won't like it if anyone from outside the family is around on Christmas day, particularly if that anyone else is you…").

He saw her as mysterious, complex, and stronger than most would take the time to acknowledge. She filled the cracks of his moral foundation and rounded the rough edges of his vast, unpolished potential. She was blunt – at times brutally so – and Ben came to rely on her candor as a safe haven in which he could invest without limit, in doing so catapulting himself to unanticipated heights.

She was struck by the fact that he saw past her exterior, to where her hopes and dreams lived in quiet abundance. She was like a baby bird relying on the efforts of its parents, building strength in the spring and preparing to depart the family nest when the warmth of summer arrived. She held her innermost designs on life deep within, well behind the boundaries she created to keep her parents and friends at bay.

Their meeting of eyes opened the portals to each other's soul, sending them spiraling into a private retreat where their relationship took seed and flourished.

"I feel as though I've just learned to walk," Ben shared with his mother one evening. "Everything seems so fresh, so sound and solid, yet unfamiliar, when we are together. But sometimes I feel as though I can't breathe when I'm close to her." His mother smiled softly, placed a knowing hand on her son's arm, and quietly relinquished the exclusive relationship she had had with Ben to welcome the young woman she believed he would marry.

Yet his mother worried, and with good reason.

Ben and Brenda's origins from different walks of life might have scattered them along separate paths, particularly if Brenda's parents had had their way. They assessed others from a perch of scripted power and faux superiority, holding in contempt anyone who wasn't from a socio-economic class at least equal to theirs. By their standards, Ben simply failed to measure up to what they envisioned for their daughter.

The mayor and his wife viewed themselves as Chateau Lafite Rothschild; Ben's family as Boone's Farm.

Ben enjoyed a typical working class upbringing. He earned excellent grades, worked his way through the Boy Scout ranks (falling just short of achieving the rank of Eagle, mostly due to other commitments that diluted his time and focus) and always held a part-time job to earn pocket money that he religiously squirreled away for his higher education.

None of this mattered to the mayor and his wife, who held firm to their elitist views and dismissed the young man as inadequate.

"He is doomed to mediocrity," the mayor judged, brushing a cigar ash from his vest. "A boy like him is a product of his environment. What good could possible come of his future? He is a wormy apple from an infected tree."

Both of Ben's parents worked blue-collar jobs; his dad as mechanic for the city's Department of Public Works, his mom as a line cook at the middle school Ben and Brenda attended. Since both of them labored on the city payroll, that firmly placed them in the class of "dependent, handout-reliant nothings" the mayor loathed. That Ben's father served as union steward for the city's Municipal Workers' Association led the mayor to hold him in special contempt.

"Miserable, ungrateful plebes," the mayor scoffed to his aides, but never within earshot of an electorate largely populated by those he despised most of all.

Ben, quick to see the mayor's contempt for his mom and dad and others of the working class, objected aloud to his parents.

"How dare he judge you...me...all of us!" Ben railed, full of youthful outrage that his parents found amusing. "Who does he think he is, regarding us as pariahs, parasites? Why can't he appreciate what honest, hard work creates, for us, this community, and even for him, as mayor? And how can he and his wife pretend to love their daughter while they stomp on her potential every day?"

His parents laughed, did their best to mollify their son, and privately pledged to vote for anyone who ran against the mayor.

They simply got on with their lives.

"The best revenge to attitudes from jerks like *hizzoner*," said Ben's father, strutting through his living room, thumbs thrust into phantom suspenders, imitating the mayor in a mocking tone, "is to live as happily and well as possible."

So they did just that.

Smiling, contented people, they worked hard, played sparingly, socialized when time and life allowed, and dutifully went to church on Sundays, happy in lower-middle class lives that Brenda's parents found pointless and contemptible.

"As for you and Brenda," Ben's father wisely counseled, "I think the two of you are old enough and smart enough to find your own way without interfering parents. ANY interfering parents – even those who occupy the loftiest perch in the city's pecking order and ought to know better than those of us stuck in steerage. My best advice: listen to your heart, and follow it with boundless enthusiasm by making wise choices."

The mayor and his wife claimed the privilege of Bedford Heights' tiny upper class: he as the city's erstwhile town father; she as his first lady. He bragged about having a law degree from a "prestigious university" that actually was a modest state college, and she about her membership in "all the right" clubs, associations and social aid societies. They were the quintessential overstated big fish in a small, stagnant pond of Midwest unremarkability. True to the hubris of the nouveaux riche and members of suddenly powerful elite, they were intolerant of those who toiled in lower classes.

A skeptical electorate or probing local press would have revealed the mayor as a fraud: a contemptuous, small-time ideologue bent on cementing his authority by denying opportunity to anyone he perceived as a threat. But he was a deft player in the chess game of politics and power, and anyone who dared question the mayor's authenticity or authority soon found themselves outside his sphere of influence – dismissed and abandoned.

"Fear is a potent motivator," the mayor loved to say. So he kept his foot on the throat of detractors and opponents, and his eye on enterprising upstarts who might challenge him. He retained control over the underclasses through deft budget manipulation and by liberally deploying eager, underpaid staff to appear in his behalf at an endless stream of "constituency service opportunities" that made him look good.

Anyone who emerged on the local scene with money, power or connections was quickly corralled into the mayor's inner circle, then pawned off on staff to cement the relationship and guard against dilution of the city's political power base.

"Squelch dissension by choking off revenue sources where the problems lurk, and keep the herd happily grazing by making sure there is always a bale of fresh hay for them to peck at," he said to his aides, referring, as was his wont, to the general population as "sheep," "cows," or, in his most vile moments, "an unwashed, incapable brood of chickens." The awkward metaphors confused the mayor's staff by their raggedness, and stunned them with the contempt in which he held those who put him in office and paid the taxes.

Typical of small-pond big shots, the mayor bad an inflated opinion of himself, and he ruled with ruthless abandon. His willingness to strike at "naysayers" was chilling, and his venom was legendary.

Political opponents, aspiring business leaders, opinionated pundits and bold "doubters" soon felt the sting of the mayor's attacks and impenetrable defenses. He meted out punishment by deploying one of his bagmen to do the dirty work, using intimidation and isolation to get his way.

Lesser elected officials who opposed his pet programs found themselves iced out of power circles. Opponents who peppered the local papers with flavorful quotes castigating the mayor and his minions watched helplessly as would-be voters slammed doors in their faces during elections, withheld promised contributions, and abruptly cancelled fund-raising garden parties.

Like an old-style union strongman, the mayor had a tightly woven network of sycophants eager to gain his favor, and he had no problem turning on those who "don't share my imaginative vision for our beloved community's future."

To deal with larger-scale problems, the mayor denied desperately needed budget dollars to programs advanced by anyone who crossed him. He bullied his political allies into shunning those "who are not with me," and politically marginalizing movements before they could take root.

"There's a guy making noise in Ward 3 about inadequate after-hours policing of the business district," one of his aides advised in one of the staff meetings that felt more like a war council than a forum to discuss city business. "There's talk that voters think he makes sense. I hear he's forming a committee to explore a run for your office."

The mayor scratched his chin as he thought for a moment, then ordered the closure of the ward's popular day care center.

"Announce that we are shifting budget from day care to policing for the next fiscal year in response to calls for more cops on the street," he said, knowing the public outcry would be immediate and furious. "And make sure people know it's because this guy opened his gob. Make him responsible for this mess. If we connect this dope to working parents having to scramble to find someone to watch their kids so they can work, he'll die a death by a thousand paper cuts."

Such moves left him widely despised yet dutifully re-elected by fearful voters intimidated by his capacity to do harm. He was ruthless, singularly powerful, and had allies and spies carefully placed to warn him of any ripples of dissension. Overworked, voiceless and afraid to assume the risk of mounting a serious challenge to his role, voters and would-be candidates alike retreated to the safety of the status quo than the promise of someone who might represent something just, fair and new.

The mayor's autocratic, imposing demeanor kept the city in his grip, year after predictable year.

Similar behavior at home succeeded in keeping his wife in line, as she avoided her husband's glare, his bullying, and endless tirades as he stormed around the house, finding fault and complaining. She simply did his bidding as a matter of self-preservation, adhering to his rigid agenda in a spiritless act of compliance. She fully intended to pass along to her daughter what she believed was the only appropriate strategy for a successful homemaker's life, with her husband's approval and encouragement.

But in a rare but serious miscalculation, they both underestimated the strength, determination and will of one crucial constituent who remained outside of their control – Brenda.

"You remember!" Ben exclaimed edging his chair closer to Brenda's. He grasped her hand in his, imploring. "What, my love? What do you remember? Trust … honesty … fidelity… our vows. You remember!"

But Brenda had slipped into a quiet slumber, the warmth of the room and a full stomach causing her to nod off.

"Please, Brenda. Tell me," Ben softly pleaded, and then realized the futility of expecting her to awaken and continue.

He settled back into his chair to wait, hope.

Nothing.

"Until soon, then," he sighed, left alone to recall their past in silence. He sat in the waning light of yet another afternoon, watching Brenda sleep, as the memories tugged him into their embrace.

Ben's parents were unique in their willingness to speak openly about the mayor's regime. While most of their friends and neighbors held their tongues but voted with conscience, Ben's parents outwardly championed the candidacy of eager challengers to the mayor, and twice went so far as to post campaign signs on their front lawn. The couple's "big mouthed whining" always reached City Hall with impressive speed, though their complaints - usually critical of whatever policy du jour threatened the peace and well being of the community they loved - were always rooted in fact.

The mayor seethed at their outrageously disloyalty.

"And to think….these…these cretins are the parents of the boy who would presume to have my daughter's favor," he fumed to his wife. "This simply cannot happen. They…they are so…so…substandard, inadequate. So…*SO* much less than we are."

Like all the other facets of his myopic and selfish life, the mayor defined personal quality in terms of wealth, influence and power.

Ben was cast from a different mold.

He was defined by the Protestant work ethic, and he expertly charted the river of life as though on a mission. Ben's quest was to exceed his own considerable potential. Brenda, who was raised in the calm yet troubled waters of entitlement and affluence, set out to survive, and then escape.

Had the mayor taken the time to look closer at Ben's values, commitment and achievements, he might have anticipated the developing problem of Ben and Brenda's relationship. But myopia's gift - an intoxicating sense of false security – prevented the mayor from heeding the warning of Ben's rising star – particularly in the eyes of his only daughter.

Brenda watched closely as Ben worked, persevered, and succeeded. She smiled as his confidence and reputation grew, and her commitment to him solidified in kind.

He was the ideal son and potential partner: respectful, reliable, and hard-working, completing his homework before supper every night and saying his prayers before bed. An only child – as was Brenda – he piled into the back of the family sedan each Sunday to attend Methodist services with his mom and dad to express faith in a deity he believed would look out for him.

In his early years, he expertly managed a paper route, rising before daybreak to fold 72 papers for delivery and then pedal his bike around the neighborhood, tossing the morning news with sharpshooter's accuracy into the gray daylight - and into his customers' lives. Throughout high school, Ben worked three afternoons after school and Saturdays at a hardware store on Main Street, increasing his hours during summer months to full-time employment so he could bolster his college savings. There was little time for sports or hobbies, though he learned to golf one summer while caddying Sunday afternoons at the local country club where Brenda and her parents often held court.

His was a life formed around the equation of work and results, a pragmatic guide to success built on a dream that still existed in middle of the USA in the 1950s and 60s. *Work hard to get ahead,* his dad taught him; *you're limited only by your ability to dream, and to commit to what you envision.*

Ben perceived his future as an open route for him to navigate, and he accepted responsibility for paying his own way through college with a shrug.

"You've given me everything I could wish for," he said to his parents with a brand of homespun realism that became his hallmark during one of their dinnertime talks about how to finance his further education. "It's up to me to provide for my own education after high school, and to make you proud."

His draft number never came up, and he watched with a mixture of concern and frustration as some of his older classmates either enlisted into the armed forces or were drafted and disappeared into the jungles of Vietnam. His middle American values, Methodist teachings and Boy Scout experience suggested that "God and country" required a stint in the Army, but his faith's commitment to social justice informed him otherwise.

Though morally opposed to the war, he kept his head down, focused on work, and outside of his parents and Brenda, kept his opinions to himself. He was too young to qualify for the draft, which was ended by an act of Congress just as he turned of age.

In contrast, Brenda's life was one of scripted solitude designed to prepare her for placement in adult life as an opinionless observer of a world dominated by men positioned to care for what her father referred to as *"the vulnerable, weaker sex."*

Her educational and social life were carefully structured and meticulously monitored. Studies were intended to give her adequate skills to hold a reasonable conversation with her eventual husband and perform volunteer work, not to pursue a career or "rabble rouse," he chafed. School was part of a social contract, a necessary component in a young woman's life yet a source of great worry and consternation for her micro-managing father. He viewed Brenda's intellect as a box to be ticked on the report card of her social worthiness.

She saw her developing intellect as a way out.

Bullied into acquiescence by her overwhelming parents, she joined the sewing club and home economics lab, her wishes to join the debate team and take typing lessons squelched by her father and his rigid idea of what constituted an "admirable young woman."

"You must accept your lot as a function of your husband's success," her father lectured.

"He truly does know what's best," her mother agreed, offering an opinion only when out of her husband's earshot. "Just look how contented I am."

Brenda's voice sank into the mire of her parents' designs.

A lesser soul might have gone lost.

Not Brenda.

She spent days in school, afternoons and weekends under her mother's watchful scrutiny, evenings and nights alone in her bedroom. On the surface she appeared to be preparing for a life of marriage to a man from a higher social class who would provide well for her and elevate her family's profile in Bedford Heights. Quietly, on the side, she sharpened her intellect and formed well-shaped opinions that developed her character and strengthened her resolve to be anything but what they envisioned.

She read (the Bible, Good Housekeeping, Ladies Home Journal and whatever repressively conservative propaganda her parents left on her bedside table), sewed and cross-stitched while she patiently awaited the opportunity to decide her own future. In her early years, Brenda accepted the fact that her father and mother would make the choices – including her eventual mate. As she matured, and her body and mind took on shapes her father feared and underestimated, a simmering feud developed over who should determine what was best for Brenda.

"She'll make someone a fine wife," her mother said.

"She must bring honor our family," added the mayor.

"I want out, to experience the world on my own, and to live as far away from my parents as possible," Brenda dreamed with vivid determination.

Ben was surprised one day when Brenda launched into a perfectly articulated critique of the war in Vietnam. The two had often spoken of the conflict, as had most teens of the era, but usually they framed their comments by the vernacular popular among their peers.

This was different.

"The war is a political response created by the military-industrial complex to send thousands of disadvantaged Americans to their deaths to advance a deeply flawed foreign policy driven by economic interests," she ranted. "It is elitist, racist and stupid, and the fools in this country who blithely turn out to serve or, worse, send their sons to their deaths, simply aren't paying attention.

"This conflict is based on a lie. A complete fabrication that Vietnam somehow poses a threat to western security by its alignment with Communist doctrine.

"It's also blatantly sexist, the thought that only young men should face the bullets as a result of our government's horrible political choices."

He stared at her when she was finished, and for a moment she thought she had offended his values or expressed a view he found objectionable.

"Have I said something to upset you?" she asked unapologetically.

"To the contrary," came the answer. "You have perfectly summarized how I have felt all along about this stupid, misdirected war. In a few beautiful moments, you made clear what I have been unable to express."

Thus began their regular analysis of Washington's futile moves to dominate the Southeast Asian conflict, keeping their opinions between another and away from their peers and parents, in particular her hawkish, domino theory-espousing father.

"He wouldn't understand," she told Ben. "He and his friends all want us to drop a nuclear bomb on Hanoi, as if that would solve the problem. The wonderful, visionary mayor and his world views. As if lording over this miserably damaged city would give him any experience in geopolitics. What a joke."

Brenda's childhood fear of her father and his intransigent views morphed into quiet contempt as she read, learned and developed opinions that conflicted with his.

Her father – whom Brenda never referred to as "dad," "pop" or "father," but simply "the mayor" - toggled between his law office, City Hall and the vast study in the familial home. The latter was the lion's lair, a sanctuary of pomposity and faux-grandeur that perfectly encapsulated the life of the biggest fish in city's minuscule pond.

One of the room's walnut-wainscoted walls featured cheap reproductions of English hunting paintings by Lionel Edwards and Peter Biegel (whom the mayor often inaccurately referred to in writing as Peter B-e-a-g-l-e). The mayor liked the paintings because by being British they conveyed a tone of superiority and a pedigree that went well over the collective heads of the Bedford Heights electorate. Only if he had spoken with a fake British accent could the setting have been more fraudulent.

The other wall boasted floor-to-ceiling bookcases that displayed leather-bound classics: the complete works of William Shakespeare, a dusty Chaucer collection, and ostentatiously displayed tomes by Milton, Lawrence, Hardy and Eliot. There were imposing law books, atlases and biographies of the world's most loathed despots – all the literary accoutrements of an intellectually superior being displayed in an austere setting constructed to advance the man's image while intimidating lesser beings who dared to enter.

The mayor claimed to have read each book in his collection, though most of the books had never been opened. In fact, he hadn't read so much as a page in many years. The gambit worked as a repressive ruse - who would challenge him? – the room conveying an 18th century British look that defied the mayor's working-class Midwestern heritage.

Along with the rest of the house, the study was kept in order by Brenda's mother, who spent her days ordering the family's aging maid around, micromanaging the woman's labors to ensure that she strictly adhered to the mayor's ridiculous cleanliness standards. When she wasn't bossing the maid around, Brenda's mother hovered over her shoulder, making sure that Brenda was tending to her needlepoint, or reading, or resting, or taking her to attend Women's Guild luncheons at the country club.

When she was 12, Brenda's eyes fell on a lanky caddy struggling to shoulder a golf bag nearly his weight as Brenda and her mother entered the country club for a luncheon. She laughed aloud, causing Ben's face to flush as he hauled the bag onto his shoulder and skulked away. Both remembered the encounter, which led later that year to the fateful school dance.

During summer months in her mid-teen years, Brenda attended an all-girls camp that promoted "homemaker skill development for young ladies". She was placed there partially to sequester her from Ben, whom her father viewed as an unfortunate distraction and a potential blight on the sole branch in the family tree. At home, the mayor ordered Brenda's mother to cram her schedule full of benign tasks and duties, as though overwhelming her with busy-ness would quell Brenda's ideas and discourage Ben's determined pursuit.

"A busy girl has no time for such nonsense," he reasoned, then demanded: "Make sure her days are so full there's no opening for him and his stupid parents to influence our daughter."

Their vastly different upbringings – Ben's, bathed in love, support and promise, and wrapped in Protestant-ethic respect for hard work and values; Brenda's, a childhood steeped in fear and emotional passivity, as though she'd been raised to apologize for her existence and passively accept what crumbs life might offer – might have kept them apart, had the young couple not found the courage to persist.

As months crawled past, they wrote desperate, feverish notes to one another when separated, expressing their undying love with promised whispers of what was to come; she on scented, themed paper with matching envelopes, he on cheap scratch paper with envelopes he recycled from the hardware store.

"Until soon," each closed their letters, a promise of more that they would repeat throughout their lives.

Brenda returned from camp late each August and their romance would begin anew, though mostly out of view of Brenda's parents. The mayor was many things, but a fool he was not. With his antiquated notion of propriety and his reputation as a control freak, he knew he needed a new battle strategy. Three years after the first dance and transfer of Ben's Boy Scout tie clip to Brenda's dresser drawer, her father gave up the battle and with a shrug permitted his daughter to make her own choice.

"Why fight it? She'll find her way, and realize the folly of pursuing such a worthless young man on her own. It's infatuation, though God knows I can't imagine why," he puffed to Brenda's mother one evening, thumbs in vest pocket. "A young woman of her upbringing is worthy of far better. Let's give her free rein; as much rope as she wants. She will grow out of whatever she sees in him, and he'll be nothing but a faint memory.

"Let her see him, do what she will. Time and genetics will resolve this matter, and it is far better for her to figure things out on her own."

Free to explore one another throughout high school, Ben and Brenda dated, walked, talked, shared syrupy banana splits at the McClellan's counter and kissed beneath smoky moons on many Midwestern nights. As time passed and their commitment seemed more permanent, the mayor and his wife began to remind her that marriage was for life.

"A flawed choice of spouse is like inviting a cancer into your bloodstream," the mayor opined. "The notion of love as a reason for marriage may sound inviting to some, but a well chosen partner pays dividends for years. Marry upwards."

35

"Your father knows best," was her mother's stock answer. Her mother rarely spoke her own mind – if she had independent thoughts - bowing her head in deference to the master of the house and scuttling off to check on the cake baking in the oven or scold the maid for missing a spot of dust on the dining room sideboard.

Determined and committed, Ben and Brenda defied her family's objection to her choice of a partner from a lower social class.

Brenda, headstrong, smart and determined, was in love with the tall, angular wizard who dazzled her with his knowledge of calculus and European history. He was everything she was not: grounded, empowered, with a strong voice that equaled his strength of character, and truly spiritually free. She saw in Ben a chance to escape the controlling grasp of her overbearing father and capitulating mother. All she wanted to leave their small town, explore the world, and cultivate a life larger and broader than either of them could envision as graduating high school seniors.

She yearned to stretch her mind, and explore the possibilities. What better way than to marry a man she loved who would make it all possible?

Ben foresaw his role in ensuring that her future would be expansive, unlimited; as though he alone could release her from her parents' grip and let loose the wonder of her potential. He was no fool, and he saw the benefits he would enjoy as her life unfolded.

Besides, he was deeply in love with the dark haired beauty who visited his dreams every night.

"She is so much more than I am," he acknowledged to his father. "So much wisdom, grace, resilience, and power."

Ben's parents adored Brenda nearly as much as he did. They welcomed her into their home, the four of them picking at pot roast and gravy-smothered potatoes on Sunday afternoons. Conversation was easy and laced with laughter, giving the gatherings a comfortable normalcy unfamiliar to Brenda but a foundation of Ben's life.

They seemed to love her mind as much as her spirit, and Brenda beamed and flourished in their presence.

When Ben visited Brenda's home, he was ushered into the "sitting room" by her mother to wait for Brenda to appear. He sat there, uncomfortable in the silence under glowering portraits of the mayor's forebears, willing away the sweat that gathered in his armpits and on his forehead as he anticipated the cool breeze of Brenda's presence.

Her father occasionally stopped by to intimidate the visitor. He would express a curt hello, scowl at Ben and demand an update on the boy's educational and occupational intentions. He often dropped hints of other young men who had shown interest in Brenda, smugly admiring their superior pedigree, intelligence and potential as he droned on about Brenda's dating and marital options. He hoped Ben might be frightened off by the threat of competition, but Ben was far too smart to fall for the mayor's ploy. He sat through the insults, silent and respectful, and simply waited for the old man to run out of gas to he could take his daughter by the hand and grant her a furlough from the prison of her home.

Ben was never invited to share a meal at Brenda's parents' table and was restricted to the sitting room. It was a line of demarcation the mayor resolved would permanently declare his intentions to make his home – and daughter – off limits. He would tolerate this awkward teenage romance, but – just like all failed uprisings throughout history – it would fail in due time.

"You are taking calculus and chemistry, son. Good for you. On the road to be a pharmacist, or maybe a nurse. Something semi-professional. I'm certain your parents would be thrilled with that. Big step up from their stations in life," the mayor puffed, attempting to unsettle Ben.

It didn't work.

"No, sir. I am going in to finance; accounting and corporate finance, to be specific. But I want to have a well rounded education so I don't fall into the trap some people do by failing to keep a broad perspective and diverse skills.

"Some people misjudge a bit of success as a lifetime accomplishment. Anyone who isn't constantly improving is missing the point of it all, seems to me. People with limited potential stay in one place. I want to constantly evolve and grow, and that'll probably mean getting out of Bedford Heights."

The mayor was too self-absorbed and arrogant to know when he'd been insulted. Ben delighted in dancing semantic circles around Brenda's father as he uncomfortably waited for Brenda - sometimes for as much as an hour. These testy mental sparring matches became a routine between the two. The mayor made Ben sit and fidget, as if to test the young man's resilience and perhaps bore him into giving up, so Ben retaliated with calm verbal parries to the man's awkward jabs.

The stalemates would end when Brenda bounced into the room and rushed to Ben, seizing him by the hand and leading him to her father's side, where she dutifully pecked the befuddled man on the cheek. Ben would shake the man's hand before following Brenda out the door and to freedom.

"Finally, I can breathe!" he exclaimed one day as he and Brenda sprinted away from her home. "It's as if the man can suck all the oxygen out of an entire room with his pontificating."

"What did you do to torment him today?" Brenda pressed.

"I told him I'd joined the Ohio Youth Democratic Committee," Ben laughed. "You should have seen his face. It was like I'd told him I'd contracted a rare infectious disease, and he might have been exposed."

As Ben and Brenda matured, so did their love for one another. They spent more time at his home than hers, a fact that became a joy for Ben's parents and a growing problem for Brenda's.

"We have to do something about this," Brenda's father worried to her mother, who agreed and caved to his cold authority while shrinking from the latest tirade. "I had thought she would see the folly of this relationship, and by giving her latitude she would come to the obvious conclusion that this simply cannot be! Lord only knows what those two are getting up to while his parents leave them alone in that horrible little house."

The mayor saw that his hand had been called, and that he had grossly misread the situation and underestimated Ben and Brenda's commitment to one another. Brenda and Ben had formed an alliance against family history and reason, in his view, and he resolved to once again take firm steps to end the charade of a union that simply could not be allowed.

But influencing an independent young woman was a far more difficult task than bullying a voiceless teenage girl, and the mayor struggled with the simple logistics.

"How can we expect to influence her development when she's rarely here?"

Facing limited options, they grounded her. She pouted and waited for the embargo to end, slipping into the parlor late at night to breathlessly convey her love to Ben in brief, whispered telephone conversations that were pre-arranged to the minute.

They took away her extracurricular privileges. She retreated to her bedroom to read, sneaking "subversive" books by Doris Lessing and Virginia Woolf from the library into her home in the bottom of her needlepoint bag. Her curious, questioning mind expanded as she read words written by women who seemed to understand the repression she had felt her whole life. She began to write, poetry, at first, and then short stories.

Hours spun by long after dark each night as Brenda conjured up stories of resilient heroines who overcame male-imposed obstacles. She crammed journal after journal with gripping tales wound around survival and gender conflict that mirrored her own struggles.

She gave her protagonists strong, enduring names - Victoria McAfee, Becky Knopf, Margaret Downtree - and painted vivid portraits of their superior character, resolve and intelligence. Murder mysteries were a specialty, and Brenda delighted in having her protagonists outsmart legions of hapless male investigators whose best efforts were swept away when "the weaker sex" showed up to crack the case.

She kept the journals in a locked suitcase in her bedroom closet, stowing the key between pages 104 and 105 of the Bible her parents had given her on her 13th birthday. October 5 was Ben's birthday, a fact that her parents refused to acknowledge but that Brenda regarded as one of the year's most important events. She delighted in knowing that the key was held close to the number that represented the day Ben came into the world – ironically protected by the Book of Holy Scripture her parents had provided, but for which Brenda had little use.

Now and again her parents would broach the subject of other eligible young men as potential suitors, usually the son of someone who was of political use to the mayor.

When Brenda refused to date others or agree to stop seeing Ben, they bombarded her with warnings of failure, poverty and misery.

"Your capitulating acceptance of this young man places you directly in harm's way!" her father boomed one night when reason completely abandoned his normally measured approach. "If you get pregnant you will be on your own, believe you me. I won't have a bastard child in this family!"

Brenda didn't bother to inform her parents that sex wasn't part of her and Ben's relationship and wouldn't be in their immediate future. They had discussed the matter but decided to allow their relationship to develop slowly, and to delay the physical aspect of their relationship until they were independent of their parents.

She punished them by not speaking to them. and often was sent to her room during dinner when her father became enraged by her silence.

Eventually Brenda won such tests of will, and the mayor allowed Brenda to return to her normal daily activities with a dismissive wave of his hand.

Winning these battles lifted Brenda's spirits and strengthened her resolve.

"I think he sees, now, how powerless he is over my choices," she beamed, clasping Ben's hands in hers. "It must be driving him completely mad, and that alone gives me more joy than I should admit."

The mayor again predicted Brenda's relationship with Ben would end when he pulled some strings and got his only child into a prestigious private university in western New York. He clucked his tongue in annoyance and growled, red-faced, when he learned that Ben had been accepted on a full scholarship to nearby Cornell University: "What is it going to take to drive a permanent wedge between these two?"

The mayor wasn't often outmaneuvered, but Ben was evolving into a shrewd young man.

Ben believed that intelligence, determination and patience would earn rewards. One of them was Brenda.

Though situated 100 miles away from one another, the two spent nearly every weekend together, riding buses and borrowing friends' cars so they could alternate Friday-Sunday commutes to maximize their time in each other's company. They spent Brenda's allowance on hotel rooms so they could savor every second, renting two rooms to maintain a veneer of propriety but never so much as opening the door to one of them.

They were in love, young, free, committed and eager to explore one another. Right on cue from their emancipation from Bedford Heights and the looming presence of Brenda's parents, sex became an important part of their weekends. They researched and discussed birth control methods with openness and honesty, determined to avoid an unwanted pregnancy.

"Can you even imagine?" Brenda laughed.

"Frankly, no. For many reasons," Ben shuddered as they settled on birth control pills as the best possible option.

They hid these weekends from both sets of parents, writing lengthy letters full of details from campus activities, demanding exams and exciting weekend sporting events and social activities. They often penned these notes while lying in bed next to each other, unashamed by their nakedness, offering suggestions to one another of what to tell the parents.

"Tell your father about the business women's club event on campus," Ben suggested, "that would drive him wild: the thought of women thriving in the business world."

"Your mother would love to hear some details about dining hall food," she encouraged. "Tell her she could teach the cooks a thing or two about pot roast, and how to make a decent omelet."

As weekends drew to a close, they would part, always with the same promise to one another:

"Until soon, my love."

Graduation meant the end of their weekly commutes and the beginning of the rest of their lives. Shortly after matriculation, cap and gown returned to the rental companies and dorm rooms packed for return home, Ben celebrated by proposing to Brenda. She promptly and joyfully accepted.

An emerging non-traditionalist and a pragmatist who usually pursued a straight line toward what he wanted, Ben approached Brenda's father to seek the man's blessing well after Brenda had accepted his proposal. In a rare act of magnanimity – though miscalculating the purpose of the meeting - the mayor surprised Ben by receiving him in his study. He expected the young man to ask him for a job, or to perhaps write a recommendation.

He responded with silent disapproval when Ben explained what was on his mind, though he wasn't completely surprised.

Brenda's father was a pompous blowhard, ruthless small-time politician and disinterested, unloving husband and father. But he was also a realist who owed a successful political career to his ability to read situations and anticipate problems. He saw a certain advantage to marrying Brenda off, if even to Ben:

having her permanently out of the house would mean an end to his financial obligation to Brenda and would end a decades-long series of skirmishes that had become tedious and predictably unwinnable.

A skilled politician and modestly talented lawyer, he also recognized the finality of defeat.

So he gave his permission, and then surprised Ben by sending the maid to ask Brenda to join them in his study.

He assessed the couple as they held hands before his oak desk. They stood in silent, awkward moments as the mayor scratched his chin and avoided eye contact. Finally, he nodded them into uncomfortable straight-backed chairs that left them several inches below his line of sight behind the oaken moat of his desk. Looking down on visitors was part of the man's power play. This was his personal battlefield designed to impress and overwhelm visitors whom he graced with his presence as though a king granting favors to powerless supplicants.

His only child and her betrothed would be treated no differently.

After several more uncomfortable moments spent drumming his fingers and fingering his necktie, the mayor rose from behind the desk, a looming apparition in black worsted. He clasped his hands behind his back and paced behind them, chuffing and harrumphing as he gathered his thoughts. He stopped, placing one hand on each of their shoulders.

"I shall give you my permission to marry," he at long last granted in the booming baritone voice normally reserved for City Hall, "as it seems there shall be little opportunity to dissuade you from this absurd course of action."

He stepped around the desk a faced them, scowling over the top of his spectacles as though assessing a discarded piece of chewing gum on the sidewalk. They returned his gaze, expressionless.

"You surprise me, to tell the truth. I thought you lacked the stomach to survive as a couple. Both of you. Perhaps I misjudged you. Perhaps you are made of stronger mettle than I had thought. Where I once saw two impertinent, love-struck teenagers, I now see two young adults with undetermined promise and potential, yet not unsubstantial determination."

The mayor was a big fan of double negatives as a ploy to confuse and disarm people. He had learned early in his political career that most people found it hard to respond when confounded by what's being said. Long-winded, pompous speech patterns, verbose declarations and endless monologs became his preferred method of communication, as though overwhelming a visitor with a confusing verbal fusillade was the best way to make a point or impose his will.

Dialog was never an objective in his day-to-day dealings with lesser beings. He was content to overwhelm people into compliance or bore them into submission. This meeting would be no different.

The mayor again stepped in front of Ben and Brenda and sat on the edge of the desk. He scowled at them, looking down into their eager, fresh faces.

"Your future will be determined by what success you can create in business (nodding to Ben) and what sort of a home you can create for your family (to Brenda). Although it's not inconceivable to envision success for you, one could only do so with unbridled optimism and faith, and with profound gratitude for the blessings of good fortune that surely would need to visit you should this unlikely coupling somehow flourish and survive. It's not unimaginable to envision something less than abject failure, but we shall see. Your job begins now to make what you can of a life together."

Ben and Brenda exchanged quick, uneasy glances. Was this a blessing, or a curse?

The great man cleared his throat in a noisy demonstration, as though the phlegm being cleared from his epiglottis should to make way for the full weight and wisdom of what he was about to say.

"I can assure you both that this is going to the far more difficult than you imagine. Your age, inexperience and idealistic wishes will work against you, in a deck already stacked to your disadvantage. You truly have no idea what you're facing."

He thumbed his vest and strolled to his side of the desk, glaring at them as he gathered himself for his closing argument. Ben and Brenda shifted in their chairs with stony countenances and stiff backs. Both knew better than to speak. They barely breathed as they prayed for the man to wrap it up and release them.

"I shall do my very best to help you understand and to prepare you, as is my duty as your father, Brenda. You may think marriage is about love, and shared ideals, and other nonsensical notions the common man inappropriately seizes upon as they try to make sense of their meager, insignificant lives.

"Yet they – and you, too, if you are foolish enough to embrace such silly ideas – are mistaken.

"Marriage is a covenant, a contract. It is a means to an end. It is what human beings do to continue the species, to evolve. A good marriage creates growth, prosperity and opportunity, not just for a young, impressionable couple of dubious value and quality, but for the entire extended family that has every right to flourish like a well-fertilized field, and to benefit from the product of your union.

"There will be the possibility of improved social standing, of wealth of some measure, of responsibility to your family and community, and there's the likelihood of children and their incumbent challenges and responsibilities. To accomplish all this requires persistence, talent, skill and good fortune neither of you could be expected to understand, let alone possess. But you can improve your chances by behaving and acting as you must."

His voice rose as he built to a climax. Ben and Brenda sensed the end was at hand and leaned forward, eager to be released. The mayor interpreted their body language as genuine interest.

"As of now, you are running mates, or co-CEOs of your new company. Your future depends on your performance, day in and out. You must conduct yourselves – within and without your marriage, without pause or failure – with duty, integrity, probity - and with honor. You must bring joy, respectability and pleasure to your families by creating a marriage worthy of respect.

"You must see: this marriage is as much about *us* – your mother and I, Brenda, and your parents, Ben – as it is about you, and I certainly hope you take this responsibility to heart.

"Marriage is an extension of your families. It is an expression of the values upon which you were raised, Brenda, and hopefully you have learned as well, Ben, though one would certainly not be unexpected to forgive you for having failed to have been well instructed, given your relatively unfortunate circumstances.

"But never the mind. Now, together, you represent the potential for return on your parents' investments."

Ben and Brenda again shifted anxiously in their chairs.

"You will face challenges that will test a marriage not constructed on a solid foundation and managed with care. Many fail; so may yours. Frankly, I hold little hope. But it is your path alone to navigate this course toward respectability or ruin, failure or success. It is no longer my job to decide for you, but to observe and advise, without responsibility, remorse, or culpability. I am no longer the principal architect of that which makes you safe, happy and provided for, Brenda. This marriage is the provenance of what will either be or not be. And since I am but a witness, I will tell you what I see before me.

"Where I once saw hopeless, fawning infatuation, I now see a modicum of possibility," the mayor opined, voice rising to a crescendo as he assessed their value and rained judgment upon them. "Your potential is yours to exploit or destroy; your salvation will be in each of your ability to overcome the other's weaknesses as you follow the path toward happiness or misery, fulfilled potential or unhappy failure."

He paused for maximum impact.

Ben and Brenda breathed deep sighs of relief: the end of the soliloquy was at hand.

"What I see in you is the potential for a reasonably viable marriage."

5

Eager to begin married life on their own, they found an affordable, two-bedroom house in Bedford Heights within walking distance of Ben's parents but well away from Brenda's. They cobbled together a down payment from their savings – able to meet the bank's standards thanks to a cash wedding gift from Ben's parents – and settled in to tackle 30 years of mortgage payments.

Ben and Brenda would have been happy to forego a wedding, but their parents objected.

"I have always dreamed of dancing with you at your wedding," Ben's mother said through tears.

"What would the city think? Probably that you're pregnant," groused the mayor.

Brenda and her mother got to work planning the event while Ben began his career as a corporate accountant. He landed his first job at a small manufacturing company on the outskirts of town and started a lifelong tradition of being the first to show up at work in the morning and the last to leave at the end of the day. Ben remained living with his parents while Brenda moved into the tiny cottage to make curtains, paint and polish, and ready the home for the couple after the wedding.

"Best to keep a public veneer of propriety to protect your father's delicate image," Ben joked. "I'll stay with my folks until we're legal."

Their marriage would be constructed along traditional roles - provider and nurturer - and each embraced their job with pleasure even before they were married and had moved in together.

Ben would earn the money, tend to their aging car, manage the home's exterior and keep the lawn neatly mowed and trimmed.

Brenda would take care of the household finances, oversee the vegetable garden and handle the grocery shopping, cooking and cleaning. Brenda presented a proposed budget for household expenses, and after a brief discussion, Ben reached into his worn black leather wallet, sifted through the bills – carefully separated by tiny cardboard tabs that separated the ones from the fives and tens – and counted out the precise amount they agreed upon.

"Our first joint decision as co-CEOs," Ben quipped, eliciting a disapproving grimace from Brenda as she recalled her father's dismissal of their relationship as a business deal.

Money would be tight, but they were thrilled to face the challenge of managing the household budget together. Meeting the financial demands of owning a home gave them a truly independent collective voice for the first time, and they rose to the challenge with quiet resolve and genuine happiness.

They spent their days apart and evenings together, usually eating dinner at their home-to-be, or sometimes with Ben's parents. Brenda's parents rarely invited the young couple to dinner, a snub that Ben and Brenda accepted as more blessing than slight. Her mother was an appalling cook, yet she insisted on preparing dinner on the occasions when Ben and Brenda joined them. Cooking allowed the poor woman to isolate herself in the kitchen and avoid the uncomfortable silences between her husband and the young couple. Ben and Brenda would have preferred that her mother join them and leave the cooking to the aging cook, whose fare was also, at best, pedestrian.

"If my mother doesn't cook at least we'll have someone to talk to," Brenda said. "Besides, it doesn't matter: the food will be terrible regardless of who prepares it."

The promise of an awful meal – and endless servings of unsolicited advice from the mayor – made Ben and Brenda dread the periodic command performances.

They focused on wedding plans.

Caught between Brenda's controlling parents - one with a sharp, critical eye on the wedding budget, the other stewing about linen colors for the reception – Ben and Brenda were bystanders to the planning process. They wanted their wedding to herald an authentic, traditional marriage, born of genuine love and commitment to spend a life together.

Thanks to her parents' selfish micromanagement, Ben and Brenda approached their wedding day as a necessary yet mildly distasteful rite of passage for their union. Ben joked that he looked forward to his wedding day as he would a final exam or a military induction physical. Brenda likened it to the financial review they had endured before their mortgage was approved.

Her father's suggestion of "reasonable viability" notwithstanding, the young couple believed that their love would cement their relationship and protect them from the buffeting storms of marriage. True independence would arrive after the last slice of wedding cake had been eaten. Until then, they remained at the mercy of her domineering parents.

"We may be co-CEOs of Tremblay Unlimited," Ben joked, "but your parents are most assuredly our board of directors and majority shareholders. And your father is chairman for life. I fear it'll require a hostile takeover to unseat them and pry their cold fingers from our throats."

They acquiesced to Brenda's mother's preference for a buffet for the reception, and caved to her father's insistence that passed hors d'oeuvres were "an unnecessarily garish expense".

"Put out a few cheese boards," he instructed. "Why pay all those waiters to hand out canapés?"

They nodded in agreement over her mother's choice of nasturtium rather than lilies for the wedding flowers, and for her parents' insistence to handle the seating plan for the reception - without Ben and Brenda's participation or approval.

Ben's parents – and their wishes – never entered into the conversations.

Ben and Brenda exchanged wan smiles as the mayor and his wife decided on the music (DJ rather than live band), the toast (cheap sparkling wine instead of reserve champagne) and the number of attendants ("Keeping it small makes it a more exclusive event," judged the mayor. "It would be politically disastrous for me to include some but not all of the legions of supporters eager to be present. Besides, any more than 200 guests would be ostentatious.")

Since Ben and Brenda had few close friends, the attendee headcount mattered little to the young couple. They left the mayor to fill the ranks with campaign supporters and political cronies, reserving a handful of seats for Ben's parents' friends and some distant relatives.

When it came time to choose a cake, though, they resisted.

Brenda's mother wanted a towering pillar that exuded purity and murmured edible grandeur: layers of rich white cake covered with luxurious swirls of beige butter cream frosting highlighted by elaborate florets. Her father pressed for a sheet cake from a local supermarket "like we always serve at neighborhood fundraisers."

Ben and Brenda wanted a chocolate sheet cake with mocha frosting with a simple inscription: "Ben and Brenda, together, perfectly, like chocolate and coffee." Anticipating a showdown, they directed her mother's attention to the other details she agreed were much more important, celebrating their minor victory with an extra slice of chocolate cake the baker offered as a sample. They cemented their preference by suggesting to her father that the more lavish cake would cost ten-fold what they had in mind.

"Our choice is the same price as the large cake at Super Duper," deadpanned Ben.

That did it.

"Celebrate the small victories," Ben said, deploying two more aphorisms that would become part of his regular verbal repertoire, "and cherish the small graces."

During quiet moments alone, they spent much of their time working on their vows.

They wanted to construct a life together on the principles they held dear, bound together by customized expressions of love and commitment. They met with the pastor for his blessing on the unconventional approach and decided to leave their parents out of the discussion. Involving them would yield predictable outcomes: Ben's parents would be thrilled; Brenda's, appalled. So why bother, they reasoned?

They read, thought, drafted ideas apart from one another, and discussed their innermost wishes. Over the course of several weeks they compiled a list of values to use as a foundation for the ceremony – and their life together.

Trust.

Honesty.

Fidelity.

Openness.

Acceptance.

Partnership.

Commonality of purpose and values.

and Love.

They wove these threads into the fabric of their love for one another, each drafting a short speech they would hold with shaking hands and read aloud to each other on their wedding day.

"I think that does it," Brenda said one night as she concluded work on her text.

"Me, too," answered Ben. "What perfect values to set us on our way, my love. Maybe my mother will make a needlepoint pillow for us inscribed with our vows."

"Maybe my father will incorporate the thoughts in his next acceptance speech," Brenda added, causing them both to slump onto the sofa in laughter.

They looked forward to a quiet period after the wedding as they settled into their new life in the white cottage with its picket fence. They would work, nestle, and save to prepare for what might come next. Expanded social network? Civic obligations? Family gatherings? Children? A honeymoon – a luxury that fell considerably beyond the limits of the couple's meager budget – was on hold until there was sufficient time and money.

"Who needs it? We have each other, and our home," said Brenda.

"One day, my sweetness, I shall spirit you away to the finest New York hotel and shower you with champagne, oysters, and rose petals," he promised.

#

The wedding was a conservative, pleasant affair that some said lacked the polish and pomp befitting the mayor's only daughter. Hizzoner was glad the event was produced under budget with a minimum of fanfare. His wife worried about the food and complained about the cake maker's abomination, a single-layer mesa bathed in thick brown frosting she felt was more suitable for a child's birthday party than the occasion of her only child's wedding.

"And that inscription," she groused, "so, well, common. 'Coffee and chocolate!' Good lord! It is indeed the sort of cake one would find at a Super Duper."

Ben's friend Adam gave a terse Best Man's toast followed by the couple's first dance, and the mayor made perfunctory, unemotional remarks. Ben beamed as he whirled about the dance floor with his mother, and Brenda tolerated her father's stiff embrace as they waltzed to "Daddy's Little Girl." The entire affair seemed truncated, rushed and contrived, rushed to discharge the requirements of ceremony as quickly as possible and release the reluctant revelers.

Everyone – except Ben and Brenda – seemed eager to get on with it so they could return home to their easy chairs, crossword puzzles, and televisions. Most attendees made obligatory pilgrimages to the mayor's table to offer their congratulations, and mostly ignored Ben's parents. Guests ate their food, drank with reserve, and left early, and the room was half empty not long after the cake had been cut and distributed. The caterers, thrilled by the premature exodus, snapped into action, clearing the tables of dishes, flatware and glasses as the bride and groom looked on in quiet amusement.

Most couples might have been upset by the early departures of their guests, and by the perfunctory nature of an event that had required so much planning and expense.

But a premature close to the festivities was perfectly fine with Brenda and Ben, and they withdrew into an intimate bubble as the crowd dissipated and the folding chairs and tables disappeared into the caterer's waiting trucks.

They lingered after the last guest left, sipping champagne, chatting and laughing at the last remaining table as Brenda's mother scavenged leftover dinner rolls and the mayor repeatedly glanced at his pocket watch.

The mayor and his wife soon left, soon followed by Ben's tearful parents, who held the newlyweds in a lengthy group embrace that provided the afternoon's most poignant moment. Ben and Brenda were left alone in the middle of the dance floor, slowly twirling to imaginary music as the caterers waited to take up the parquet.

Soon after, alone at last, they drove from the country club as the sun set over Bedford Heights, casting a warm glow over the town and their first hours together as Mr. and Mrs. Benjamin Franklin Tremblay.

# # #

Nature responded soon after the Tremblays abandoned their strict adherence to the rhythm method of birth control. Brenda breathlessly shared the news of her confirmed pregnancy with Ben one Saturday morning as he cracked the shell of a boiled egg. He dropped his fork mid-stroke and rushed to her side, engulfing her in a hug and stroking her hair.

"Oh, my beautiful, sweet honey bun," he cooed, envisioning the wonder of becoming a father.

The couple took the weekend to celebrate the significant life change. Then they got to work.

Brenda decorated the tiny second bedroom in pinks and muted pastels, anticipating the arrival of a little girl based on "my mother's instinct that it's a girl, and by my fear of raising a son with a grandfather like the mayor as an influence."

Ben's salary barely covered the couple's living expenses, so he fretted about the costs that would come with having a child. To bridge the financial chasm, he picked up weekend hours at the hardware store where he had worked in his youth, yet he nonetheless elicited a disapproving chuckle from Brenda's father when they shared the news of impending parenthood.

"I should think you would have waited until you could afford it," he lectured, as though a child and its incumbent complications was just another budget line item to manage. Having provoked no response from the couple, he changed tactics. "I trust you will not expect any support from us. You – just as everyone else - must learn to live within your means."

Ben publicly tolerated but privately loathed Brenda's father, and he had become sphinx-like in the man's presence as an effective strategy of non-engagement. Hate was an unfamiliar emotion for Ben, and quiet contempt for the man became his chosen tool as he suffered through every moment in his presence. Ben refused to give the mayor the pleasure of becoming angry, surveying the man with a slight smirk on his face, unblinking, dispassionate. He kept answers to direct questions clipped, and rare unprovoked comments offered with an overarching tone of detached obligation.

It was an effective chess game that Ben came to relish as he perfected the art of riling the mayor with his stoicism, self control and calm, quiet self assuredness.

"I can almost see his blood pressure rise as he tries to bait me into an argument," Ben chuckled to his approving wife. "I hope I don't cause the old so-and-so to have a stroke, but I'll be damned if he'll rattle me to the point of engaging on his terms."

All this didn't deter the mayor from heaping judgment, unsolicited advice and criticism on Ben, but the endless lectures only fueled the young accountant's drive. He studied for the Certified Public Accountant exam nights to position himself for further opportunity, looking up from his books with adoration as his wife washed the dishes, her expanding belly pushing her further from the kitchen sink as each month passed.

Magic soon arrived in the form of Belinda Margaret Tremblay, a pale pink brown-eyed waif who appeared at birth with a shock of her mother's chestnut hair atop her egg-shaped head. She instantly took to her father when he received his daughter from the hospital nurse, nestling into his chest and nuzzling as Ben spoke quietly to his daughter. Belinda's cries subsided as Ben cradled and cooed her to sleep while his exhausted wife beamed from her hospital bed.

"How could our life be any more perfect?" Brenda whispered as she dozed off to sleep.

"Just you wait, my dear," Ben responded, full of hope, confidence and love. "Just you wait and see."

6

"I remember."

Ben woke with a shudder from his uncomfortable slumber in the chair next to Brenda's bed. He squinted at his wristwatch dial. Two hours. He had been asleep for two hours, meandering along a path of memories that faded as he returned to the present.

From the bed, again: *"I remember."*

He rushed to her side, scooping both her hands in his and staring past the wrinkles into alert, shining eyes. Moments of clarity between them had become rare, but for her to recall details such as their marriage vows was unprecedented.

"Yes, she breathed. "I do. I remember. So much…fun…love…goodness."

"Oh, my dear. I remember, too," he whispered, craving more. "All of it. So very, very much. And you? What do you remember?"

She smiled; he beamed. Would they have a normal conversation like they used to? Would the colors, textures and aromas of a life rich with significant moments come back in three-dimensional splendor, or would she drift back into a fugue-like haze?

"We had a good life, didn't we?" she said.

"Yes, my sweetness. We certainly did. Such a life. And such a love, ours. Still do, in fact."

"We did. Our house…our little white house, with the picket fence and garden in the back. The kitchen, just off the dining room where we ate our Sunday dinners," she said, shocking him with accurate details.

"I remember our first car…the black one…was it a Buick?" she asked.

"Yes, love," Ben agreed, lying, "it was a black Buick sedan." Their first car had been a used red Pontiac, but Ben wasn't about to correct her. There had been a black Buick, years later, but he wouldn't quibble over such details. Anything to keep the conversation alive, the memories flowing.

"I remember Sunday afternoon drives, after dinner, pot roast, or pork loin," Brenda continued. "We would pack into the car and drive through the countryside, stop along a stream and put our feet in the cool water."

"Yes, my love. We did. And sometimes we would take a picnic for an early supper, cold drinks and snacks in the sunshine. The three of us."

She tilted her head, confused.

"Three of us?"

Ben swallowed.

"Yes, dear, three. You, me and Belinda. Our daughter."

"Ohhhh….Belinda. Belinda. Whatever became of her? Where is she now?"

The afternoon, a Saturday, had been hot and muggy. The sun baked Bedford Heights in a relentless heat wave that drove its residents into the shade and onto the tiny beach on the river that dissected the city. Brenda was attending an afternoon tea to benefit the Hospital Children's Aid Society, so Ben was in charge of childcare. He would keep one eye on Belinda and the other on his accounting books, he reasoned, as he studied for advanced accountancy exams and his daughter played.

A precocious, active child of seven, Belinda soon grew hot and restless in the cramped house, so Ben packed his papers and books and moved to the veranda at the back of the house. There he could be close to her while she played on the metal swing set tucked into the corner of the tiny back yard. Belinda toggled between the swing and the see-saw, occasionally skipping into the home for a drink of water, then meandering around the front of the house, softly singing to herself, chasing butterflies, and day dreaming away the sultry afternoon.

The boredom and repetition of accounting theory conspired with the afternoon heat, and Ben dozed off. Soon he was in a deep slumber, papers strewn on the worn table before him and water pooling around the sweating glass of iced tea.

He awoke with a start – surely it had only been minutes – and he scanned the vacant backyard for his daughter.

"Belinda?" he called out, expecting her to rush around the corner from the side of the house with a clutch of daisies in her tiny hands.

Silence, and no Belinda.

Ben circled the home's exterior, calling her name again and again, and then strode through the house. He looked under the beds, in the closets, calling her name.

Alarmed, he grew cross.

"Belinda! Are you hiding from me? Please come out. Right now!"

Panic set in.

He rushed to the street, standing in its center in the late-afternoon sun, spinning in frightened sweaty circles, his eyes darting one way and then another for a glimpse of Belinda's chestnut curls or gingham dress.

She'll come back any second now, he told himself. *Any second now.*

But seconds turned into minutes into an hour as he rushed about the neighborhood, pausing to ask passersby for a sign of the little girl, but with no results. Returning home, he snatched the keys from the kitchen counter and widened his search from his car, leaning from the window and calling her name as he circled street after street with the empty seat beside him and a heavy, guilt-stricken heart.

As dusk approached two hours later, Ben returned home and considered his choices: wait for his wife to return and engage her in the search, or go to the police for help. He deliberated for anxious, wrenching moments, and then decided to wait for Brenda.

Ben paced the house's interior, rushing from time to time to the living room to pull back the curtain and wish his wife into view.

"She'll know where she is," he promised himself. "Brenda will know what to do."

He heard the sound of wheels crunching into the driveway as Brenda's friend arrived to bring her home. Then a closing car door, two friends exchanging farewell words, and Brenda's footstep on the back stoop. He met her at the door.

"I…she…I mean, she was there, and I fell asleep, and then she was gone…."
The words spilled into the empty space between them as he related what had happened.

All color left Brenda's face. She dropped her handbag on the sofa and rushed from room to room, shouting Belinda's name and searching under the beds, as though Ben somehow might have missed his daughter in his own search. Leaving the home by the back door, she surveyed the backyard, eyes darting in frantic arcs as her hands clutched at her throat as though she were suffocating, or drowning, and then to the front of the house, where she fled into the street, crying Belinda's name through sobs and gulps of air that did nothing to ease the pain in her chest and pounding in her head.

Gone.

Brenda's energy slumped as her anxiety swelled. She stood in the intersection as the day's light abandoned her, arms limply at her side, tears painting shiny rivers down her cheeks, spinning in a slow circle, again and again calling for Belinda and begging her to come home. After a time Ben was able to coax her back to the house and into the car so they could drive to the police station.

"We need more help," he reasoned. "The police will be able to find her. You'll see. They'll find her."

Her only words to her husband during the drive:

"How could you?"

Twenty minutes later Ben and Brenda – her eyes red, jaw clenched, and voice taut with worry – sat before a desk sergeant at the Bedford Heights police department, providing a description of their daughter and details about when Ben had last seen her.

"I fell asleep while she was playing in the back yard…it must have been three o'clock, perhaps three-thirty…"

Casting an anxious glance at his expressionless wife, "I only fell asleep for a moment. Certainly no more than an hour…."

Brenda refused to look at her husband. She provided perfunctory answers to the sergeant's questions while staring fixedly into space, what tears she had left to cry pooling in the corners of her eyes.

Bedford Heights' police department consisted of four patrolmen, two cruisers, one sergeant and a chief who had received limited training in Cleveland but had no experience investigating missing persons. Police activity in Bedford Heights mostly involved petty theft, an occasional drunk and disorderly charge, and minor accidents to investigate for the benefit of insurance companies.

The chief called in deputies to aid in the search, which involved street-by-street canvassing and knocking on the doors of concerned neighbors. As evening became night they issued notices over the local radio station and an All Points Bulletin through the State Police.

As the search stretched into the night, the chief's wife brought coffee and sandwiches to help fuel the department's efforts.

Morning brought a return of the brilliant sunshine and searing summer heat, but no sign of Belinda.

Members of the church where the Tremblays worshipped gathered after the Sunday morning service and then tacked hand-made "Have you seen this little girl?" posters around town. The mayor, grim-faced and visibly shaken, made a public appeal over local radio and television stations for information regarding his granddaughter's whereabouts. Ben's mother appeared on their front step, slack-jawed and silent, and then retreated to her home to wait when words wouldn't come and she realized the futility of trying to help. Brenda's mother holed up in her own home after placing a call to her daughter with an unhelpful promise: "Children do these things from time to time. She'll turn up."

Ben's father, who used example to teach Ben to be a competent, reliable man, often used humor to motivate him. He once again gave his son a lesson in appropriate human behavior the younger Tremblay would remember forever when he turned up in Ben's living room:

He wept.

Deep, wrenching sobs surged from the man as he draped his arms around his son. Ben stood erect and silent, uncertain how to respond as he consoled his father. Then, everything changed in an instant, as Ben slumped to the floor, regressing from competent executive, husband and father to a helpless child reliant on his dad for protection. He melted into his father's embrace, sobbing as he released the pain of Brenda's disappearance. There they rested, two men huddled on the barren wooden floor where Belinda once played.

Days and weeks passed, and the phone calls from concerned friends to Brenda and Ben's home slowed and then ceased. The last of casseroles dropped off by sympathetic neighbors were either eaten or tossed into the garbage. Awkward Hallmark messages of support were read and discarded. Ben and Brenda spent sleepless nights facing away from another in their bed, often still dressed in street clothes, curled in longing fetal positions.

After Belinda's disappearance all color drained from Ben and Brenda's lives. Their marriage became a bland, obligatory march of functionality in a parallel co-existence. They went to the supermarket, and to church, and collected junk mail and paid bills, often in unison, but never touching. They rose in the morning and exchanged curt greetings, cleaned their teeth and bodies, ate what would be required to sustain them for the coming day, and left one another to fulfill their independent duties with silent resolve.

They exchanged few words and even less physical contact, avoiding one another in the cramped, hot kitchen. One of them would wash and dry the dishes while the other would cover yet another uneaten meal with plastic wrap and return it to the refrigerator.

"Sorry," Ben confessed one night as his hand brushed Brenda's when he reached for a dinner plate to put away in the cupboard. Apology unnecessary; she had turned her back as she recoiled from his touch.

Brenda's view of the world was monochromatic. The daisies Belinda had so loved to pick, and the polished red fenders of the McFadden's new Pontiac, and the soft, welcoming blue sky all seemed ominously, spiritlessly gray to her.

Brilliant colors of spring, the glistening yellow forsythia, pastel hues of tulips, and vast beds of yellow daffodils blossomed and then faded into the mist of their empty, spiritless lives. In autumn, the crisp red leaves of maples fell to the ground, were swept into small mountains and then hastily discarded, the reminder that Belinda once would have glued the prettiest of the leaves to sheets of paper to be proudly displayed on the refrigerator too painful for her parents to endure.

Beauty that once brought appreciating smiles to Brenda's mouth and eyes now elicited little more than a glance, as though acknowledging the world's palette would pry her from the purgatory of omnipresent loss and somehow make Belinda's disappearance more real, more present.

She became committed to the still grey solitude, and then lost all ability to consider anything else as her spirit collapsed.

Ben's perspective on life had always been more black and white than Brenda's, but now the boundaries were more rigid, unforgiving, presenting sharp, orderly borders with razor edges.

There was work, and there was home.

Work revolved around avalanches of black numbers and blizzards of white paper, all wrapped around endless hours in the office and punctuated by downcast gazes from colleagues who felt his pain but avoided his eyes and left plates of macaroni and cheese and sandwiches for him to ignore at lunch time.

His was a manic pursuit of labor as a convenient panacea; a one-dimensional, exhausting cycle of productivity that created a ton of output but meant nothing to him.

Home was a place to eat sparingly, sleep fitfully, and wait until it was time to go to work again.

Police, meanwhile, continued their efforts. Their search widened and grew more desperate, yet the pace of their investigation became less frenetic as time passed.

All the effort – the searching, probing and watching – yielded nothing until a part-time Bedford Heights deputy interviewed landscaper Bill Hutchins and stumbled over the first break in the case. Hutchins mowed lawns, tended gardens and removed trash for the few Bedford Heights residents who could afford the luxury, and he did the same for enough families in neighboring communities to call it a living. As such he was a fixture throughout the county but rarely in the same community more than a few days each month. He had been in Bedford Heights the day Belinda went missing, cutting the Gordons' grass on Mayberry Street, he told the deputy, when he saw an unfamiliar car drive by "a little too fast for my liking."

It was a Chevy beach wagon, he reckoned, "what I'd normally call a family car, but with the back windows all blacked out..covered with paper on the inside or something. Struck me as odd." Hutchins didn't happen to note the license plate number, though he described the car in detail: "brown, mostly, with white trim and shiny silver hubcaps. Ain't seen a vee-hicle like that around here ever, no, not once."

State police put out an alert on the car. Two days later police in a nearby town found it, abandoned on an empty lot adjacent to a vacant factory on the outskirts. Glum-faced state police detectives gave Ben and Belinda the bad news: they had found bits of tattered blue gingham in the back of the car and one black shoe beneath the driver's seat that was the size and color Belinda was wearing the day she disappeared.

But no body.

Brenda confirmed the gingham as identical to the material on the dress Belinda had worn that day, and police sent swabs and samples from the car to the State Police Crime Lab for analysis, hoping a thumbprint would turn up on the state's criminal database. The results came back as inconclusive, but police quietly acknowledged that circumstantial evidence pointed to a random abduction and murder.

"I want the shoe," she told police with bland resolve. "It's all I have to remember her from that day."

"Sorry, ma'am, but it's evidence, possibly in a murder case," came the response. "I'm afraid that's not possible."

More months passed and the police efforts subsided as other cases replaced the missing child on the newspapers' front pages and in coffee shop gossip. Ben and Brenda somnambulated through life, inconsolable and dysfunctional, isolated from one another in their grief and unable to accept the permanence of their daughter's abduction to achieve closure. Without a body to bury, they would never know what had become of Belinda. They would always hope, stuck between a misery that consumed them and a horror they feared above all.

7

"We lost her, my dear. We just lost her," Ben said, as usual defeated by the memory; one of the silent torturers of his sleepless nights. "She was there...and then gone."

He studied Brenda's face for a reaction, or a response; was it asking too much to hope for forgiveness?

But Brenda had retreated once again into dementia's grasp, and she turned from her husband and faced the window. There was a bit of sun now, and it cast growing shadows across the lawn as Ben held Brenda's hands. He sat in the cruel silence and remembered what happened next.

# # #

An ominous stillness enveloped their home. Where once had existed an uncomfortable impasse that kept them separate yet allowed them to co-exist now became so thick with tension it was difficult for them to be in one another's presence.

Their lives were on hold.

Interaction between them, which sometimes had been businesslike but always grounded in love, mutual respect and common purpose, now had become perfunctory, discordant; two lives bound only by history, routine, and defaults to habit.

Food became a necessary moment, their dining table a pointless venue for the brusque exercise of acquiring sustenance. Roasted, tender meat might as well have been oatmeal; shirred eggs and bacon dry toast. What alcohol Ben drank affected him little except to deepen his sadness. Brenda avoided it altogether: Why waste an inebriant on the terminally numb?

Words had little meaning, an embrace from a friend, or a relative, did nothing to alleviate the pain and move them beyond the cycle of suffering.

Ben and Brenda danced an uncomfortable ballet of stubborn avoidance and awkward co-existence. Day in and out, in repeat performances that left them both empty, unsatisfied, and deeply, hopelessly sad.

Belinda's absence and the events that led to her disappearance became a shapeless demon that tormented them with equal fury yet prohibited them from discussing – let alone resolving - that which threatened all they held dear.

They became mechanical in their movements and silent to one another.

Brenda cleaned Belinda's room each day. She polished her shoes, fluffed her pillows and smoothed the wrinkles from her bed as though expecting her daughter to bound through the door at any moment and wrap her in an embrace. Brenda fulfilled her household duties with detached resignation. She shopped, cooked, and stared at her food while her husband pushed his food around the plate and read the evening newspaper. She went to bed long before Ben, turning her back to his empty space to add extra chill when he slipped beneath the covers hours later, their bodies molding into separate clumps beneath the woolen blankets.

He worked longer and longer hours to occupy his mind and minimize the quiet marathons at home, which became a source of anguish and added misery. It was as though the human who took their daughter had conspired with the forces of evil that torment people, heaping pain on the young couple as a cruel reminder of their fallibility and exposing them to the worst of each other. Belinda's absence created a vast chasm of suffering, blame and guilt that Ben and Brenda seemed unable to bridge. The distance between them – even more than Belinda's disappearance itself - seemed capable of consuming them.

Brenda, angry and resentful, treated Ben with contempt, laying the blame for her misery on his slumped, defeated shoulders. Ben, with no ideas to help them survive the loss or salvage their relationship, accepted Brenda's sentence and offered no appeal.

He could only watch as he lost what remained of his wife, and of his marriage.

Brenda retreated further within as the weeks sped past. She regarded sunny days of brilliant blue skies the same as she did gray, rain-swept afternoons - with dull disregard. All meaning fled, and the hours hung cruelly on her as did the un-ironed dresses that draped her shrinking frame. Eating had become a chore. Food had no taste, words had little relevance, and the love she once felt for guilt-laden husband of no consequence or value. The more Ben tried to engage her, the further she disappeared into the loss of her only child.

Ben lost weight, too, but not from lack of eating. He was constantly in motion, rushing from work to kitchen to yard work to studying to cleaning to the bank and finally to bed, though for only two or three hours a night before rising in the bland, gray dawn and repeating the process.

Ben's manic behavior sought to backfill the widening void Brenda carved out of their relationship by subjecting him to benign neglect, disinterest, and occasional outbursts of verbal abuse.

Even a harmless gesture of normalcy could be an incendiary trigger for conflict.

"What would you say to a nice pork loin for Sunday?" he asked one Friday morning as he prepared to leave for work. "I could pick one up on the way home today."

"Honestly, Ben, who gives a good God damn what we have for Sunday dinner?" she snapped. "Buy what you want. I'll cook it; you'll eat it. Happy? Now leave me be."

She blamed Ben for ruining their lives. Her hostile responses to his efforts to reach her gradually caused him to give up. Soon, they talked sparingly and made little eye contact. Ben at times made an effort but was silently rebuked with every attempt. Theirs became a sad co-existence: two humans once steeped in love, life, laughter and the promise of the future, reduced to sharing a home they neither loved nor wanted; a prison packed with reminders of failure, and of loss.

He became the sad, fawning sycophant; she, the stubborn resister.

Brenda allowed no physical contact, other than a quick peck on the cheek when Ben left for work in the morning, and another when he returned at night, greeting her with a small smile and "Hello, my love..how was your day?"

She turned her back on him when he arrived home from work, spent hours behind the closed door of their bedroom, and sought solace in a nightly hot bath, the door locked as she sank into the steaming waters as darkness swept into the unlit room, and into her soul.

One day she stopped cooking.

Ben, as usual, adapted.

When he arrived home from work, Brenda would disappear into the bedroom while he absorbed the kitchen responsibilities in desultory acts of duty. When he put dinner on the table and called her to join him, she would sit across from her husband, avoiding eye contact while dissecting meatloaf and mashed potatoes with her knife and fork.

There was little conversation unless the subject was the business of being married: Paying bills, when to replace the roof and how to pay for it, who should take the car in for an oil change. They declined dinner invitations from friends, or to join neighborhood barbecues, or to accompany Brenda's parents at the country club for lunch.

They stopped visiting Ben's parents, too, so they didn't notice how the elder Tremblays had suffered. Belinda's disappearance had stolen the joy from Ben's parent's lives, and the pain of loss – and watching their son and daughter-in-law shredded by the event - seemed to sap their minds and bodies as though riddled with virulent cancers. Their swift declines went unnoticed by their only child, who was too consumed with grief, concern for his wife, and career pressures to recognize their rapid descent into ill health. When his father and then mother passed away days apart, Ben and Brenda exhumed their mourning clothes from storage, sat in the front pew and tearlessly said goodbye.

Once buried, his parents went into the back of Ben's mind, along with memories, hopes, dreams, and such lavish gifts of life as joy, laughter and fun. Work became the only positive factor in his life, and he poured more energy and dedication into his job as a matter of salvation – and survival.

His efforts were rewarded by a series of promotions and pay increases that relieved the couple of financial pressure. He was named controller two years after Belinda's disappearance, and after he completed his CPA certification exam, he changed careers and work venues, accepting a new job as Chief Financial Officer for the Pureton Chemical Company.

"Change will do both of us good," he said, telling Brenda of the new job and of their further march toward financial security. She nodded glumly and rose from the table, leaving behind a plate of grilled flank steak, roasted potatoes and mixed vegetables, and a husband desperately yearning for a moment of humanity with his wife.

"I'm sure it's good for you," Brenda dismissed as she retreated to the bedroom. "I'm also sure I do not care one way or another."

The job came with a high rate of pay – nearly double his former salary – and an impressive list of perquisites and benefits. One of them was travel – some of it to international destinations to curry favor with investors and manufacturing and distribution partners – and Ben began to spend as much time away as he was at home.

This suited Brenda perfectly well. Ben was responsible for the loss of her daughter – and for ruining her life. It became her unspoken truth that kept them in a parallel existence; connected yet separated by an impassable distance. Her resolve, once the source of foundation for the structure of their relationship, became her private cache of weapons that she used for one purpose alone: to punish Ben.

Her parents fed on her misery and heaped blame on Ben.

"I only wish you had listened to my advice when I offered it," her father admonished. "You were always headstrong. Always had your own ideas. You chose an incomplete, unworthy man to marry, against my advice.'

Then, cruelly, "Perhaps this is the price you must pay."

Her mother piled on: "If only you had listened, Brenda, and *obeyed....*"

Brenda would turn away or hang up the phone after her parents' harangues. She resented them for their harsh words, yet in her heart she agreed with the message: *this horrible incident is Ben's fault, and I brought it on myself by marrying him.*

She spurned Ben's attempts – for conversation, or to accompany him on one of the many company functions or trips that were part of his work. Sex was out of the question, and he had long since abandoned all hope for intimacy of any kind.

At first Ben gently suggested that Brenda join him on his trips to some of the more exotic lands – Hong Kong, Munich, London – but she rebuffed him each time with the same excuse: "Easy for you to go off and travel the world. Who would look after the house? Besides, Ben, it's not as if we're comfortable in each other's presence. I mean, *look* at us."

He stopped asking her to join him. He would tell her when he was leaving and when he would return, then haul his suitcase from the attic and begin to pack. She would dutifully get to work, ironing enough shirts to last the trip and making sure he had enough extra shaving lotion.

He maintained a robust balance in their joint bank account by shrewdly saving and investing, though for what purpose he would have been hard pressed to explain. She spent little other than what was required, so their separate lives rarely intersected and never conflicted.

She would leave notes for him when unanticipated household expenses would arise.

"Washing machine on the fritz again. Repairman said it was on its legs last visit. Time to replace. Brown's has a Maytag sale on - $249, with 3 years service. I'll buy it while you are away."

This was his signal to make sure there was ample money in the checking account for the extraordinary expense – a sterile cash management scenario that was precisely like what he dealt with at work.

So he scrawled "Done – thanks" on the note and left it next to the sugar bowl on the kitchen table – just where he had found it when he had entered the kitchen an hour earlier – and then left for the airport. Brenda would see it when she rose and would tend to the details without further exchange.

Problem addressed and solved.

Necessary communication completed.

And their parallel lives resumed.

Neither had the strength or capacity to bridge the silent gap that widened between them; two rudderless ships bobbing in opposite directions on swift, conflicting tides.

Ben was shocked when he returned from a 15-day Far East trip to find a "For Sale" sign on his home's front lawn and a seller's agreement awaiting his signature on the kitchen table. "You've sold the house? While I was away? Without talking to me about it? I have so many questions, Brenda...."

A stunning response:

"It's time we got out of this ridiculous town and away from my horrible father and pathetic excuse for a mother," she said, packing tea towels and crisp white sheets in a box, a premature, frenzied swirl of activity. Her parents had seized the opportunity of Ben's extended trip to launch a particularly venomous assault on Ben and their marriage that wrested Brenda from her ongoing fugue.

"This is your chance, Brenda, to rid yourself of that man," her father advised. "Come home, and let us help you rebuild your life."

She stared at him, unblinking, and delivered her judgment: "I cannot stand this any longer, father. I really can't. I have had enough."

She left her childhood home without further comment. Her father was certain that he had finally won the argument and that Brenda would soon return home. But Brenda strode from his office having made a decision that would soon remind the mayor how powerless he was over her life. She went straight home, called a real estate broker she knew from the country club, and by the end of the next day had the property listed for sale. A week later, she instructed the agent to accept the offer the nice couple from Missouri had made.

"I don't care that it's under the listing price. I want you to accept it and schedule the closing as soon as possible."

All this had happened during Ben's two-week absence.

Now, surrounded by unpacked suitcases, his briefcase on the floor next to him draped by his overcoat, Ben approached his wife as he always did – gingerly, cautiously – as he struggled to understand the moment.

He wanted to ask her to explain how she had sold the home in such a short period, and how long she had been contemplating such a dramatic move. Ever the pragmatist, he assumed the sale of their home – securing a broker, determining a selling price, advertising, and then house tours, open houses – had to have taken months to organize.

He longed to address the issues that lay beneath: to talk to her about Belinda, his culpability in her disappearance, and what they might do to resurrect their marriage. But silence had replaced openness as the guiding principle of their relationship. The stain of profound loss had ruined what once was innocent and pure.

"Don't you think it's a bit early to start packing, Brenda? I mean, the house isn't sold, and we have no place to go."

She glared at him and shoved a stack of towels into another box.

"We can start now. It won't hurt," she snapped. "Feel free to go to bed. I can handle this myself."

Ben shrugged, shoved his suitcases to the side of the kitchen and tossed his suit coat over the back of a chair. He began to help pack, taping together a box to make it ready. He threw a pillow case into the trash when Brenda noticed a tiny stain on it and clucked her tongue in disapproval.

"No use keeping something that's stained," she said, "like friendships, barrels of apples, and marriages, once it's tainted, it's not worth keeping."

Such condemnations always hurt, but Ben was conditioned to ignore them. This was just one more example of his wife laying blame at his feet for "ruining their lives." Such remarks had become the norm, and the effects of her passive aggressive attacks on Ben diminished as he rationalized their origin and got back to work.

"If you say so, my dear," he said, avoiding eye contact. "We can buy new ones when we find a new home."

Ben had no energy for the tiresome game of verbal chess his wife had perfected. His job had become the antidote for his diseased life. While Brenda's days were empty and spiritless, Ben's had become marathons of meetings, deadlines, pressures and always, always more. When not at his desk, crunching numbers and building complicated macros into vast financial analysis spreadsheets, he was in motion throughout the office, inquiring, directing, resolving. Gone from his demeanor was the affable, approachable side that his colleagues had once found endearing and now missed. His mechanical presence yielded the same precision and reliable results Ben was known for, but his monotonous voice and pallid complexion – and the absence of his trademark boyish grin – were discomfiting reminders that Ben was a miserable, lost man.

Work sustained him as the weeks flew by, and as his colleagues grew more uncomfortable with Ben's omnipresent misery, Ben foresaw trouble and made a move before the problems at home created yet another issue to be resolved.

He reached out to his network of business contacts, and by the time the ink was dry on the purchase and sales agreement of their home, he had secured a new job in San Diego, California, this time as CFO for Stepley Pharmaceutical, a private company that was preparing an initial public offering and looking for a steady financial hand to guide the process.

Brenda accepted news of his new job as though Ben had bought a new pair of shoes. She turned from him to continue packing and expanded her attack: "New job, more money, new home in a new state… yet nothing changes. Ben Tremblay – vertical climber taking care of himself. How wonderful for you."

Ben's mind raced as he considered his options for a response:

"It's good for you, too, Brenda! This is about us, not me! Why can't you stop punishing me, and give us a chance to move on and reclaim our life?"

Or,

"How dare you! What claim can you make to help us move onward, to forget, to survive?"

Or,

"Please, Brenda. Stop. Just stop. I am tired of being your foil, and the cause of our misery. I accept responsibility for my part in our situation. Isn't it about time you did the same?"

But he said nothing, shelving his thoughts and stifling his emotions. He allowed the silence between them to consume yet another piece of their hearts, minds and souls.

Ben left for San Diego first, two suitcases in the luggage hold and his leather attaché in hand, on a flight from Cleveland through Chicago. They agreed that Brenda would follow after she closed bank accounts, canceled contracts, sold their car and concluded all the other facets of the life they so desperately wanted to escape. She would move into a short-term rental apartment, remaining in Bedford Heights long enough to close the unhappy chapter in Ohio, then would join Ben in California to attempt to rebuild their lives.

"This is just what we need, my love. A fresh start. Please. Let's do our best to make it work," Ben pleaded.

Brenda stared at him and then shut the door as he once again left for an airport without her.

The company installed Ben at a nice hotel near Balboa Park. His expense account provided for food, transportation and entertainment. Ben eased into a comfortable yet unfamiliar pattern of long hours at the office followed by dinner in the hotel dining room and a few hours of sleep.

One month into his new job, he received a letter from Brenda informing him that she was delaying her trip west. *Odd that she wouldn't call. It's not as though we can't afford the long distance charges,* he thought as he read the missive, and then quickly realized why she had chosen to write. He should remain in San Diego, she wrote, while she "sorted out some things" and "laid plans for her next steps", which she failed to identify, explain or quantify.

Ben worried that the message meant he was permanently losing his wife to the overpowering negativity of her father and the simpering neediness of her mother. Yet he was still incapable of questioning her or demand an explanation. He sent a cursory "as you wish" telegram and worked longer hours, often asking his secretary Stacey to order a takeout dinner for him from the nearby 24-hour diner.

Unfailingly efficient, eager and friendly, Stacey became an extension of Ben's work life – managing his hectic schedule and anticipating his efforts to run the office. They developed an easy, amiable relationship, often exchanging casual banter throughout the course of the day. They frequented nearby restaurants for working lunches that sometimes stretched into the afternoon.

One night, in need of a break from the tedium of balance sheets and consolidated statements, and starved for company, Ben asked Stacey to join him for an evening meal.

"No work; just a bite and a quiet dinner," Ben suggested. "It'll be nice to have someone to listen to, other than the foolish television."

They drove in Ben's car to nearby diner, which was attached to a motel frequented by fatigued travelers in need of rest and lovesick couples in search of a discreet place to spend a few hours. They eased into a corner booth by the diner's window, leaning into one another to share a menu, a few laughs, and a quiet meal.

Not long after they pulled into the diner's parking lot, another car eased to the curb across from where Ben parked. Its occupant remained in the late model Oldsmobile, monitoring Ben and Stacey through the diner's window with a pair of binoculars and a single-reflex camera with a powerful telescopic lens. Now and then the man took a series of photos and then rested the camera on the car's front seat to scribble in a notebook.

8

Ben rationalized why Brenda's move from Ohio was taking so long.

"She will be here soon," he theorized. *"It's taking longer than she expected to pack everything and coordinate the move with the shippers."* Then, as weeks passed, *"I'll bet her mother is giving her a hard time about leaving. They're probably spending some extra time together."*

Finally, as weeks expanded into two and then three months, he became concerned, then angry.

"It's her father. He is running her life, as always, telling her it's a mistake to move to California, and in her weakened state she can't resist him."

Ben fretted and worried as the days passed, tapping his fingers on the sole armchair in the hotel room as late night talk show hosts cracked jokes to which Ben paid no attention.

Fruitless telephone conversations with Brenda yielded neither explanation nor resolution. He pleaded with her to join him. He asked her to explain herself, or at least justify the change of plans – and of heart. At first she danced around the issue, but her refusals soon became more adamant, pointed.

"I am contented here and you seem perfectly happy there, so I think it's best we leave our circumstances as they are for now, and perhaps for the foreseeable future," Brenda startled him one night. "Perhaps you have forgotten how unhappy we were under the same roof, but I have not. It's clear to me, now: We both need some time."

Time? Time for what? To heal, alone? To divorce? To find someone else?

Ben fretted through more sleepless nights, and then decided to fly back to Ohio to assert himself and bring his wife to California. He telephoned to tell her he was coming, then smelled trouble when Brenda declined to meet him at the airport and told him to meet her at her parents' home.

He was ushered into his father-in-law's study. With his suitcase on the floor beside him and with dry mouth and pounding pulse, he waited as Brenda hovered behind the mayor, eyes lowered and her hand on her father's shoulder as he sat at his enormous oak desk.

This was a posture Ben knew all too well – a classic conciliatory scene that reeked of capitulation.

The patriarch spoke, the picture of pomposity.

"Brenda is in need of her family's comfort and care as she mourns the loss of our granddaughter," the mayor began, excluding Ben from the circle of sadness that arrived with Belinda's disappearance. "It is clear to all – except you, apparently – that she is better off with us, in our care. We alone can give her the solace and comfort she so desperately needs, and that you are incapable of providing.

"Besides, you clearly prefer work over family."

Over the years Ben had silently chafed at the mayor's officious behavior and stern, insulting interference. He loathed how the mayor treated subordinates, the public and his family, how he viewed them all as inconvenient distractions. Now, though, Ben was reminded of the man's true essence: an inappropriate, invasive control freak, a selfish monster bent on destroying Ben and Brenda's marriage so he could regain control of his daughter. And worse yet: a hypocrite. For a man who cherished his office and power above all to question Ben's role as husband was too much.

Years of repressed anger from the mayor's criticism, passive disapproval and animosity brought a flush to Ben's face. He bent to rest his attaché case next to the suitcase, then slowly rose. He clenched his fists.

Ben saw himself act. He crossed the room in three strides and punched his father-in-law in the mouth, breaking the mayor's lower jaw and a bone in his own hand. The punch forced the older man to the floor, where he sat, jaw askew and blood dripping onto his white shirt, while Ben slumped into a straight-back chair and nursed his hand. Brenda, forced to choose, rushed to her husband's side, worrying over his injured hand and fretting over him while her father leaned against the wall behind his desk, bloodied, defeated.

The fugue dissipated as Ben's head cleared. He stood, enraged yet powerless and voiceless, as what he imagined he might do once again faded into his chronic inability to act. He wasn't a swashbuckling savior at all, but a middle-aged accountant on the verge of losing his wife; an impotent weakling unable to compete with his father-in-law's power and aggression, forced to accept his wife's silent judgment. He was an ineffectual, pliant suit of rumpled gray polyester against a contemptuous, rock of black worsted wool with sharp, well-pressed creases.

Ben did as he had always done. He gave in. He said nothing, quietly accepting his father-in-law's will, and his wife's capitulation. Brenda silently validated her father's wishes, staring at Ben with expressionless eyes and tight lips.

"You let someone steal our child from us," she spoke at last, "and then you abandoned me. Now I find out that you have cheated on me, too. With your secretary. How could you? After everything else?"

Brenda's wrongful indictment stole the breath from Ben's lungs and ripped a fissure in his soul. His mind stopped functioning as the depth of her accusation overwhelmed his ability to think, act or speak.

Empty seconds passed, and he mumbled a protest to challenge the lie and proclaim his innocence. What emerged sounded like begging, or an objection; a vague explanation that might also have been an apology.

"I...I...never..I mean, I would never. I mean, what is the basis for this outrageous accusation, Brenda..."

Brenda interrupted.

"Save your breath. My father suspected you would be unfaithful to me...that you would break our vows once you had time alone on the West Coast. Perhaps you've been unfaithful all along...on your business trips. I don't know. And I no longer care. It is the final dishonorable act, the ultimate insult to me, Ben."

She snarled: "How despicable."

The mayor puffed his chest. He cleared his throat as if to begin a speech to the city council, or offer a blessing at the Thanksgiving table.

"You have been exposed. You're a fraud, and a liar. Even worse: a philanderer. I hired a private investigator to follow you, at first out of curiosity but then with a growing sense of mistrust," he began, reaching into his desk drawer for a sheaf of papers as he spoke with a booming voice loaded with derision. "I'm sure the name Stacey McGaffigan is significant to you," referring to Ben's secretary.

"My investigator saw the two of you enter the Fern Motel together on several occasions, but one night in particular. Honestly. A seedy, cheap motel. With your secretary. How tawdry, and in such poor taste. And such a cliché among people of your class: shacking up with your secretary. How utterly, astonishingly predictable that you should sink to such an obvious low."

Brenda drew closer to her father.

Ben again tried to speak, to object, explain, but she waved him away.

"Just shut up and leave, Ben. Please. Haven't you done enough damage?" Angry tears came, and she left the room.

"You have hurt my daughter for the last time," said the mayor, returning the papers to his desk drawer and closing it with force that caused the desk shudder as he rose to dismiss Ben. "And you have darkened my door for the last time as well. Go. And do not return."

Ben stared at the man and finally spoke.

"You know this is untrue..." he protested. The mayor waved him off.

"I know nothing of the kind, but I do know that if you don't leave this moment I'll have you forcibly removed. We're not interested in your lies, or your empty words. So unless you would like to face a criminal charge of trespass as well as having to deal with the end of your marriage, you will be still and be gone. Right now. You are done here. Forever."

Powerless in the face of the mayor's venom and unable to speak to his wife, who had retreated from the room into the dark recesses of her childhood home, he gave up. He retrieved his briefcase and suitcase and slunk out the front door.

Ben went straight to the airport. He fidgeted in the airport lounge for six hours waiting for a flight to San Diego, and then spent the cross-country flight worrying, fretting, and contemplating his next move to find a way to prove his innocence and bring Brenda away from Ohio - and back to his side.

# # #

Ben dove into work with renewed fervor, having no choice but to set aside the personal crisis that otherwise would dominate his days. There was always too much to do, and now the endless piles of paperwork provided a welcome distraction. When not at work, Ben obsessed with strategies to disprove his father-in-law.

He considered asking Stacey to speak in his behalf. She would confirm that they had had dinner together several times but that there had been nothing untoward.

But he knew that Brenda's father would poison his attempt to explain.

"What would you expect a woman who engaged in an illicit affair with her boss to say in her own defense," the mayor would drone, fraudulently to Ben's ears, but convincingly to Brenda's.

Ben could demand to see the proof, meet with the investigator and submit to questioning to prove his innocence. He'd take a polygraph, he vowed, if that would help clear the record – and his name.

Alone and despondent, he wrote to Brenda with heartfelt pleas in the middle of the night as solitude forced the words he preferred to say to her into imploring, desperate missives.

"I miss you," he wrote, then, *"you know me. You KNOW I would never..."*

and

"THINK about it: this is yet another of your father's assaults on our marriage,"

and

"What can I say? What can I do? How can I convince you, if not to take my word against your father's, then to at least agree to talk to me about it. Face to face. Just us."

But his letters went unanswered.

He telephoned, only to be turned away.

"If you persist in calling, I shall have no choice but to obtain an injunction to stop your harassment," the mayor warned the last time Ben called.

The Lie, as Ben came to refer to it – that Ben had compromised their marriage by having an affair, a fabrication that imposed immeasurable cruelty and devastating impact on Ben and Brenda – loomed with greater authority than Ben could battle alone. His linear mind saw only one way to expose The Lie: to diffuse it with the truth and bring Brenda back to his side.

"I'll prove my innocence, however long it takes, and whatever it requires. I will demonstrate my faithfulness, and prove him wrong."

So he wrote more, penning letters that were sometimes terse, direct and pointed but more often laden with pain, loss and remorse.

He explained.

He objected.

He begged.

But there was no forum for the truth, no room for Ben's plaintive explanations and appeals for reason. His quest for acquittal in Brenda's court of judgment was as lost as was he.

Finally, after weeks of sleep-deprived nights and anguished days, Ben gave up. He stopped writing. He worked, and fretted. And waited.

9

The sun was sinking low on the horizon, dusting the landscape with a yellowish tint that reflected on Brenda's face as she stared across the valley.

Ben glanced at his wristwatch: 6:57. Time to go home.

He moved Brenda's dinner tray to a small table by the door where it would be retrieved by the nurse's aide who would soon arrive to help Brenda to bed. Ben had asked for dinner to be served in her room, hopeful that she would continue the moment of lucidity. But her food had remained mostly uneaten, in defiance of their collective belief that food must never go to waste. Though hungry, Ben – hopeful that his wife would abruptly change course and eat the food placed before her – resisted the temptation to eat it himself. Even institutional food - tonight sliced turkey roll with bland stuffing and coagulating gravy surrounded by a small moat of gray-green boiled peas – deserved to be consumed, rather than thrown away.

"Never mind," he told her. "I'll make a bite for myself when I get home."

He leaned forward and gently kissed Brenda on the cheek.

"Until soon, my lovely honey bun."

He struggled into his raincoat and opened the door to leave, turning to glance once again at his wife's frail image by the window. The setting sun cast half her body in a shadow now. Ben sighed.

"My goodness. You're half gone. Literally."

He spotted his umbrella leaning against the wall, then seized it and breezily joked, "Gotta keep the landing strip dry for all incoming flights!" deploying one of the standing jokes about his receding hairline they had shared throughout their marriage.

"You can't grow grass on a busy street," he would quip when Brenda made note of his fading hairline while he was still in his 30s.

"Yes, and you also can't grow it on a concrete block," she would retort.

Theirs had been a relationship of happy banter built on understanding. Strengths and weaknesses, fears and foibles; all were fair game in the whimsical word games they played. Point, counterpoint. Thrust and parry. All in good fun.

On a good day, Brenda would point out the lunacy of dressing in a rain coat and carrying an umbrella in arid New Mexico.

"Unless you're hiding from the sun or expecting a rainstorm that hasn't visited this place in centuries this time of year, you're overdressing," she would have chided.

Not long ago, this would have led to a spirited exchange of wit and will.

"Oh, my love, how you carry on. I will invite you to do a bit of research on the issue. Facts matter, you know. You will learn that July through September are the rainiest months of the year in this part of the country," he would have shot back. *"And the weather can change in an instant. I choose to be prepared."*

"Which is akin to saying you once thought about voting for a Democrat, and therefore might again," Brenda would have effectively countered, winning the sparring session, as was often the case.

These days Ben carried both ends of the conversations in listless one-way exchanges of point/counterpoint, questions and answers, all delivered in his quavering monotone. Dialog with himself was unsatisfying, depressing; monologs doomed to brevity in pointless exercises that filled the emptiness of solitude but left behind gaping emotional voids. Any reasonable human soon loses interest in a talk with himself, and Ben was no exception to the rule.

As he expected, Brenda didn't acknowledge the joke about the umbrella, or even Ben's preparations to leave. He sighed, blew her a kiss with a second "Until soon, my love..." and closed the door behind him, strolling down the corridor toward the fading sunlight of the day and into the emptiness of another night.

He slowed his pace to lengthen the 20-minute walk from Stonybrook to his condo. What was the hurry? It was a lovely, quiet summer evening. The sun angled low over the mountain range to the west and would soon sink behind its peaks. The cool desert air sank into the valley as the sun conceded to the night's chill.

"Even the mighty sun is powerless against the creeping, inexorable darkness that surrounds us at the end of the day," Ben observed aloud, pausing to appreciate the metaphor. Then, scolding himself: "Poetic, romantic old fool!"

Ben stopped and slowly spun in a half circle, taking in the quiet landscape and absorbing the stillness painted in the waning day's soft tones. It seemed as though the entire world had retreated to its edges so he could be alone with his thoughts. What automobile traffic occupied these streets now was absent. Even the twilight birds were silent, and the lack of even a slight breeze created a stillness that was perfect for remembering.

When he was not with Brenda, Ben mostly thought and reflected. He remembered, too, recreating a billion moments in his life that had led him to a sidewalk in New Mexico on a quiet summer evening bathed in muted twilight colors, drowning in his own company. Occasionally at times like these – when nature gave him reason to appreciate his surroundings, he would smile, and occasionally laughed out loud in spontaneous delight.

Mostly, though, he regretted.

This evening would be full of regrets.

He fretted about the awful moments, decisions and events that had destroyed his role as father and imperiled his marriage. Ben had boundless capacity for doubt, self-criticism and regret. Extra grist from guilt fed spiteful mental demons that skewered him with daggers of recrimination. Memories, whipped into looming, hovering specters, ground him into submissive dust with punishing reminders of mistakes made and wrongs committed.

Ben's life had been about making decisions. Making smart, informed choices, he had built a reputation for clarity, precision and wisdom that created positive outcomes for his company, colleagues, and family. Except for one fateful afternoon in a Midwest summer when he lapsed and took a nap, Ben had carefully plotted a life course that ensured success: Reliable, positive results that ought to have led to happiness and a measure of peace.

When able to fairly assess his work and career, Ben felt at ease, happy, and contented. He had amassed considerable wealth over decades of labor, and he left the working life with much more than a gold watch and a reliable 401(k) balance. His work yielded far more than financial security, and Ben was proud of decades of respectable professional conduct.

An admirable legacy by any measure, Ben would remind himself, *"far more than reasonably viable,"* as he compared his work life to the marriage his father-in-law had predicted. On days like these, though, his decades of work felt insignificant compared to the rubble of his personal life.

The memories refused to let him to walk undisturbed. Though the event was well in their past, the raw pain of Brenda's rejection left Ben's wounds open and festering, unhealed. As he strolled the sidewalk, using the umbrella as a cane as the sun dipped below the mountains, Ben sank into familiar despair as he remembered what had come next.

# # #

Weeks passed with no word from Brenda. No notice of divorce. No telephone call agreeing to reconcile. No messages from an intermediary, trying to help them resolve their differences, together or apart, or providing Ben with third-party confirmation that his marriage was over.

"Not knowing is the hardest," he reasoned to himself. *"I'd almost rather know we are finished."*

Not knowing fed on Ben's insecurities, self-criticism, and all his life's challenges: his nerdy, bland early years, his awkward courtship of the intelligent beauty from a branch of the social tree well beyond his reach, Brenda's father's disapproval, their silly, contrived wedding and pathetic attempt at a middle class life in Ohio, Belinda's disappearance.

Normally a positive, upbeat man whose rational abilities guided his decisions, Ben became sullen, defeated, his thoughtful demeanor morphing into something more impetuous, unpredictable, mildly angry.

Minor problems at work became unsettling distractions. A low-level clerk who made the slightest error became a target for Ben's public criticism and rebuke, and on more than one occasion, ridicule. Where Ben once imbued the workplace with his steady hand and calm reassurance, he now infected his colleagues with fear and apprehension as his job performance reflected the torment of his personal life.

One night six months after their separation, Ben was seated at the hotel restaurant during his dinner break – a solitary figure with a sad routine that drew deferential attention from the restaurant's kindly waitress and accommodating kitchen staff. Often he was the sole diner in a restaurant attached to a hotel frequented by travelers, transients and couples in who registered in embarrassment, scurried off to their rooms, and then quickly left an hour or so later.

Stacey appeared at his table, a sheaf of papers in her hand.

"These need your signature. You left them on your desk, and I thought you might want to look them over while you had your dinner," she said. She hovered near his shoulder. He could smell her perfume. The overhead light glistened on her finger nails, painted a deep red. He looked up at her. She had touched up her rouge and lipstick, Ben noticed, wondering why she was still at work at 7:30 on a Tuesday night.

"Have you eaten your supper?" he asked.

"I have not."

"Care to join?"

"I would."

She sat across from him and ordered a ham steak and mashed potato – the same as what rested uneaten on the plate before Ben. He waited for her food to arrive, considering small talk but deciding he hadn't the strength.

Their eyes met, and held.

"You are so sad, so lonely," she said. "I want to help."

She reached across the void and laid her hand on his. "Any way I can."

Ben straightened, contemplating her words and questioning their intent. He recoiled from their potential, and from the problems that would come with one more bad choice made in a moment of weakness.

"I appreciate it, Stacey, but I can't. I mean, you're lovely, and thank you, but I just can't. Or at least I shouldn't. Mustn't." Stacey brought her hand back to her side of the table. Gripped the edge as if holding on for stability.

He looked at her, appreciating the slight smile and eager, receptive eyes. They looked at one another in lingering hesitation, each weighing the consequences of the awkward, hovering dilemma that required one of them to decide.

Ben chose.

He pushed his plate into the center of the table, and retrieved Stacey's hand from its neutral, safe place.

She pushed her plate next to Ben's; joined her fingers with his. Food would not satisfy their hunger. "Perhaps we should go," she said.

"Yes," Ben replied, leaving a $20 bill on the table. She followed, not to the restaurant door and to their respective cars to return to work, but he to the hotel registration desk and she to the ladies' room while he secured a room.

Moments later they met at the elevator and silently rose to the eighth floor, faint pings from the elevator marking their ascent past each floor and interrupting the awkward stillness, and then falling silent as the doors opened into the dimly lit corridor.

Once behind the closed door, they fell into one another's arms and into bed as the months of hurt, anger, rejection and fear erupted from Ben and met with Stacey's wishes, hopes, imagined pleasure and genuine affection. Afterwards, they rested aside one another, naked but untouching between the threadbare hotel sheets; parallel miscreants fraught with guilt, silently staring at the ceiling as if searching for an answer to a hopeless conundrum. Sensing the awkwardness, Stacey rose, dressed quickly with her back to Ben, ashamed at her nakedness and fearful of his.

She moved to distance herself.

"I understand that this can never be discussed, nor repeated," she said, hand on the doorknob, eager to leave. "I'm sorry, Ben. I shouldn't have come here. This never should have happened. It's…it's not what I thought it would be. Not what I imagined. I was mistaken. I wanted to …help. To…well…."

Ben pulled the sheet to his chin, as much for protection from Stacey's words as to hide his nakedness. He remained silent, so she spoke again.

"I can see that this has done you more harm than good as well, and that we may have unwittingly added to your difficulties. I am so, so sorry….for all of it. "

She steeled herself, waiting for words assurance that never came. She adjusted her skirt and patted her hair into place. Draped her purse over her left wrist and drew her hand across her waist as though enveloping it in a protective cocoon.

"See you in the morning."

And she left.

Ben lay in the bed for long moments, tangled in doubt, guilt and remorse.

"Sorry...for all of it...."

Stacey's parting words – and their irony: *more harm than good* - spoken to a man whose soul was already steeped in sorrow and regret, caused the empty room to collapse around him, the silence too close, horribly imposing. The bed threatened to consume him. He smelled Stacey's perfume and was repulsed by its aroma and the reminder of its proximity to his naked, flawed self.

His rational side took over. He strode to the bathroom for a hot shower that would purge the moment, the smell of Stacey and his descent into infidelity.

At once the horror of their actions forced him to his knees and then into a fetal ball on the shower floor. He wrapped his arms around his legs, water running over his body in rivulets that carried away Stacey's scent but not his guilt and regret. Hot water pounded on Ben's back, tears blending with the water and into the drain as he sobbed and begged for the pain to ebb.

He had done the unthinkable.

He had stomped on his own code of behavior, ethics and morality, violating the deepest, most valued trust in his life.

He had insulted his wife, their marriage, and the memory of his daughter.

He had broken his vows to a woman he loved, who surely would now be lost forever.

He had become what his father-in-law predicted, and in doing so had sealed his own fate.

10

Ben struggled to fit the key into his front door. A slight tremor caused his right wrist to pivot, and the key jangled against its mates, uncontrolled. It bounced against the cast bronze fob, a wedding gift from Brenda inscribed with their marriage date and the word, "Forever."

Clucking his tongue in frustration, he switched hands to gain purchase. He leaned the umbrella against the exterior jamb and opened the lock using his left hand, then scooped up the umbrella and entered, closing the door behind him.

Darkness swept over him; stillness, too. The nightly ritual of entering space he and Brenda once shared that was now his alone overwhelmed him with a feeling of undiluted loss. Television and radio would fill the silence but not mitigate the fact that he was alone.

The phone would not ring.

The doorbell would not buzz.

There would be no one to talk to, or even talk *at*, and he would spend the evening in the awful company of Brenda's absence. He would cook a quick supper and eat it at the kitchen table, kept company by talk radio or a TV game show under a glaring fluorescent light that would force back the shadows but not dilute the gloom. He would read for a bit, don his pajamas and brush his teeth, and then slip into bed around 10, to retreat to the side that had always been his and attempt to ignore the mocking void next to him.

Alone in those moments, Ben felt the empty side of the bed expand. Its engulfing presence threatened to consume him – an invitation to a merciful end?

"What a relief that would be," he at times mused in the dark.

He missed Brenda's presence, and as he stood in his hallway, a lonesome, stooped figure, memories of Brenda's peculiar traits coursed through his mind. The things about her that only he knew; the habits and foibles humans collect in the course of a life.

The half-used facial tissues she would store beneath her pillow, ever the conservative pragmatist, placed there in case she should need one in the night. They collected in abundance as she added more to the cluster every few nights, kept out of her commitment to conserve. They rested there even now. Ben couldn't bear the thought of removing them.

Her worn light blue slippers, tattered by years of use, now lay expectantly in the waiting position on the floor near Brenda's side of the bed, never again to envelop her foot in the early morning light. He vacuumed around the slippers, as if moving them or even touching them might somehow imply something deeper, more awful, about Brenda's absence.

He missed her smell.

Her voice, her laugh, her messy makeup bag, with its contents spilling over the bathroom shelf in a constant state of disarray.

Her specificity.

Her routines.

Her flaws.

Her tiny bowls of yogurt with four carefully sliced rounds of a banana each morning. Her lack of spatial awareness, which often left her blocking the aisles in stores, or sidewalks when she strolled, and which caused the destruction of vast amounts of dinnerware over the course of their marriage.

"The dropsies," she called her affliction with a smile, dismissing the significance of a dinner plate or cup that rested in shards on the floor, a reminder to both that the tangible contents of a home have little to do with the lives they serve.

He smiled as he recalled things about Brenda that only he knew. Personality characteristics that at times annoyed him but that he grew to love in increasing intensity as the years swept past and dementia claimed more and more of her.

He clung to these memories in desperation, to keep Brenda close, vibrant, alive.

The crumbs of food that collected in her hair, or in her eyebrows, when, as a younger woman, she would enthusiastically tuck into a croissant while talking excitedly and playing with her curls as they sat in their favorite Saturday morning cafe. Ben would listen as she spoke, regarding her with a soft, knowing smile, and wait for her to finish. Then he would sweep the buttery crumbs from her hair, often with a standing joke: "I suspect you were saving that for later, but you do have a reputation to uphold. I guess you'll have to find sustenance elsewhere."

Her detachment from possessions, like the earrings Ben gave her for Christmas the year Belinda was born but, like Brenda's sharp mind and keen wit, now were gone, no longer part of their bond. They were gold with an elegant cut of green tourmaline stones. Ben had saved for months, and presented her with the gift as she nursed Belinda in her hospital room. She wept; he beamed. She wore them for special occasions: for dinner out with friends, to company functions, and always on Christmas Day.

Returning home one night six years after he presented her with the earrings, Brenda met him at the door with tears in her eyes and hands clasped together at her waist, the picture of a confessor about to reveal a dark sin.

"I've lost the earrings," she cried before Ben had even set down his briefcase. "Your earrings. The ones you gave me when she was born." Tears flowed as rivers of remorse, and Brenda's shoulders shook as if to release the angst of an awful deed. "I've looked everywhere but I can't find them. Your earrings."

Ben smiled and took her hand, gently prying apart her white-knuckled fingers to insert his in hers.

"No, my love. YOUR earrings. I gave them to you as a symbol of my love for you. They were yours to wear, to enjoy. They also were yours to dislike, though I seriously hoped you would not, or to give away. Or to lose."

He pulled her close, absorbing her angst.

"Some things are with us only for awhile; others, forever."

The next year, Belinda was gone, too.

There were differences between them, and he remembered those as well.

He liked his soup hot to the point of boiling; she liked it tepid.

He rolled the toothpaste from the bottom; she squeezed the middle.

He liked the toilet paper hung with the paper cascading from its top; she preferred it upside down, and her preference only strengthened when Ben found an item on the internet that showed the paper hung *his* way in the original sketch by the man who designed the toilet paper dispenser.

"It's simply a functional preference," she retorted when he showed her the drawings. "Besides. My father always insisted that toilet paper in our home be deployed the way YOU prefer. So, far as I am concerned, that makes your way incontrovertibly incorrect, boorish, and stupid."

After that, Ben always hung the rolls upside down – just as she liked it.

Such memories tormented yet sustained him in a constant march that rose and fell out of his control.

Sleep, he knew, would come at some point, but not before the memories did their worst, as they always did in the dark of night in the fertile fields of solitude where loneliness grows in abundance. Food, and TV and radio, too, would have to wait.

"First things first," he sighed.

He hung his raincoat on a hook, slipped the umbrella into its stand by the door and eased onto the straight-back chair. He stared at the wall across from him, elbows on knees, fingers locked beneath his chin to form a cradle.

A deep sigh. Of reconciliation? Remorse? Acquiescence?

He let the memories consume him as he gave in to the darkness, and to the quiet.

###

Six months had passed since Ben's "transgression," as he sometimes termed the evening with Stacey.

"Thing," "fling", "liaison," he reasoned on other occasions as the memory haunted him. He searched for a word that would provide emotional distance from the event while minimizing its importance; it really wasn't an affair at all, but a mistake; a simple, physical release. Insignificant, forgettable. There didn't seem a label that sufficiently allowed him to compartmentalize, marginalize, and isolate his practical self from the reality of infidelity.

"Best to put a mistake into context, learn from it, and move on," he reasoned. To get to that point, though, Ben needed the right word, the right turn of phrase, to place the experience in a sealed emotional box and hide it.

"A dalliance," he settled on one day with fixed jaw and folded hands, neatly confining the event to lesser status, as if redefining it made it abstract, perhaps someone else's problem.

He had not returned to the hotel restaurant since that night, often driving out of his way so he would not have to see the building.

At work, Stacey and Ben kept their distance, his requests brief and impersonal, her responses clipped, professional. They mostly interacted on the phone or on the office intercom system. Theirs was a dance of cautious avoidance, both partners careful not to step on the other's toes, respectful but wary and guarded against the possibility of repeating the error.

One month after the "dalliance," Stacey did them both a favor: she resigned.

"I am leaving so I can breathe again," she told him, speaking through a slight scowl that that conveyed resolve. "It's as if I've been holding my breath for weeks. I simply can't take it any longer. So I'm leaving, and soon. Where I'm going is of no consequence, so don't ask. I am simply going.

"We both have a right to a life, to happiness. That can't happen – for either of us - if we remain in this place, this close to one another. Silence, permanent separation and distance is the only solution.

"I want you to know, Ben, that that night provided the most excitingly glorious, yet painfully malignant moments of my life. It was fabulously, deliciously, predictably wrong, and I am both grateful and sorry that it happened.

"It's odd, really," she said softly, with a slight smile, "it's as though I knew what I wanted, yet also knew it would end my time here, and perhaps for you as well. A bit like tucking into a peanut butter sandwich even though I'm allergic to nuts. And now that I've tasted it, I must suffer the consequences of a reaction I should have foretold. There's no going back. Only onward. So I'm going to move on and put it behind...all of it. I hope you can do the same.

"No," she said, wiping away a tear, "No more peanut butter for me."

Ben made no attempt to dissuade her. He shook her hand, accepted her two weeks' notice and notified the company's human resources department that he would need a replacement. He watched her turn from him just as Brenda had in her father's study months before, mindful that once again he was incapable in the presence of a woman whose power and authority rendered him incapable of engaging.

Ben, the strong, silent professional male, reduced to a simpering witness to a woman whose strength, courage and candor was beyond his comprehension, yet shaped the contours of his life.

So be it, he accepted.

Besides, there was work to be done.

Stepley Pharmaceutical was in hot pursuit of its rival, Benson Chemical, in a hostile takeover that required more effort and focus than ever from Ben. He worked nearly around the clock as he prepared financials, investor packets and labored with other senior management team members to develop a strategy to bring Stepley out on the winning side.

It was stimulating, demanding and draining work, and Ben had little time to dwell on Stacey's departure, the disaster of his marriage, or his solitary life. He was at his desk before 5 each morning and rarely left before 10 at night, except for a quick sandwich in the company's cafeteria for lunch and a bowl of soup or takeout at his desk at dinner time.

Stepley tendered an offer of $27.50 per share of Benson stock, an attractive premium on the security, and that meant more meetings with investment bankers and external consultants to complete the deal's financing. Ben joined Stepley's senior management team at the podium in the company's board room when they announced their purchase of Benson and a timetable for the acquisition.

Ben rounded out recruitment for an investor relations team and set to work to address the countless issues and nuances of managing the finances of the merged company. There were financial disclosure requirements to be met, stock exchange filing deadlines, shareholder communications, earnings reports, and conference calls with the market and institutional investors.

Ben cherished the challenge and worked harder. He slept less than three hours a night, ate sparingly, and rarely was away from his desk unless he was in meetings. His suits hung looser on his slight frame, leading the CEO to suggest he take some time one day to visit a tailor to take in his trousers and suit coats.

"You look like an elephant on one of those fad diets," the boss told Ben, who appeared in his office in a gray worsted wool suit that appeared two sizes too large. "You have more wrinkles than a Council on Aging luncheon. We can't have the financial face of the company look like a man dying of cancer AND starvation at the same time."

His skin developed a worrisome pallor that revealed a deficiency in Vitamin D – as well as nearly every other nutrient necessary to power the human body.

Ben had his suits taken in and took vitamins. Work intensified yet again as the tender offer approached. It was an exhilarating yet exhausting time; the journey, though finite in its length, seemed endless in its demands.

Returning to his hotel room after one particularly long day, he found a telegram peeking from beneath the door.

He shoved the door open with his shoulder and tore the telegram open, cradling his briefcase under his arm. He stood in the pale hallway light, halfway between the reality of work and the discomfiting sterility of his hotel room, as his life took yet another bizarre twist.

"I arrive 7 p.m. tomorrow. Stop. San Diego. Time for us to speak. Stop. Will be at hotel by 9. Stop. Brenda."

Ben's briefcase slipped from beneath his arm. It crashed into the door and sprung open, spilling its contents across the tattered hallway carpet. As he bent to retrieve them the door swung closed, smashing into his forehead with enough force to plant him on his backside. His back slammed into the wall across from his room and the door shut as he realized he had dropped his key card inside.

He sat in the hallway, confused and stunned. He was locked out of his own room, surrounded on the floor by sheaves of paper with a red bump growing on his forehead.

Yet he sported the grin of a man about to reap a long-sought reward.

11

The words defied each other, juxtaposed in a misfit pattern that made no sense.

Will be at hotel by 9. We must speak.

They scrolled across his mind like a ticker tape display, teasing him through the sleepless night with uncertainty, anticipation and fear, as he speculated what Brenda's arrival could mean.

In the morning, he informed his boss that he needed to take some personal time, though he kept the details to himself. He hurried from work around 6, showered, shaved, and dressed in a clean suit that hung loosely on his lean body, and took a taxi to the airport.

No way am I going to wait for her at the hotel. But it wouldn't do to drive, he planned, *it'll be easier for us to talk in a cab.*

The drive took an eternity, and Ben fretted, smoothed his suit and silently rehearsed in the back of the cab while enduring the last streams of rush hour traffic.

"Brenda. My love. You're home…"

Or

"Just come here," followed by a lingering embrace.

Or

"Shall we wait to speak until we are somewhere quiet?"

"Please wait," he asked the cab driver, rushing to the arrivals gate.

And then there she was, somewhat slimmer but otherwise unchanged – a vision of familiar beauty to Ben that instantly filled a void whose magnitude he had not fully acknowledged. Her jaw was fixed, her freshly painted lips giving nothing away. When their eyes met, hers were dispassionate, cold.

He approached her cautiously, fearful of her reaction and terrified by what she might say:

"I told you I would meet you at the hotel. What on earth are you doing here?"

Or,

"I have come to serve you notice of our divorce."

Or,

"You must sign these papers so we can legally and financially separate."

Or,

"I am flying to the Far East and wanted to see you one last time before I leave – probably forever."

But he did not expect:

"Oh, my dear, dear Ben. I have been such a fool, so wrong, so misled by my horrible father. So much pain, and so many lies. I am so sorry. So incredibly sorry…"

She collapsed into his arms, softly crying. The tears flowed faster when she felt his ribs through his suit coat, and his thin arms through the sleeves. Wrapped in one another, they blocked the terminal's exit. The other passengers flowed around them like river currents around a midstream rock.

She assessed him at arms' length.

"Oh, what have I done to you?"

With a wan smile and slight waggle of the head, Ben swept her under his arm, took her suitcase in his other hand and led her to the waiting taxi.

They rode wordlessly together through the warm, soft night as she collapsed onto his frail shoulder. She fit comfortably as ever despite his slighter frame, two puzzle pieces at last conjoined. Easing into one another soothed them, but it was an awkward reunion; familiar, yet strained.

At the hotel, they hurried to Ben's room, eager for the isolation that would allow them to speak at length, and from the heart, for the first time in months.

He poured glasses of water for both of them from the bathroom sink, wishing the trickle to quickly fill the plastic glasses so he could return to face Brenda.

He sat on one bed and she on the other, facing one another but avoiding eye contact. Ben waited as a convict would anticipate his final supper. He fidgeted with his tie, then removed it. He played with the collar of his shirt, then loosened the top two buttons. He rolled up his sleeves. Sipped water. Took off his shoes.

"If you don't say something soon, I'll be down to my boxers," he said with a nervous laugh.

No response.

Brenda sat in prim silence, knees pressed together and her purse on her lap. She played with the clasp, opening, closing, again and again. Her downcast eyes kept secrets incubated by months of separation.

More seconds passed.

"I have much to say to you, so very much," Brenda at long last began. "I only ask that you just listen to everything. Please don't interrupt me. If you do, Ben, I don't think I'll be able to start again. So please. When I am finished you can speak, but for the time being, just listen."

Brenda had spent days organizing her thoughts, rehearsing for this moment. All the planning and preparation made it no easier.

"Firstly: I love you. I always have, though I doubted that for a long time; for too long. I am sorry I forgot that, and how vital you are to me. And I have missed you, and us, in spite of it all."

A deep breath, gathering her thoughts.

"Not long after you left…after that horrible meeting when my father told what turned out to be the biggest lie he ever told me, or anyone else, I was devastated. Despondent, really. I felt betrayed, lost. I wanted nothing to do with you, but I also wanted to hurt you, to cause you the same level of pain you had caused me when I learned that you had violated our marriage."

Ben started. "Brenda…"

"No. Please. Just listen.

"How could you have an affair, sleep with another woman? I thought. It tormented me, the idea that you would do such a thing.

"This pain was different than when we lost Belinda. Losing her left me empty, in a deep, bottomless void. But the pain of losing you, of your supposed infidelity, was a different brand of torment. It made my heart pound, my lungs ache. I couldn't eat, or breathe, or think, really. It is a mystery to me, how a pain so deep as losing a child could be surpassed by the loss of the trust with one's life partner.

"Perhaps it's because you were all that held me together, Ben, through all of it. The years of dating in school as my parents fought to separate us, then college, then living in Bedford Heights under their presence, and then Belinda…

"You must understand. After Belinda was gone, you were all that held me in place, despite my anger. I blamed you – I suppose I still do, partly – how else could I handle the fact of our daughter being taken from us? Then it got worse, when you took the job here and told me we were moving.

"Yes, I said it was a good idea. Yes, I was eager to separate myself from Bedford Heights, our history there, memories of Belinda. But the idea also shredded my last tether to…to…myself. It was though your leaving for California put my life into a spin. I had no sense of being. I was lost, incapable of approaching a day with any sense of purpose or self worth, and when my father told me you had had an affair, it shredded the last bit of my sanity ….

She shook her head. *This was not what I came to say. At least not yet.* She shifted on the bed and changed course. *Get it over with.*

"There was a man who frequented the house…one of my father's business associates. It seemed that he was in our home every other day, for quite some time, though I know that couldn't be possible. It's such a blur…

"He and my father would meet in his library for hours on end, discussing their important matters, plotting business deals and political strategies, or whatever they did."

Brenda's voice was edged with bitter sarcasm and irony, and with hatred directed at her father. She spoke faster now, eager.

"One day when my father was out, the man – his name is not important, it is as meaningless as is he – came to our home. I answered the door, was surprised to see him, actually; why would he visit when my father was not there? I was uneasy. It all seemed untoward, somehow wrong. He said he would wait in the parlor for my father.

"My mother was at the club, as was her habit on Wednesdays, and so I knew she would not return for some time. We sat in the parlor and talked, I, as the dutiful daughter fulfilling my role as the respectful hostess until my father returned. It was quite proper and, well, acceptable."

She squared her shoulders.

"Eventually my father returned, and he dismissed me so he and the man could retreat to his office to conduct their business.

"But not before I had accepted the man's invitation to accompany him to a fundraising dinner. At first it shocked me: how presumptuous! But then I thought: Why not? I am a free woman. My marital status was a formality at that point: we were divorcing, in my mind. Months had passed. You had violated our vows, and I felt such anger toward you. I felt no call for loyalty: Why should I? Besides, he was good company, and it was just a dinner.

"He was very convincing, and persistent. And I thought, 'Am I to spend my days entombed in my parent's home with no interaction with the outside world?'

"But it was not just one dinner. There were others, too. And then one night, after yet another fund-raising dinner...."

She paused. Locked her fingers together and stared at her hands as though seeking guidance, or strength.

"It was for release, and also to punish you, and perhaps myself as well," Brenda said blandly. "We went to his home for coffee, just coffee, I said to myself, but I knew what I was doing. It was conscious. I wanted another man, to hurt you, and to soothe my wounded soul, as if sex would resolve problems of such magnitude."

Ben stared at the floor, limp, lost. She saw the pain etched in his face and began to reach across the void that separated them, then thought better and returned her hands to her lap.

"I want you to know that I felt nothing. Nothing. It's as if I wasn't there. I could see myself, as if suspended above, an empty vessel, not participating, unaware."

Silence engulfed them as Brenda again paused. She sighed deeply, searching for a way to continue.

"Afterwards, I just left. We never spoke again, and he had the decency to not call, and to never visit our home again. It's as if we both knew how wrong we had been, and though we had been too weak to prevent it from happening, at least we had the courage to let go of the moment as a mistake best forgotten.

"We both knew it was a mistake. A horrible, misguided moment by two stupid, greedy people. Greedy, yes, but with disparate motives. I've tried to rationalize the moment, to grant it the insignificance it deserves. It was nothing, really, Ben. A foolish mistake. A meaningless moment of weakness. It was nothing more than a tryst, a release: a dalliance. Yes, a dalliance, that's all it was."

Ben recoiled over her word choice.

His word.

Brenda leaned from the bed to take Ben's hand. He offered no resistance, which she took as a sign of hope; perhaps acceptance.

"So there it is. It was one night, a few hours, actually, but just that once."

She stared at her husband, unable to read face. So she continued.

"I have condemned myself more than even you could for what I've done. How could I be so foolish? As if an affair would resolve anything: Belinda's disappearance, my parents' calculated manipulation of my life, your absence – all of it! I had no idea how much being with another man would complicate it all…how much pain it would bring to me, and make it all so much worse.

"I promise you, Ben. I swear. It was one time. I swear to you that it will never happen again. The agony, afterwards…was indescribable….and that was before I learned the truth. When I learned the truth…well, that's when the pain truly began in earnest. When I realized what I had done, and my father's role in my misery."

Brenda stepped to Ben's side and sat beside him on the bed, close but not touching.

"I know the truth. It was all a lie, a ruse; a complete fabrication my father concocted to deceive me and keep me in his control. He orchestrated the entire, cruel course of events."

He tried to speak, but Brenda stopped him again.

"I am not finished. Please.

"I was working on a scrapbook one day, and I went to his office to look for a pair of scissors. I opened the drawer to his desk, and I saw the file from the private investigator. It was just resting there. My father would probably have been furious, would have ushered me straight from the house, if he knew I had been in his office, let alone sifting through his private papers.

"But I took the file from the drawer, and I read it. Why shouldn't I? It was as much mine as his, wasn't it? I sat at my father's desk, as self-important and judgmental as he, expecting to read the sordid details of your affair, to cement my hatred for you and justify what I had done. I thought, by reading the file, that I would be able to really separate myself from you. Commit to a divorce. Let you go from my life.

"How better to rationalize my own indiscretion by knowing the full details of yours? I wanted to punish myself with the details of your affair, to be branded with the knowledge that *you* had taken the first permanent steps away from our marriage, not me. I welcomed the pain of knowing, so I could write you off and get on with my life. Easier to blame you for it all than take my share of the responsibility.

"Everything changed when I read the file. I realized what a fool I had been, what a pawn I had been for my lying, horrible father, and how cruel and misjudging I had been.

"Such a fool!

"He made it all up. The truth was in the report; you did nothing wrong. My father used that file as a prop to manipulate you, and me. The investigator hadn't seen you in a hotel with a woman, only in the restaurant for dinner. You were there for an hour, and you remained within sight the entire time. The report said the woman was your secretary, and that the two of you sat by a window, ate dinner, and that you left in separate cars, and moments later were back at your office.

"There were even photos of the two of you, sitting across the table from one another and sharing a meal, but that clearly was all. There was no intimacy, nothing untoward. Nothing but two colleagues taking a break together.

"But no. That wasn't what my father wanted. Oh, no. He wanted you to appear the serial philanderer – untrustworthy, immoral. He wanted to make it easy for me to reject you once and for all. Such a liar!

"After that, I no longer cared. About him, and his self-important righteousness, or his lying, or manipulation. About me, or my feelings of abandonment, loss. It's as though my father made a mockery of my entire life in one, hateful act.

"After I read the file, the enormity of what I had done consumed me. That's why I didn't answer your calls, or write, or respond to your letters. I became proficient at hating myself, and deservedly so. I was – am – ashamed, humiliated; to think I could be so gullible, so malleable at the hands of my hideous father…

"I was lost. That's all. Lost. Hopelessly, pointlessly lost.

"That's when I knew I had to leave Bedford Heights. For good. And I knew I had to come here, to face you, and to beg forgiveness. And to accept what comes next. Whatever you decide."

Brenda returned to the other bed.

"So that's it. This is what I have done, to you, to us."

Brenda slumped on the edge of the bed, shoulders rounded as though under a great weight.

"And now our future is in your hands, Ben. I accept your decision. If you want me to leave, I'll go. Right now. I won't blame you if you never want to see me again, not after what I've done to you. Whatever happens, I will never go home again, and I will never forgive my father for what he has done to both of us.

"I hope you can accept me, and perhaps begin to forgive me. But you must know…I am sorry. Truly. I see what a fool I have been…"

Ben had been staring at the floor, unmoving, impossible to read. Now he looked up. Lifted his hand to silence her.

"Stop. Just stop, Brenda. Please. It's my turn now."

He thought, struggling. There was a truth to share, a confession of his own. How to proceed?

Seconds passed. Clarity arrived.

"You have done no more to me than I to you," he began, again waving Brenda into silence when she began to protest. "You and I are bookends, Brenda. We always have been. Mirror images of one another, a human parallelogram; together, but apart, but in perfect alignment. In every way; good or bad.

"In this case, it's bad. Terrible, really. It should be no surprise that our actions, though separate and under different circumstances and far, far apart, were once again as if we were one. Mirror images. That's us.

"The actions…the timing….the circumstances…", he paused, with a sad smile and slight shake of the head, "apart but identical in our imperfection. Even the word. Dalliance. That's what you called it; a dalliance.

"Yes, a dalliance.

"Your father was correct, but his timing was wrong. I had not committed adultery when we met that day in his library. Not then. But later, soon after I returned from visiting you, I did. I did as you did. Felt as you felt. I, too, attempted to fill a void with an act so empty, so stupid and insignificant that it insults everything about us with its mere existence. My actions discredit you. Me. Belinda. All of us.

"Like yours, mine was no affair. It was an act, indeed, a dalliance. And your father was right in one regard; it was with Stacey. It was one, entirely regrettable moment; a senseless, desperately wasteful and selfish act, but it was my choice, and I must live with the consequences. It also was without question the worst decision of my life. Even worse than allowing myself to doze as someone took our daughter from us, because this involved a conscious decision on my part.

"You used the word I sought so desperately to describe what I had done: a dalliance. How ironic that you and I should settle on the same description for similarly destructive acts.

"I understand your pain, and the pain I caused to myself, and to us. More than you could know."

Brenda stared across the room.

He continued.

"What you just told me. The feelings you had, the circumstances of your, well, indiscretion, they are a perfect replica of what happened here, in my own life."

Ben tended to be vague when under extreme duress, spewing confusing verbiage rather than his typically concise speech. Brenda had endured many much moments. This conversation required more of him if he hoped to make Brenda understand, and Ben struggled to find his way to the most important words of his life.

He rose and began to pace, fighting - for the memory of a daughter lost, to restore happiness that had dissipated under pressure, and for a marriage that hung in the balance of what he was about to say.

"I've been empty. Lost, Brenda. Even more than when Belinda was taken. It's as though some external force reached down within my soul and pulled out the core of my existence. Look at me! I'm a shell of the man I once was, and in many ways.

"I, too, was angry, and lonely, and....well, it doesn't matter. It happened, and the regret and disgust I have for myself has made clear what DOES matter to me. "

Moments passed.

"I am sorry, Brenda. Sorry for being less of a man than you deserve. Less of a father than Belinda deserved, too. I'm sorry for the mistakes, and misjudgments, and thoughtless moments where my confused priorities got the better of me.

"My foolish priority of work above all else. My selfish objectives, and my neglect of you and what you have gone through.

"Mostly, I'm sorry for fulfilling your father's prophecy. Perhaps he was right. Perhaps I have never been good enough for you."

He sat again on the bed. Months of guilt, remorse and frustration joined with Ben's pragmatic instincts.

"I forgive you for your transgression, Brenda. I do. I understand, and I forgive you. Fact is, I am partially to blame. I turned my back. I left you, and your misery, in the hands of your parents. How foolish of me to leave you with so much unresolved, and in such uncaring hands. All for what? My work? How stupid. So I forgive you.

"The question is: can you do the same for me?

Ben usually played the role of peace negotiator in their relationship. It was left to him to take the initial step to settle differences, to negotiate compromise, advocate reconciliation, and to resolve conflicts. This, though, would require more to move them forward.

Brenda was impossible to read.

"This is ours, Brenda. We own it; all of it. The horrible and good, miserable and positive.

"We have attacked the fortress of our marriage on both sides. It's as though we have chipped away at the foundation, bit by bit over the years, by not discussing what needed to be discussed. We have both been derelict in our duty.

"It began when Belinda disappeared, and by failing to truly take care of each other in the years that followed. We failed, both of us, by not listening to one another and seeking ways to connect, to support, and heal. And we failed worst of all by each making two independent, awful decisions that threaten the structure of our marriage.

"You failed me by not forgiving me when Belinda was lost; by not understanding that what happened could have happened to you, too. And I failed you by not being strong enough, man enough, to find a way to help you through your own pain.

"I failed you by walking away, leaving you to resolve it all on your own. But I believe our marriage is still sound. There is much yet to preserve. We both violated the vow of fidelity, but what about the rest of our vows? Aren't most of them still intact?"

He paused to think for a moment.

"Remember commonality of purpose and values? Openness and acceptance? We forgot about trust and fidelity for a while, but can't we restore them as we re-commit to one another? Or do we let these wasteful acts, these horrible choices born of temporary madness end our marriage?

"I think we're stronger than that. At least I hope so. I want to try. I want to rebuild what we have destroyed. We can reinforce the wall around our marriage that will protect it forever – rebuild what we have destroyed and reconstruct a life together.

"That is what I want. What about you?"

He stared at his feet, Brenda's figure reflected in his polished black shoe.

"We can hold each other accountable for what we have done – to ourselves, and to one another. If we can forgive. And move forward.

"What was it your father said about us? 'A reasonably viable marriage,' he called ours, as if describing a business deal that would pay dividends. Leave it to your father to trivialize something he could never appreciate or understand.

"We deserve this victory, Brenda. Over the challenges we have faced, over the loss of our daughter. Our acts of infidelity. And, importantly, over your father, and his determined, awful hatred of what we represent.

"Our marriage is much, much more than viable, Brenda, and if we can find the courage and strength to overcome this latest disaster, your father will never encroach upon our union again. Even our own flaws and weaknesses will be no match for the power we have together.

"What a wondrous victory for us, and what a fitting tribute to the memory of our daughter."

He took both her hands in his.

"You are what matters to me. Together, we are the center of my life, and you are the nucleus. Perhaps, with time, we can find a way to move forward. I'll try, if you will."

Ben looked deeply into Brenda's eyes. He saw hope, and yearning, along with loss, grief and isolation, and sadness and defeat, and wanting and acceptance. For the first time in months, he allowed himself to hope.

His optimism dissolved as Brenda fixed him with a cool, blank stare.

"There's more," she said. "Something horrible. It's about Belinda."

12

"Belinda? What about Belinda?"

Ben sat up, alarmed. He tried to speak, to ask questions, but failed. He nodded, encouraging Brenda to continue.

"There was a man…arrested in a county near Bedford Heights several months ago…for child molestation. He took a young girl from her front yard on a Sunday afternoon. Just like Belinda. But this time someone saw him and called the police. They stopped him not far from her home, arrested him, and returned the girl to her family, safe.

"He hadn't hurt her. She was the lucky one.

"At first they thought it was an isolated incident. He claimed to just want to take the little girl for ice cream; a harmless act of kindness on a hot afternoon, he said. After they questioned him, they became convinced that it wasn't the first time he had done something like that. They circulated advisories to other police departments, and word got to the Bedford Heights police department. When my father learned of it he demanded that Bedford Heights police join in the investigation, at least question the man. He thought he might have taken Belinda. For once in his miserable, selfish life, he did something positive.

"He was right."

Brenda spoke around sobs that choked her words. Ben rose to comfort her. She waved him back to his seat.

"It was him. They found a diary – the police – the man kept a *diary*, for God's sake!…extensive notes, photos…horrible details of all the children he had stalked, molested and….abducted. Ten children, perhaps more. All under 12 years old. Boys and girls: he was indiscriminate. All gone missing.

"Belinda was one of them. Photos of her among the ones police recovered. Polaroids, they said, kept in sort of a family photo album. They wouldn't show them to me. Too explicit, inappropriate, they said, unnecessary. So I'm left to imagine the horror he put her through.

"Police charged him with abduction and assault based on his diary, but they couldn't charge him with murder, because there was no body.

"That man took our daughter, Ben, and probably did unspeakable things to her before he discarded her like a damaged rag doll."

Ben stared at a spot on the wall behind Brenda as though envisioning safe haven behind the tattered wallpaper, or an escape route into the watercolor that depicted a quiet country lane. Tears painted salty rivulets from the corners of his eyes to the curve of his jaw. He shifted his gaze back to Brenda.

"Go on."

"It's all in the diary, Ben. He stalked Belinda. Watched her for weeks, with you, me, us. At my parents' home; at yours. He coveted her like a carnival prize, and wrote of his obsession. He watched, and waited…for weeks, it seems.

"He watched others, too, but it seems that Belinda was his primary focus.

"And then the day you were watching her. He saw you fall asleep, saw you nod off from where he was parked on the next street, watching you and Belinda through our back yard with binoculars. There's an entry in the diary. In specific, awful detail, of enticing her from the swing set in the back yard. They let me read it. I wish I hadn't.

"He told her I had asked him to come and get her, to take her for ice cream. He told her to let you sleep, that you were so tired from all the hard work, and that you needed to rest. He goaded her into his car by telling her to keep quiet. He knew she'd want to please you by letting you sleep.

"He preyed on what a good little girl she was. How kind, considerate and trusting she was. She *trusted* him. Remember how trusting she was? She was just like you. She had your soul, your kind, trusting heart that would give anyone the benefit of the doubt. And it cost her her life."

Brenda wiped her eyes with the back of her hand.

"It wasn't your fault, Ben. He was determined to take her, and it could as easily have been me as it was you.

"Do you hear me? It wasn't your fault.

"I spent all this time – all these months! - hating you, resenting you, blaming you for what I thought was your doing. *You* fell asleep. *You* let her go. *You* did this to her, to us. Oh, how I resented the fact that you were still here and she was gone. I'd have traded your life in an instant, if I could just have her back.

"I needed to blame you, or else I would have lost my mind. Honestly. Holding you accountable was the thin thread that kept me from going completely mad."

Brenda folded her hands.

"But I was wrong, Ben. For all these months. While I should have been comforting you, relieving you of guilt, sharing the loss with you and trying to find a way to continue together, I piled it on, adding more misery to the burden you already carried.

"I spent all my energy pushing you away, and the more you tried the harder I pushed.

"Yet you remained, somehow. You put up with my selfishness on top of your own feelings of loss and responsibility. I will never understand why you stayed with me. Or how. I never considered how you might have felt; what losing Belinda took from you. I was too wrapped up in my own loss to think about you.

"You carried on. Holding us together, working, providing, caring for me even as I ignored you. And then, when I went silent on you, my contempt fueled by my horrible father's determination to drive us apart, you just waited. Patiently, endlessly. My dear, wonderful Ben. How kind, and forgiving, and patient you have been.

"I am so…so very sorry, my love. For all I have done. To you. To us."

They sat unmoving on matching double beds, heads bowed, staring at an equidistant point on the floor, a neutral spot, as they contemplated whether to remain a couple or retreat into private, hopeless loss.

Ben's mind reeled.

"This is not what I expected. I don't know what I expected, but this? It's too much to absorb. So much I can barely breathe.

"I need to think," he said, rising from the bed and moving to the door. He picked up Brenda's suitcase, opened the door and stood in the doorway, his slight figure framed by the hallway light.

"Perhaps you should get your own room for the night. No more talk tonight. I am exhausted, and confused, and … I just need to think. And sleep. Yes, sleep. We should both sleep. Anything we will say, or think, will be clearer, more helpful, in the morning."

He glanced at his watch.

"Besides, I must be at the office in just a few hours," withdrawing to the confines of his work schedule.

She nodded in silent acquiescence, rose, and left, the door closing with a shudder that Ben felt deep in his core. The room collapsed around him, pulling him into cheap polyester silence that held him in sleepless embrace throughout the night, worried, uncertain, and once again, lost.

13

Ben squinted at the clock in the hallway, its iridescent numbers piercing the thickening dark.

"8:11. Late for dinner," he admonished himself. "I've been sitting here for more than an hour. Ruminating. Good lord."

If he ate at this late hour, he would lie awake throughout the night, tormented by indigestion and more memories. Solution: He would eat a light supper. *Eat late, won't feel great; Eat a lot, your belly's shot,* was his motto. He'd endured more sour stomachs from sleeping on a full stomach than he cared to recall, and had learned to dine accordingly.

"Right," he said aloud: "That's enough thinking for today. Time to refuel. But with what?" Then, "Eggs it is," and trudged to the kitchen.

He switched on the kitchen light, welcoming the glare from the overhead bulb as it chased the darkness from the room.

He removed two slices of brown bread from the loaf stored in the countertop breadbox. He scraped a green dot of mold from one and then popped both slices into the toaster and put a pan of water on the stove to a boil. Dinner would be two poached eggs, the yolks well done; firm, but not completely hard. That was how Brenda always liked her eggs, and Ben had adopted the standard. He flipped on the radio, spinning the dial to a talk radio station in search of a soft voice to keep him company.

He ate, serenaded by droning radio personalities whose words came and went without notice or impact. He heavily salted the eggs, as was his preference, imagining Brenda's scolding as he chewed *("If you persist in using that much salt you'll have a stroke. You'll wind up in diapers, drooling and unresponsive, as I force feed you oatmeal!").* He reserved a bit of buttered bread crust to mop up the last bit of yolk, herding pools of congealed egg in a broad circle around the plate to catch every last bit.

Finishing his meal, he washed the plate, pan and cutlery and put them away, then poured a glass of water to sip while he watched television. He paused at the sink, and his gaze took him through the kitchen window up the hill to Stonybrook.

He poured half of the glass of water into the sink.

Not too much before bed, or I'll be doing laps to the toilet all night long.

Wheel of Fortune repressed further memories until he heard 10 chimes on the clock in the hall.

He shut off the television and living room light and limped to the bathroom. He did his best to hurry from the dark, fleeing the gloom as if from a prison of horrid memories, stiff from sitting, and foggy-brained from television programming that absorbed the hours but did little to stimulate him. Most evenings he forgot to move while watching "the squawk box" and struggled to rise when bedtime arrived.

The apartment always seemed bigger at night, emptier. Footsteps echoed more loudly, faint creaks of the walls settling were more ominous, the dark more looming, invasive. Every shadowy corner threatened with memories, and heavy, reeking loss.

He changed into his pajamas and brushed his teeth, scanned the bathroom for order, and then eased into his side of the bed and reached for his waiting book, "Elizabeth is Missing," by Emma Healy. "A few pages'll help bring sleep," he reasoned, though the painful story of a woman afflicted by Alzheimer's was hardly the best bedtime story for a man desperately in need of a lullaby, the rhythmic sound of waves washing ashore, or a gentle poem to guide him to slumber.

"No rest for the wicked," he reasoned when he considered the unwise choice of bedtime reading, but still he read on, page by horrifying, mocking page.

His right hand shook as he balanced the book on his chest. He rolled to his left side and braced the book with his left hand. But his mind was elsewhere, and his concentration failed. He slid the bookmark into the spine, closed the book, and returned it to the bedside table. He shut off the light, and with a deep, mournful sigh, surrendered to the dark with open, searching eyes, and permitted the memories to fill the silent room.

#

Ben strode into the hotel dining room at 6 a.m., his habitual breakfast hour as long as he could remember. Brenda remembered, too, and she was waiting for him at a table by the window. She nodded him into the empty seat across from her. Two cups of steaming coffee rested on the table. A salt and pepper shaker, ketchup bottle and sugar dispenser formed a straight line that separated their place settings; sentries on watch in the marital demilitarized zone.

Both showed the effects of a sleepless night.

"I ordered for you," she said, fiddling with the napkin dispenser, her eyes flashing to meet Ben's, assessing and searching, and then out the window. "I knew you would want to eat quickly and be off to work. And I have a full day, too. I'm going to contact realtors so we can find a place to rent, short term, until we can sort out whether to buy or remain in an apartment."

All Brenda, again: All business, and having made so many assumptions. She would encounter no resistance from Ben.

"I have checked out of my room and will move my things to yours. There's no sense in spending money on my own when the company is paying for yours. You just need to stop by the desk on your way to work and ask them to add my name to the register and give me a key."

Ben cocked his head with a confused look at his wife.

So that's it? No mention of last night? There'll be no closure to all we discussed; no answers to the countless outstanding questions?

He considered broaching the subject of all that had happened during the previous weeks and months, to continue the previous night's talk, resolve unanswered questions.

Ben felt the power within their relationship swing back to Brenda. She sat before him, stoic, with clenched jaw. Firm, resolute, committed. She had moved on.

At once he recognized her approach as the wisest and only solution: *What's past is done; we only have here and now, and the future. We must proceed. Move on.*

He took a sip of the black coffee, bitter and scalding. Brenda broke the silence, acknowledging the awkwardness as only she could as she addressed Ben's unspoken worries.

"What's the point, Ben? Let it go. I think we understand one another, so let's focus on what's in front of us, not behind us."

And so, chapter closed. She breezily shifted focus.

"Our furniture is being stored in Ohio, but it's all packed so it can be shipped here when we are settled. I left our bank account open but with instructions to wire what's left in it to an account when I contact them. There's the proceeds on the sale of our home to consider, too. We have a limited amount of time to reinvest it in a new home or pay taxes on the capital gains."

She had done her homework.

"You should tell your payroll staff to stop sending money to the Ohio account right away. What must we do to add my name to your account here, to make it a joint account?"

Brenda's brisk attention to life's details confounded Ben. He had come to the dining room expecting to talk and perhaps resolve, but equally prepared to find Brenda distant, unapproachable, or worse, emotionally and intellectually absent. Yet here she was, organizing their life, as if the previous night, the lengthy separation, and all the events that had dominated their lives had never happened.

Brenda: back in control. Brenda: as he had always known her, stiff backed and neatly coiffed, fussing over his breakfast to help speed him on his way so they both could get on with their days. Roles re-established and agenda for the morning made clear, Ben relented, the balance of power once again clearly in Brenda's capable hands.

This was their comfortable place, a merger of common interests and shared values bound by history, familiarity and predictability.

Organized.

Competent.

Viable.

And what of love?

He sat across from her, hands drawing warmth from his coffee cup; silent and still, a sphinx in black pinstripes. She sensed his unease, and addressed it with a soft smile and slight squint that revealed steely resolve. Brenda had made up her mind – for both of them.

She reached across the table, pushing the salt and pepper apart to create a lane so she could reach his hand. She took it in hers, soft and accepting.

"It is as you said last night, Ben. Though we cannot forget, we can forgive. We must move on, together. We have history, and much that binds us together. That must be enough for now. No matter how flawed we may be individually, we are stronger, and far better off, if we are together.

"That's what's important. Together. We'll form a partnership, if you will; a marriage partnership to bring back some semblance of meaning. To get our lives back.

"There were many vows in our marital contract, and most remain intact, despite…well, in spite of all of the rest of it. There's so much, so many years, memories, so much good…it can bind us together, if we allow it. Trust, honesty, fidelity, openness, acceptance, partnership, commonality of purpose and values, and love."

She squeezed his hand.

"Perfectly viable. Remember?" she said, displaying something between a smile and a grimace. "My father's greatest insult." She puffed up her chest, mimicking the man in a mocking tone, 'What I see in you is a reasonably viable marriage…' " A shake of her head; smirking laugh. "What a damning, horrible thing to say. Or perhaps a challenge. Maybe with prescient insight that is more relevant to us right now than we would care to admit. Maybe viability is all we can expect at this point. Maybe that's enough. For now.

"So here we are. Viable. Can we find strength in what he created together? Is there enough left to salvage? Is there enough amid the rubble of this horrid mess for us to forge a new partnership?"

She sat back.

"Or do we give up. Go it alone. Convict each other for our transgressions and walk away. End it. Here and now. That's not what I want, and judging from what you said last night, I don't think that's what you want, either."

He nodded.

"Partnership. A partnership..." came his words. They slipped from his mouth as though describing a lengthy sentence in an unthinkable prison, or, perhaps, reconciliation. The future would reveal whether this moment would lead to incarceration or emancipation. He wrestled with the implications of what Brenda proposed.

"How clinical, sterile. Where once was a marriage built on trust and love has devolved into a partnership, as though it were negotiated in some boardroom for the benefit of some abstract group of shareholders. So that's what we are? Shareholders in a partnership? Survivor's rights for the chronically imperfect?"

He paused, head tilted to one side; assessing. Ben, in his element: cerebral, pensive, analytical and practical, and then decisive.

"Yes, I suppose that's us. Chronically imperfect survivors."

She took a sip from her coffee, leaving a thin deposit of red lipstick along the rim.

Brenda took Ben's assessment as a sign of capitulation, or agreement. She would accept either, but she had made her choice and was committed to her preferred outcome.

"Fine, then it's settled. We build a new life here together – far from my parents, the horrible memories of Ohio, and our past. We made mistakes...both of us, and many of them. We mustn't waste our time talking about it."

She picked up her coffee cup, blowing across the top to cool the inky liquid before taking a soft sip. She replaced the cup on the tabletop and centered it before her. She nodded as if to agree with herself and cement the possibility of a new beginning.

"So this is what you were looking for this morning, wasn't it, Ben? Some sort of closure, or understanding, or agreement? Something to put into context all that has happened over the past months? A cozy, heartfelt conversation to bring some sort of resolution? So here we are. Yes, let's put it all behind us, and never again speak of the whole sordid mess.

"Why would we? Why flog ourselves with our own imperfections?" She smiled softly. "As if we need the reminder. Perhaps the pain of our errors will inform our behavior going forward. What a wonderful gift that would be, wouldn't it? If we emerged from this mess intact, together, and perhaps even better and stronger. It is possible, isn't it?"

In that moment, Ben remembered why he loved Brenda so much, why he had remained hopeful of a life with the woman of his boyhood dreams who had become his wife, why his mistakes had caused him such intolerable pain, and why he found her own imperfections so easy to overlook and accept. This, an understanding reached between flawed humans with shared interests, in an acknowledgement of something bigger than either of them, was without question worth the effort of one last chance.

He took her hands. He realized that this diluted version of love and marriage that once formed the center of his universe was his only chance at redemption, at happiness, and at a fulfilling and contented life.

Cherish the small graces, he reminded himself.

Ben believed that conscious acts of acceptance imbue humans with quiet comfort; they give a warm, acquiescent glow of being at peace with circumstances beyond mortals' control. Acceptance is the antidote to conflict, and to emotional unease, giving grace to the most tormented of souls, and gifting even the most deeply flawed with a grounded sense of being.

Acceptance is the forward in the book of forgiveness.

For Ben, and the wrenching, soul-shattered loneliness he had endured during their separation, acceptance meant salvation.

"A merger. A partnership? Why not? We'll be co-CEOs. We'll do it the old-fashioned way: start with a sound partnership and let the love return in due course."

"Co-CEOs, then," she replied, just as the waitress arrived with two orders of poached eggs on dry whole wheat toast, the yolks cooked through fully, firm, but not to the point of being too hard. The presence of an outsider brought finality to the exchange. Something resembling normalcy returned to their lives, punctuated by eggs done to their liking and a quiet breakfast shared by a two friends who had navigated dangerous waters in the sea of marriage, and somehow emerged with a clear, unobstructed view of a new horizon that lie ahead.

#

Ben and Brenda looked on two weeks later as movers unloaded furniture and boxes, unpacking their history into a small rented bungalow. Their sofas, chairs, beds and kitchen items reattached their discordant lives, as the stuff of life

114

provided restorative glue to a fractured relationship. It took Brenda four days to organize their things and add the details that make a house a home. Ben got lost on his way home three days in a row before mentally recording landmarks to guide him to his garage.

They eased into a routine as a suburban couple, gradually mending emotional fences that separated them while projecting a public image of comfortable affluence: he, a pedigreed, respected corporate executive of substance with a master's degree in finance; she, college-degreed, eager volunteer and skilled homemaker who presented their socially affable, approachable side. On the surface, they appeared a childless, contented upper middle class couple with considerable upward mobility, respectability and potential. They were hot commodities in a culture that placed enormous value on projecting a certain pedigree to attract the right friends.

In the transient world of suburban San Diego, friendships were often built on arms-length awareness of social position rather than through heartfelt connections between people with much in common.

It was perfect for Ben and Brenda, as they worked to rebuild their life together.

As a college-educated woman with no career or children, Brenda was an anomaly. Most women in their social circle had high school educations and multiple offspring. She would listen attentively as her friends bemoaned their husbands' long hours at work, their children's reluctance to behave, and the pressures of balancing after school activities with the endless loads of laundry, PTA bake sales and social obligations. She would sigh into the comfortable solitude of her own home as she picked up the telephone to make dinner reservations at one of their favorite restaurants.

Ben's position and title earned cautious, envious respect among the men. Though he exuded a quiet, unapproachable quality and lacked the war stories that came with fatherhood, other men liked to have him around. He was an unknown, untested presence, abruptly appearing in midlife as an addition to the southern California social construct. Intelligent, well read, and articulate, he was a hovering, cerebral alpha male with a slight frame in an expensive suit; non-smoking, light-drinking and soft of word. He stood out as a redwood among scrub brush – focused, resolute – and an important fixture at social gatherings.

Ben and Brenda became highly sought after components of the frenzied Southern California cultural matrix. Brenda kept track of their hectic social schedule, and they logged one engagement after another, benefitting from the exposure though at times struggling with the commitment required to meet the demand.

All the dinners, barbecues and cocktail parties gave Brenda pleasure and meaning. She was careful to bring along a tasteful yet not ostentatious hostess gift, and to promptly send hand-written thank you notes after they had retreated once again into their quiet existence.

Ben tolerated but didn't relish these gatherings, nursing a Rob Roy as he answered the occasional direct question and avoided small talk, softly smiling from the side of the room as his wife held court, seated on the sofa in a friends' home surrounded by the other wives.

They appreciated the conspicuous anonymity of suburban life secured by an image they did little to promote but accepted on its merit. The veneer – a solid marriage with enviable success and upward mobility - provided the perfect cover, allowing them to maintain a healthy distance from a past of which their new friends knew little and never inquired about.

Such full lives also shielded them from their history and provided an important buffer between them at home. When Ben would arrive home from work, he would shower and don the fresh clothes Brenda laid out for him, tying a perfect Windsor knot in his tie while Brenda put the finishing touches on her makeup before heading out for the evening's entertainment. Returning home late at night, she with a light head from white wine, and he, exhausted from a day of work and a night of conversational tedium, would gift each other a quick peck on the cheek, then move to their respective bedrooms and promptly go to sleep.

They were rarely alone in the same room at home together and they accepted the parallel existence with quiet resolve. Far better to be immersed in constant activity than to address what really mattered under the awful, intrusive influence of introspection, candor and honest discourse.

At first, re-entry into married life had been awkward, disjointed; like two former political opponents who unnervingly found themselves on the same ticket. They moved into the house but retreated to separate bedrooms each night, Brenda into the master en suite bedroom, and he into minimalist guest sleeping quarters by the front door. There had been little physical contact, save for an occasional polite kiss or a slight touch of the hand.

It was an uneasy truce, a negotiated settlement of superficial co-existence that left crucial needs unattended, important words unspoken, and essential matters of the heart unattended, suppressed.

They cemented their roles in separate, complimentary existences. At work, Ben reclaimed his persona as a quiet yet powerful force whose opinion was the last sought but most valued. At home, he became the acquiescent enabler of Brenda's wishes. She oversaw the house keeper and gardener's efforts while cooking wholesome meals and keeping Ben's closet full of neatly pressed dress shirts, efficiently going about her day with quiet, predictable regularity. In the evenings she kept Ben informed about important dates, purchases and matters, all conveyed with sterile precision, impersonal and unemotional.

"You're off to New York on the 10th, correct?" she would ask.

"Yes, my dear. Back in time for the philharmonic fund-raiser on the 13th," came the response.

Problems resolved.

Issues addressed.

Questions asked and answered.

Professional therapy – had they been of the minds to indulge in such self-care – would have exposed a relationship riven by guilt, overshadowed by remorse, and desperately in need of honest talks, openness, and intimacy if it were to be salvaged. Theirs was a marriage tenuously toggling between lifeless acquiescence and dissolution, and Brenda and Ben were powerless to make it otherwise.

They saw their lot as an alternative to the independent solitude they wanted to avoid. Far better to function in parallel existence that gave them the comforts they sought and the emotional separation they required than to give up on their marriage. They embraced the chance to prove her father wrong and demonstrate the immense power of their union, tattered as it may have been. History gave them a common bond and purpose; contempt for her father and his failed effort to drive them apart gave them reason to re-create a life together.

It was enough, barely, and Ben and Brenda wordlessly accepted the truce and the inherent isolation it imposed as they spent hours under the same roof.

At home, Ben was content to let Brenda call the shots, and he blithely went along with whatever she wished.

She wanted to dine out; he made a reservation. She proposed a neighborhood barbecue; he got the grill out of the garage and made sure there were plenty of charcoal briquettes. She wanted to watch a movie on television; he abandoned the baseball game with two on in the bottom of the ninth and handed her the remote control.

He never questioned or challenged her choices, motives or ideas, and he exuded a quiet calm about his life of parallel existence with his wife. Ben's chosen path had always been the one of least resistance, and he found happy comfort amiably bumping along the marital road as he watched the miles speed by from the passenger seat.

His behavior was informed by pervasive guilt, as though a giant sphere of pressure hovered over him, reducing his status within their marriage and stripping him of an independent voice. The contrast between Ben at work and Ben at home - had anyone had the insight or occasion to witness it - might have been cause for great concern.

Ben compartmentalized the fact of his dual personality. He simply switched personae when he arrived home, smiled softly, and waited for something different.

"Well, g'night, then," he said, switching off the television at the conclusion of the 11 o'clock news.

"Right," came the response. "Eggs tomorrow?"

"That'll be great," and Ben would place a furtive kiss on Brenda's cheek as she turned her face to receive the sterile peck.

Change arrived when he came home from work one day and found his bed stripped of sheets and his suits gone from the closet in the spare room. To his surprise, they had been moved to the walk-in closet in the master bedroom. His shaving kit rested on the sink in the en suite bathroom and his pajamas were neatly folded on one side of Brenda's queen-sized bed.

That night he quietly resumed sleeping by his wife's side. It was a wordless emotional journey of a million miles made in a fleeting, decisive moment when Brenda allowed her husband back into her life, her private moments, and their bed.

He joined her beneath the sheets, and with his back turned toward her curled into a semi-fetal position that mirrored Brenda's and fell asleep.

Brenda lay quietly, eyes open, listening to Ben's rhythmic breathing as the red figures on her digital clock radio marked the passing hours.

One night soon after they resumed sharing a bed, she reached across the void between them. She helped him shed his pajamas and initiated their first lovemaking in many lonely months. It was a tender, tenuous coupling they both enjoyed cautiously yet immensely before falling deeply asleep, back to back. Sometime during the night Ben rolled over, snaked a hand around her hips and pulled her close, breathing deeply of her hair and collapsing into a sleepy calm.

"Until soon," he whispered into the dark, unaware of the tears of joy that glistened on Brenda's face as she nestled next to him.

Sex became a rare but deeply appreciated part of their reconstructed marriage, and it slowly helped to restore the crumbled foundation of their relationship. Afterwards, Ben would draw her into his embrace, smoothing her hair as they talked, voices gentle and low in the comforting dark.

Openness and honesty slowly returned as a hallmark of their relationship.

They re-lived their earlier years.

They talked about their separation, and of the pain that had grown as the cold distance between them had expanded.

They spoke of Belinda, softly recalling their happy days as parents, and of the gnawing loss they both felt but could not share when she was first taken, and again when each learned her fate.

They talked about his mother and father, and how sad they were to have been unavailable to his parents as the end of their lives coincided with Belinda's disappearance.

They talked about Brenda's horrible father, and her voiceless mother.

They discussed Bedford Heights, its stubborn grip on Midwest values, and how grateful they were to be out of the city's dispiriting influence.

They talked about fairness, and inequality, and life in California, and politics, and religion, and the economy; even the fruitless point of being San Diego Padres fans.

There was no talk of their affairs. Or of the months they had wasted in voiceless co-existence.

Often Ben crooned songs of their courtship into the still night, steering them from conversation and into a happy place as husband and wife. Once she slipped into slumber, Ben, too, would fall into uninterrupted, dreamless sleep. Hours later he would awaken, refreshed, to an empty bed and the smell of coffee percolating in the kitchen.

Life was good, again.

Until the letter arrived.

14

Ben knew something was amiss when he walked through the kitchen door.

Dirty breakfast dishes were piled in the sink. The pan from the morning's poached eggs rested on the stove, encrusted foam clinging to its edge along with the slotted spoon Brenda had used to lift the eggs from the hot water. Toast crumbs littered the countertop, and a package of butter rested on the counter, open and softening in the bright, warm room. The light over the sink burned brightly, even though the afternoon sun filled the room with its brilliant yellow glow.

Clutter was anathema to Brenda's sense of order, and on days like this one when the house keeper was off she typically washed, dried and returned dishes to their orderly stack minutes after they had consumed the meal's last bite. She would wipe the countertops clean with vinegar and water, dry the surfaces with a paper towel, and snap the light off in a routine of frugality.

Such mess in the kitchen under any circumstances would spell trouble. This was more serious: An entire day had passed as Brenda ignored the disorder.

Something was wrong.

He called out to her. Silence.

He placed his briefcase on the floor by the kitchen door and called her name again, louder, as he moved with growing alarm to the kitchen's center island. His eye fell on a small stack of the day's mail. An open letter rested atop the pile. Ben picked it up and read.

Daughter...

I will come urgently to the point which must be made, lest you continue to act as a spoiled child and maintain a charade I can no longer abide, and which promises to ruin your life. I hope this letter will help you come to your senses and return to the life your mother and I always intended for you, but which you seem resolved to disavow.

Your mother and I have invested heavily in your intellectual and social development, sacrificing greatly in your benefit and never asking for much in return. We had hoped that you would benefit from what we have taught you, and that our family's sphere of influence would expand into new horizons with the addition of a suitable husband who would give us grandchildren and a full, rich life.

Now, however, we doubt that our wishes will come to fruition.

We held our tongues and tolerated your pursuit of independence as evidence of a young woman's normal development, but we now find your strong-mindedness little more than misdirected, wanton behavior that we can only interpret as intentional acts designed to cause us discomfort.

It is time for you to grow up, acknowledge your station in life, and for once do the right thing. Since you fail to appreciate the grievous error you are making, it is my duty as your father to review the facts of your poor judgment, and to demand that you immediately return to Bedford Heights.

How ironic that while most find my position in Bedford Heights enviable and admirable, my daughter alone seems to not only shirk her duties as my progeny but is committed to dishonoring not only her own potential, but also much of what I have worked hard to create.

Now, your shameful behavior is affecting my own stature in the community, and this I cannot allow. Your mother, too, is suffering, and has even stopped going to the club to avoid the tormenting looks, gossip and hurtful laughter behind her back. I suspect you care little for my wishes; I am dismayed to think you feel as careless toward your mother's comfort and feelings.

You have always failed to appreciate the opportunities of your life, but now your own failures are causing us difficulty. You have pushed us to a line which we will not cross.

We were not able to address this issue in person since you left for California in such a state of anger and disarray, and since I have such contempt for telephone conversations I am forced to write my thoughts to you. It pains me to be forced to take this extreme step. I assure you this will be the last of such missives.

So, the facts.

I know of your dalliance with my business associate Mr. Whitney. All of it. Why wouldn't I? I encouraged him to pursue you. In fact, I arranged it.

I did so with an interest in your future, as I have always acted.

Mr. Whitney is the sort of man I have always envisioned as a worthy son in law; reputable, wealthy, hard working. His business and political interests align well with my own, and he would have made an ideal partnership to help our family grow and prosper. After the introduction I arranged at our home, I was pleased to learn that the two of you had found commonality, and though I would have preferred not to have known the sordid details of your interpersonal exploits, I was encouraged to learn that the two of you had cemented your relationship in the physical sense.

I thought you would acknowledge the value of partnering with a man like Mr. Whitney, and forever turn from the sorry excuse of a "husband" you once again pursue. I thought your upbringing would instruct you at long last to make a wise choice instead of the absurd path you have followed since leaving our embrace and attending university.

Once again, sadly, your actions proved me wrong.

You shock me not only with your moral turpitude, but also by your rejection of a man far superior in all regards to the one with whom you continue to consort.

I also know you read the file in my desk drawer that detailed your "husband's" movements, and that the documents therein contradicted what I told you had happened between Ben and his secretary. I am sure you hold me in contempt for my misappropriation of facts. How typical of your self-indulgence, and of your short-sightedness.

A father's duty is paramount, a fact you would fail to understand or acknowledge, of course, since God has punished your weakness by denying you the chance to serve as mother to our poor, lost granddaughter. A father must do what a daughter is incapable of imagining. It is thankless work; far more than I had expected or envisioned, but a fact nonetheless that I shall die knowing well, having learned it repeatedly at your uncaring, misguided hand.

I should think you would value the interest and judgment I made in your behalf. Financial security is a clear path to family happiness, and it was with this fact in mind that I worked to create a satisfactory path for your future.

I see now that you lack both the capacity and interest in understanding that I have always acted in your best interest. But I am willing to give you one final chance to redeem yourself.

You must return to Bedford Heights within one month. This is ample time to rid yourself forever of the inferior man you chose for marriage, and resume the life your mother and I envisioned for you, assuming it is not too late for us to use what influence we still have in this regard to help you at long last begin acting like an adult.

Sadly, it is too late to consider Mr. Whitney as part of our family's future. He is engaged to marry another young woman whose parents will thus enjoy the increased stature of such an alliance. As mayor, I will attend their wedding, but it will be with a sense of profound disappointment that my foolish daughter will not be the lucky woman at the altar.

Perhaps another man will see the value of you as his wife and will fill the void I can no longer permit to weaken the structure of our family.

You may think you have the strength and ability to go it alone. Do not be fooled; you will fail. Women have neither the aptitude nor capacity to find independent success in this world, which is designed and organized for the benefit of men. Indeed, look at your own pathetic life thus far. What can you say you have accumulated by your own effort, versus what your floundering husband has accomplished?

So you will see the futility of choosing anything but my offer.

One month, daughter. Return, apologize to your mother, and resume your life here. Or I will re-structure my will to reflect the fact that you are no longer part of my life, and your mother and I shall turn our backs to you.

Do not call, and do not respond by letter. I will understand your intent either from your presence at our front door within the month, or by your absence from our lives forever.

Regards,

Your father

Ben dropped the letter on the table and rushed from the kitchen in a panic to find Brenda. The living room was empty, as was their bedroom. He strode to the closed bathroom door and approached softly, cautiously, and gently knocked on the door.

"Brenda, my love. Please, Brenda. Can I come in?"

Nothing.

He tried the knob.

Locked.

"Please, Brenda. Open the door. We can talk about this. It's just a letter. It's just your father. It's all right, my love. I am here."

Moments passed, then the door opened with a faint "snick" of the lock, and Brenda was in his arms.

"It's all right, my dear. That horrible man cannot reach you. Not through me. Not ever."

He took her tear-streaked face in his hands: "Nothing has changed. You are safe. Here, with me."

15

"You are safe. Here with me...."

Ben woke with a start. He glanced at the clock next to the bed, the numbers a fuzzy orange blur in the still gray of morning. The dream – nightmare, or apparition? – receded as he struggled to read the time. He fumbled for his glasses, worried that he had overslept, then squinted at the clock: 5:48.

What day is it? Tuesday?

Still early. I'm not late at all, though it's time to get cleaned up, and get breakfast started.

He rolled to his right, imagining Brenda curled in the fetal position, her favorite sleeping pose. Solitude rushed at him as he surveyed her empty half of the bed, with its undisturbed pillow and perfectly tucked sheet and blanket.

Ben rested in the stillness, gathering his thoughts as his heart pounded in rhythmic loneliness. A tear gathered at the corner of his eye. His lips twitched. Sadness, sorrow and loss returned with the new day.

"No! I will not wallow. I am not alone. Not as long as she is still with me in spirit. Not as long as I can see her. Not as long as I can hold her hand, help her remember. As long as I can be near her, there is still plenty of us to make today worthwhile. Plenty of good. Plenty of time."

Thus resumed Ben's daily struggle between fact-based reality and boundless positivism. Having been imbued from childhood with a spirit of hope, trust, and with a firm grip on "positive mental attitude" as one of life's strongest allies, Ben confidently rolled into the daily battle against Brenda's disease with commitment and focus. As the hours of each day wound past, he found his energy on the wane, his guard relaxed. Then, when he was least able to repel the onrushing truth of Brenda's one-way march toward an unhappy ending, he would withdraw to his condo, to refuel, retreat, and search for the strength to begin the battle again the next day.

Mornings had become a ritualistic challenge to fight back worries and fears, set aside memories that had visited in dreams or haunted him as he lay awake in the dark, willing the moments to pass so he could re-stock his emotional larder with ample supplies to sustain his soul through the day.

Brenda might fight through the fog, if only briefly.

Ben's belief system left ample room for a miracle.

He must be available, and prepared.

He wiped away the tears and rose, muscles complaining and knees cracking as he made the bed and shuffled to the bathroom. He stared in the mirror as he brushed his teeth.

Dark circles framed both of his eyes, the product of restless sleep caused by the omnipresent memories. His hair was in disarray, and he smoothed it with a shaking right hand. Everything was taking more time this morning. Even more than usual.

Right. Off you go. No time for poached eggs today.

After breakfast – a generous dollop of yogurt, four slices of banana, eight raisins and an English muffin sparingly painted with butter and topped with a dollop of Dundee's marmalade, Brenda's favorite – Ben washed and dried the dishes.

He glanced at the clock as he entered the hallway: 7:33. *Perfect – right on schedule.* He showered, brushed his teeth and carefully shaved the gray stubble from his chin, giving extra caution to protect his face from the razor in his quivering right hand. He splashed cold water on his face to clear the scattered blotches of shaving cream, and then blotted it dry with a towel. He looked for any small cuts and, finding one on his chin, dabbed the wound with a styptic pencil.

He dressed, scrutinizing his shirt for signs of errant bits of food from the previous night's dinner.

Would Brenda notice that he was wearing the same clothes as yesterday? Unlikely.

He sniffed the armpit of his shirt and declared it wearable.

It will have to do. I cannot be late.

Ben had always dressed in fresh clothes Brenda meticulously cleaned, pressed and organized. Unfamiliar with the skills required to keep a store of clean clothes, he had been an unconscious beneficiary of her labors. She laid out his suits and dress shirts, always careful to select a complementary-colored tie and appropriate socks, and would nod approvingly before he left for work, a quality control agent in a conservative house dress and protective apron.

He missed her efforts to make sure he was presentable.

To stay reasonably on top of the issue after Brenda moved to Stonybrook Acres, Ben committed to a firm schedule to keep his clothes clean and pressed. Friday evening was for laundry, and the night for ironing in the hazy glare of whatever game show was on the television. Without Brenda's careful guidance, Ben's dubious sartorial taste and lack of attention to detail risked bizarre combinations of stripes and plaids, earth tones with rainbow colors, and mismatched socks. Shirt collars were often left wrinkled, and handkerchiefs were clean but never pressed.

He concocted a schedule to recycle his clothes as laundry day drew near, often wearing a shirt or trousers several times before washing.

Occasionally he failed to spot food stains when he donned a shirt for the second or third wearing, arriving to visit Brenda with a blotch of marmalade on his shirt or a coffee stain on his trouser leg. He botched the ironing with appalling incompetence, and he stopped wearing white shirts after burning a deep brown stain into one with a dry steam iron. Creases often abandoned, his trousers hung from his narrow hips in spiritless displays of inattention. More than one pair bore the scar of an iron left in one place for too long.

"I am one beard short of Abraham Lincoln," he jokingly appraised himself in the bedroom's full length mirror, critically scanning the length of his lanky body until his eyes fell on the brilliant brown luster of his carefully polished brogues.

Ben cleaned his shoes every night, applying two layers of shoeshine buffed to a brilliant shine first by the brush reserved for the act, and then by the soft cloth that rested in the shoeshine kit by his bed. The spit-shine finish was achieved courtesy of an enthusiastic discharge from Ben's quivering mouth that over the years challenged his ability to aim straight.

Much of the routine of Ben's life had been torn apart by Brenda's disease.

"I'll be damned if I'll let my shoe maintenance slip into the chaos that otherwise rules my life," he groused to himself.

Ben lived in fear of a disapproving evaluation by his wife when he presented himself each day, but Brenda hadn't spoken a word about Ben's clothing since she had been admitted to Stonybrook.

"I could just as well turn up in pajamas," he unhappily mused on more than one occasion, "as much as she'd know or care."

He dressed as best as he could in a daily process that Ben struggled with but took seriously; a final, lasting commitment to impress the woman of his dreams and earn an approving smile.

He glanced again at the clock: 8:11.

"Oh, dear. Now I'm late."

Raincoat donned, hat atop his balding pate, and with umbrella in hand, he scurried out the apartment's exit and hurried onto the steps to the sidewalk below. He misjudged the top step and tumbled, missing the railing when he reached with his right hand to catch himself. He failed with his left to break the tumble, and his forehead smashed into the sidewalk, body crumpling around him in an angular pile. He lay there, unconscious, a deep head wound leaking rich red blood onto gray sidewalk, until a horrified neighbor found him moments later.

After checking to confirm he was breathing, she shielded him from the drizzle with her overcoat and rushed inside to call an ambulance.

16

It's so bright…too bright…the light…what on earth? Did I leave the lights on?

This bed…it's so hard…so unfamiliar. Where am…

My eye! Dear God, I can't see out of my right eye!

Ben lifted his right hand to his eye to determine what was blocking his vision. His arm hurt, and a thick bandage restricted its movement, but he forced his hand to the patch that covered his right eye, evaluating it with shaking fingertips. A bolt of pain radiated from a spot just above his eye to his temple and across the crown of his head. Pain shot from his bandaged arm as well as he walked his fingers up his forehead to the injured spot, shocked when he encountered a baseball-sized bump that was – like his eye – covered with gauze.

His left eye darted around the unfamiliar surroundings, assessing the fluorescent overhead light, the thick blue privacy curtain, and the intravenous fluid bag that hung from a stainless steel pole attached to the side of the bed. He scowled at the thin plastic tube that ran from the bag into his right arm, disappearing under the bandage.

He tried to sit up, but the agony in his head, arm and back forced him back onto the bed. A shadowy figure drew close. A hand extended, gently resting on his shoulder, warm and consoling.

He addressed the figure, a woman clad in blue who slowly came into focus, with scattershot questions born of confusion and distress.

"Where am I?

"What happened?

"Where is Brenda?"

"Mr. Tremblay….Ben. You are in Mercyfield Hospital," came a soft, feminine voice.

Not Brenda. Who?

"My name is Elizabeth. I am an emergency room nurse. You have had an accident, and you are in the hospital. You've had a nasty fall, but you are in good hands now.

"Do you know what day it is?"

"Tuesday. No, Wednesday. No, wait. It is most definitely Tuesday. Cribbage day. No, not cribbage day. I don't play cribbage any more. What time is it? And where did you say I am? Hospital? What time is it? I must be on my way. Brenda will be expecting me..."

Agitated, Ben again tried to sit up, but a new round of pain and the soft pressure of gentle hands forced him back to the bed.

"You fell outside your apartment. You have a concussion and head wound that required a few stitches," the nurse told him. "You are going to be fine, but you need to rest now."

"No! I can't rest. Brenda will be looking for me, waiting for me. You must understand..."

"Your neighbor...Mrs. Stinson...the woman who found you, told us about your wife and your circumstances. We have alerted Stonybrook Acres about your accident, so you needn't worry."

"But Brenda..."

"Brenda is fine, but you are not. The doctor will be in to see you in a moment but you are going to be here for a while so we can learn what happened to you. We need to run some more tests to make sure you have no other serious injury other than your arm and the bump on your head..."

"Tests? My arm? What's wrong with my arm?"

The nurse spoke softly to Ben, outlining the injuries he had sustained while reassuring him that he would survive the fall. Six stitches had closed the gash on his head. His right arm was broken in two places. The doctor had placed a temporary cast on his arm, and she would soon replace it with a permanent version. He had deep bruises on his back, shoulder and neck, but x-rays showed no additional broken bones.

"You are going to be very sore for a few days. Is there anyone we could call? Family? Friends?"

Ben shook his head, groaning at the pain that came in response.

"No. There is only Brenda. Brenda and me. Only us."

The nurse spent a few moments to reassure him, then tugged the curtains closed around his bed as she retreated, leaving him in a sterile cocoon.

Time passed. Thirty minutes? An hour? The curtain parted and an older woman with a stethoscope draped around her neck eased to the side of the bed. She smiled at Ben, inquired how he was feeling and looked into his left eye.

"Mr. Tremblay. We're going to admit you for observation and further tests," the doctor began, placing a reassuring hand on his shoulder when he protested.

"You're quite lucky, actually. Only a broken arm, and that'll heal quickly. A gentleman of your *experience* who takes a tumble like that often winds up with far worse. I want to take another look at the bump on your head once the swelling goes down in a day or so, and we'll order a CAT scan to make sure there's no damage beyond the obvious.

"But that's not what concerns me most. Your initial blood work showed some anomalies that I want to investigate…"

Admit me to the hospital? Tests? Anomalies?

"That's not possible," Ben interrupted. "I must be on my way. My wife will be expecting me, and she sometimes gets terribly agitated if I am as much as an hour late. She is a patient at Stonybrook Acres, and she is all alone there. I am all she has, and if I do not arrive on time…."

The doctor spoke in reassuring tones.

"Mr. Tremblay…may I call you Ben?" Ben nodded in assent. "Great. Ben, your blood tests revealed signs that warrant a further look. I want to look deeper before we discuss what it might be."

She continued, outlining her concerns without providing specifics. Ben pressed for more, gently at first, but then with growing insistence. The doctor's words faded into a faint haze as Ben lost focus, confused and worried.

"Neuro-muscular...progressive...debilitating...possibility of Parkinson's, or perhaps Pheochromocytoma...sorry, that's a certain kind of tumor..."

The doctor's urgent tone brought him back to the present.

"I don't mean to frighten you, and these are only suspicions, possibilities at this point, but there's enough evidence to suggest we look further. The tests could be negative, or inconclusive. We want to rule out anything serious before we send you on your way.

"So there you have it. That's why I want to keep you around for a bit. Take a closer look. Again, I really don't know anything conclusive at this point. Normally I wouldn't care to speculate, but since you insisted on knowing. Since you asked..."

"Did I?"

"Yes, Ben. You did."

Her words fell away as Ben fretted.

The thought of being in a hospital for hours, let alone a full day or more, separated from Brenda and a routine that he believed delayed Alzheimers' assault on his wife and held his marriage in place, was unacceptable. Brenda might become agitated, worried.

Would she think Ben had forgotten to visit? Fallen ill? Died overnight and left her without saying goodbye? What if she was having a good day, when they might have talked and reminisced and here he was, lying in a hospital bed, missing a moment that might be the last such chance?

His mind raced. They couldn't force him to remain in the hospital, could they, or to consent to tests if that was not his wish? He said as much to the doctor.

"No, I can't keep you here against your will, but I strongly advise you to take my advice and let us find out what's going on. You know, rule out the bad stuff. I just want to be able to give you a clean bill of health, or help if you need it," she concluded.

Ben thanked her and said was grateful for the care and concern, but he was eager to be on his way. They parried over the conflicting interests of patients' rights and responsible medical care before the doctor suggested a negotiated settlement: she would discharge Ben if he would agree to return to the hospital within a week for further tests.

It seemed as good a deal as Ben could hope for with the persistent yet kindly doctor, so he agreed, rested, and waited for her to return to put the permanent cast on his arm and sign him out.

Brenda was waiting, and he was very, very late.

He relaxed into the hospital pillow, lulled by the gentle buzz of the emergency ward activities, and let his thoughts drift.

17

The letter lay between them in the center of the table next to half empty coffee cups and plates dotted with toast crumbs from the dinner they had consumed without notice.

Ben drummed his fingers on the table as he stared at Brenda, waiting for her to break the silence.

She sat slumped against the chair, fingers steepled against her forehead as though bowed in prayer.

Ben picked the letter up and read it again.

He folded it carefully and slid it back into the envelope.

Studied his wife.

Weighed his words.

"We should burn this, Brenda," he began, watching for a sign, hoping for clarity, wanting to help. "He's an evil, malevolent man..the most selfish, thoughtless, arrogant person I have ever known...."

"Stop," came the quiet rebuke. "I am well aware of how horrible my father is. After all he has done to me...to us...my childhood, full of fear and doubt, fed by his need to control and manipulate, my school years, under his heavy thumb, and the college years, all carefully controlled by a man whose only real interest is his own stature. And then our marriage, which he condemned yet condoned when he sensed that my will might be strong enough to challenge his.

"Burn the letter?" She picked up the envelope and waved it in the air, her eyes flashing with anger. "Oh, no. We're not going to burn this. We're going to keep it; preserve it. As a reminder of my father's cruelty, and all he has done to us. After all we've been through.

"Belinda's death, which he blamed on you, of course, and then fed my own need to assign responsibility for a loss that meant more to me than I could have imagined. Our separation. Even our wedding day, which he did everything in his power to ruin.

"Honestly, Ben. When I think back on all the cruelty, selfishness, the mean-spirited interference … it's as though my father takes delight in tormenting me. It's as though he's settling a score with me; like he resents me - views me as an expensive, inconvenient impediment.

"How different our values are, as if a man like him could conceive of such a thing as values. His twisted sense of duty, his selfish way of turning what I might want into an affront upon his grand plan of 'financial security for our entire family.' How cruel. And how utterly contemptible.

"Values, hah! His values are power, and affluence, and superiority. And domination."

A pause. And then:

"How much he must hate me!"

A thought occurred to her.

"Not so much as a word from my mother, on this, or on any other conflict between us and my father. Over all these years. And now this. What does my mother think of all this?"

She raised her eyes to Ben's. Cocked her head. This was no time for him to speak, so he nodded, encouraging her to continue.

"My mother. How could my mother tolerate him? How could she live with such a monster? How could she allow him to be what he has been to me, to us? How spineless is she, and what is the limit of her cowardice?"

Years of repressed anger added a sharp edge to her voice.

"We know what kind of man my father is. But what kind of a woman is she? What kind of a mother? She never protected me, or looked out for me as I cowered in his shadow! She never stood up for me! Defended me to that horrid, sorry excuse for a father! Not once! Even when I lost my own child, when the pain of loss made my own life seen worthless, she blithely stood by and bowed to him. Oh, how he enslaved her, and how she capitulated. It's the worst form of abuse; a weak, dominated woman who failed to find the strength to defend her only child from the manipulations of a selfish, hateful man who doesn't deserve a daughter!"

Tears flowed as Brenda's words tumbled over one another.

"It's not fair! Not right! Why should she be allowed to have a child, and I denied the pleasure? She is incapable of love, both as a mother, and a wife! That's my mother: an empty shell of a human being, wed to a soulless, unloving man whose catechism is power, and position, and wealth!

"Why was I doomed to be their daughter, yet denied the chance to be parent to my own?

"What kind of God would deny me the opportunity to correct all the wrongs my father did to me by being a loving mother to my own child?"

She slumped onto the table, sobbing. Her shoulders rose and fell with each surge of pain purged after decades of torment. Ben moved to her side, dragging his chair around the table. He draped an arm around her shoulders. Soothed her hair with his right hand while his left cupped her shoulder, pulling her into the safety of his embrace. He waited for time to pass, her sobs to diminish, and to allow his thoughts to coalesce.

"There are mysteries, and there are truths," he began.

"The mystery is all you say, and more. The 'whys' and 'what if's'…all of them. And your questions are all valid, though perhaps unanswerable. All the things people like you and me will never understand. What we'd never be capable of, and which shall remain awful mysteries.

"And there are truths, too, like you, and me, and us. What we feel, what we think, and what we say. And what we do.

"In the end there is only us, Brenda. Not your mother, or your father. Just us. After all the difficulty, and pain, and the brutality of being raised by two wooden caricatures of what a mother and father ought to be, there is just us. And what we must do.

"And this, my loving, wonderful wife, is what we must do: We must go on. It's the only way to find comfort in a final separation from our pasts, from where and what we come, far away from the awful influence of a father you have every right to loathe and a mother who has done nothing to deserve you.

"We must survive, and thrive. Live well, in silent defiance of that hideous man and that dreadfully silent woman. Your mother is complicit, but it's your father we must defy. His words may hurt and his actions may cause discomfort, but we must recall the strength of what he called 'a viable marriage' but which far exceeds the power and value of his own accomplishments. We must be the living testament to a better way of living, a marriage so strong that even he cannot breach its perimeter."

Brenda's sobs ebbed as Ben spoke softly. The clock on the wall marked time as he outlined a new order for their lives that would create an emotional distance from Brenda's parents. It was a path from their tormented past and the influence of a dysfunctional family toward happiness that would follow Ben and Brenda through the rest of their lives.

"It's back to us, Brenda, and to what binds us to one another, what drives and sustains us. Our vows. Yes, our vows: Trust. Honesty. Fidelity. Openness. Acceptance. Partnership. Commonality of purpose and values. And love. Lots and lots and lots of love.

"We'll show him by acting and living well, and by rising to the challenge we set forth in our marriage vows," Ben whispered soothingly into his wife's eager ear. "And we'll show your mother, too. Yes, my love. We'll show them both. Viable marriage, indeed! We are so, so much more than viable.

"We are essential."

18

Ben closed his eyes and tried to relax as he waited for the doctor to return.

Opened them again, and scowled at the clock on the wall. 1:45.

Good lord. Brenda will have eaten her lunch, and she'll be ready to be tucked into bed for her nap. Where on earth has that doctor got to? How could so many hours have passed...the day is nearly half over!

Ben felt adrift.

"My wife is my purpose in life, my sole focal point," Ben would say when the subject of their marriage came up in the few social engagements he attended on his own. He would linger at the edges of the room, nursing a drink and minimizing small talk. Now and again, if prompted, he would open up if the subject of Brenda or their marriage were broached.

"We have a partnership, a contract of sorts, which has endured through it all. Throughout our marriage, we have shared many qualities, many values, all of which emanate from the vows we made to one another at our wedding 60-plus years ago. One of them is commonality of purpose and values. We have always had the same goals at heart, whether it's family affairs, or financial, or professional. Always.

"At first it was the simple stuff: where to live, how to pay all those bills with so little money in the till; what to have for dinner.

"Then it was tactical: who would make the money (me) and who would spend it (she, but always carefully, and with keen oversight of our savings account)? Later, our focus was on how to plan for a future of freedom, choice and comfort after the working years had passed? How we would manage the things people do to move their lives forward after work and family are no longer the priorities?

"These days, it's more about survival. Brenda depends on me to survive, and I on her for the same. We simply require each other's presence to start and end

each day. It's as though our lungs won't work after awhile if we're not breathing the same air. We are each other's essential truth. Without Brenda, I might as well not be breathing at all. She is nourishment for my soul, and the blood of my life."

The nurse had covered him with a soft, warm blanket, and he felt the fatigue and the stress of the day tug him toward gentle slumber. He let his mind float, and was soon consumed by memories of a time in his marriage that now seemed more vital, more significant, and more poignant than ever.

# # #

"Commonality of purpose and values...the seventh component of our marital vows. Remember?" Brenda asked one Saturday morning months after her father's letter arrived.

They had relaxed into their weekend ritual. Ben had retrieved the newspaper from the front stoop while Brenda made coffee and peeled two oranges – one for each of them - and they met in the bedroom to slip between the covers, share sections of the paper, sip coffee, munch on orange sections and discuss current events.

The smell of rich coffee blended with the spicy hint of orange as the rising sun painted the room with a faint yellow glow.

"Of course I do," Ben responded, removing his reading glasses and gifting her with a soft smile. "I remember every word of our vows. Why do you ask?"

"My father's 90th birthday is next month, and I've been thinking about it, and him, and us, and, well, all of it."

Since the letter, Brenda rarely mentioned her mother and never her father. The letter had destroyed what thin tether remained to Bedford Heights, and to her parents. Her parents' existence had become one more issue best left alone, a festering emotional wound too sensitive to touch, let alone scratch. Since repairing the marital bridge that joined them, Ben and Brenda had become cautious in choosing conversation subjects. Forbidden issues included Belinda, their respective forays into destructive realm of infidelity, and their separation. Now, her parents topped the list of topics best avoided.

Ben's work and his career were favorite subjects. He was nearing retirement age, and they frequently spoke of what might come next when it was time to retire. She wanted to paint; he to garden. Both wanted to travel. They loved to "motor," as Ben referred to the languid Sunday afternoon drives they often took through the California countryside, and they yearned to pursue the open road with no planned return.

"I've been thinking it might be time for you to retire. Maybe we could celebrate with a trip. A cross-country drive would be nice," she suggested, "and if we were to go through Ohio, perhaps it's time to visit my parents. They're getting old, and so much time has passed."

Ben stared at her, withholding his thoughts. He waited, expecting more. Brenda didn't disappoint.

"It took me most of my life to see my father for the evil force that he is. I grew up afraid of him, always prepared for him to disapprove, or punish me for some minor transgression, always fearful that I would fail to live up to his expectations.

"I can't recall my father complimenting me, or encouraging me, or telling me that he was proud of me. All I remember is the scolding, the disapproval; always pushing me, demanding that I do better, that I live up to his expectations. And him making it abundantly clear all along that I had failed."

Brenda's voice had taken on a cold, thick quality she reserved for discussions that involved her father. "I grew up knowing how disappointed he was in me, how angry he was that I wasn't born a boy, how embarrassed he was to not have fathered a son. I was not a child to him, but an unfortunate misappropriation of genetics doomed to disappoint and discredit him.

"Mine has always been a life of duty," she continued, easing into a monolog Ben had heard in fragments over the decades, but never in such a condensed manner, or with such detached angst. She spoke as though a witness to her own tragic history.

"I grew up required to say 'I love you, papa' and give him a peck on his cheek before I went to bed each night. I would step to his side, fearing disapproval, resentment, and his anger, say what was demanded of me, give him his kiss and slink away to bed. The gesture was never acknowledged, let alone returned. He would sit there in his easy chair, reading a paper, or listening to classical music in his attempt to appear cultured and refined.

"He never so much as acknowledged me. As years passed, that became perfectly fine by me. He terrified me. What sort of a man steeps his child in fear? And how should a child learn about love, commitment and intimacy from such a man? What choices did I have? How better to cope with such misery than to simply disappear?

"I spent an entire life on paper-thin ice around the most essential influence a girl can have. Honestly! It's a miracle that I didn't turn out to be some simpering wife of a mid-level banker who never left Bedford Heights. Alone in a house with a man I didn't care about, left to manage the meaningless details of a loveless, empty marriage."

She paused.

"Just like my mother.

"Or I might have been one of those women who spend their adult lives in therapy, drinking heavily, despising their husbands and their children, and trying to figure out why her father had focused so intently on stunting her intellectual and emotional growth.

"It took the loss of a child – and nearly the destruction of our marriage – to plant a seed of truth about what a horrible father he is, and to help me understand that it all had absolutely nothing to do with me. It was always all about him. The letter forced me to come to terms with what a thoroughly vile, malevolent bastard my father is, and to find some measure of peace in that truth.

"But I have never told him how I felt – how I truly, truly *feel* – about what he did to me…to us…and that rankles me to no end. I've allowed him to rob me of my voice for my entire life. It's as though the truth about what I think of his contempt for me, his mistreatment…my experiences and emotions…are all only vague ideas, whimsical notions, unless I *force* him to listen to how his behavior hurt. Unless I *tell* him.

"It's bad enough that he raised a child to resent herself for being a woman, and to fold his contempt for the paths I chose into everything I did and felt. That was bad enough. But what he did to us? And to you? How he mistreated you, and us, from the beginning… "

She faced Ben.

"No, Ben. No more, and no longer. It's time. Time for me to have my say. Finally.

"Before he dies, I want to confront him. Both of us, standing together, with commonality of purpose, and tell that evil, dreadful old man how wrong he was. About me. You. All of it. I want to stand before him and show how he misjudged us, underestimated us. How much more powerful we are than he could imagine, or ever be.

"I want to stand in his office, in front of his oak desk, with its big drawers full of important papers and vicious lies, and crush him with the strength of our marriage. I want to demonstrate what a decent, loving couple looks like. What a daughter worthy of a father's love looks like.

"I want to wave our wealth in his face, flaunt it, to show him that good people can achieve financial success AND enjoy genuine love, not as a byproduct, but as an essential ingredient of their, well, commonality of purpose, to steal from one of our vows. I want him to see by our example that his miserly choices have left him with only his money and his legacy as a petty, insignificant politician.

"I want to show him, not in anger or in hope that he might see the truth, or change - it's far too late for that - but in a display of clear, unavoidable reality, that when he dies he will leave this world feeling as worthless and voiceless as he made me feel my entire life."

Her words tumbled freely, released after frustrated decades.

"Then I want to laugh. Oh, how I'll laugh. I want to laugh in his face as he turns red, my defiance making his palms sweat and his temples throb, challenging him as no one has ever dared. I want to loom over him as he has done me, and assault his very essence with the power within me that he never took the time to acknowledge.

"I want to devastate him with my strength, and with our authority. Overwhelm him into silent submission. I want to see the stunned, hapless look on his face when he realizes that all his efforts to control my life have failed. I want him to see his own failure and realize the enormity of his poor judgment. I want him to feel what it's like to be crushed by our power, just as he tried to crush us with his."

She patted a wrinkle on her skirt into submission. Squared her shoulders. She raised her chin; powerful, defiant, with a soft tone to her voice that made her words all the more powerful, resolute.

"And then I want to forgive him. I want to forgive him as I forgave you for your mistakes, as I forgave God for taking Belinda from us, and as I have forgiven myself for my own errors. I want to forgive my father, not out of love and respect, but out of pity and acceptance."

She paused.

"And then I want to walk away, one last time, and take all his power and dignity with me. And then I want to never see him again."

She was crying soft tears that released the burden of the years: loss, sadness, and devastation from decades of conflict that threatened to overshadow the joys and happiness of their marriage. All the anxiety washed forth and ran in salty rivulets into the corners of her mouth.

Ben took her hand.

"Commonality of purpose and values. Of course. Yes, of course, my dear. And you're right. It's time for me to retire, and to think about what might come next for us. And by all means, let's celebrate with a drive across the country.

"Yes. Let's drive to Ohio and slay the demon within your father's hallowed office. And then on to New York, where we shall celebrate with champagne and rose petals in the city's finest hotel. Just like I promised you all those years ago."

"And oysters," Brenda added, smiling gently, wiping the tears from her face as though erasing the traces of a painful past. "Oysters, too, if you please, sir."

"Of course, my dear. Indeed, you shall have oysters. Oh, my delicious honey bun; love of my life. I please. I please very, very much, indeed."

19

Ben gave notice of his intent to retire, and in an emotional meeting with his appreciative CEO, laid plans for his departure and selection of his successor.

"Honestly, Ben. I can't fathom what I'll do without you," the CEO moaned. "I'm envious of Brenda. She gets all of you now."

As a senior manager fully vested in Stepley Pharmaceuticals stock options, Ben's retirement package ensured a post-professional life of choice and comfort. The stock options and his retirement savings provided a healthy financial portfolio managed by a wealth adviser Ben had selected. Ben's contract included lifetime health insurance - an important perk for a retired couple who could expect to spend more and more time in the doctors' offices as time passed.

Ben and his boss agreed that Ben would take the lead in recruiting his successor. He would screen the applicants and work with the company's human resource staff to schedule personal interviews, each of which he could conduct in his expansive corner office in the company's executive suite.

His boss, Bill, a man of dubious skill and limited vision, yet a micromanaging control freak, possessed a chronic disdain for details. Ben had stepped into the performance void for years, doing a disproportionate amount of the work while deflecting credit to a man who lacked talent for everything except flash, bluster and an uncanny ability to manage the politics of a diverse and demanding board of directors.

Ben likened his relationship with his boss to his marriage to Brenda.

"It's a partnership," he told one candidate who sought to replace him, an experienced woman with impressive credentials and experience, remarkable energy, and strong employment references. "We share common company values, Bill and I, which is why we work well together. It's a commonality of purpose." Ben carefully withheld an outright endorsement of the CEO for good reason. The successful candidate would have to learn how to fill in the gaps to represent the company while supporting the well-connected buffoon in pinstripes.

The woman left Ben's office as his choice to replace him, but she was swiftly removed as a potential replacement when Bill reviewed Ben's recommended shortlist.

"I want someone like you," he told Ben, "someone I can rely on. Someone I can joke with. Someone who wears pants."

Ben's efforts to soften the man's misogynistic bias failed when Bill insisted on hiring a male.

"What's the point in trying to influence him?" he sighed to Brenda over dinner. "The man is an incorrigible windbag; an overpaid Neanderthal. Without me covering his innumerable shortcomings, it's only a matter of time until he gets censured for misspeaking to investors, fired for his incompetence, or sued for being the leering, sexist fool that he is. Maybe all of the above, in fact."

Through Ben's diligent focus - and immense luck - Bill had sequestered himself on an island of unearned success in the river of Ben's effort. Ben was always on edge when the CEO engaged with the public or employees. He intervened during conference calls to explain the CEO's misguided extemporaneous remarks to institutional investors better oriented to Ben's grasp of subject matter than Bill's rambling blather. Ben interpreted Bill's narratives with concise recitation of facts and figures, reflecting an impressive grasp of details that eased investors' angst when Bill opened his mouth. He blunted Bill's sexist comments to women at work, and diverted the subjects from the CEO's lingering, lustful gazes.

"All part of the job," Ben reasoned to Brenda. "My job is to make Bill look good, and sometimes that's like putting lipstick on a pig."

Bill was the titular head of the company, and Ben more than most knew him as a philandering, shallow fop; a Brahmin with upper class genes and a private school education. With a penchant for Armani suits, dry martinis (most days at lunch, and always before dinner) and gold cufflinks, Bill was just another bloated, under-skilled white male executive whose string of good fortune had inexplicably planted him in a position of power. More dictator than consensus builder, he was accustomed to his ways being tolerated and his word regarded as law.

"They must have had Bill in mind when they created William Shatner's role as Denny Crane on Boston Legal," Ben joked to Brenda. "A drunken, leering has-been propped up by his subordinates, tolerated by his peers, and celebrated by a fraternity of like-minded fools."

Now, as he sought to preserve his own legacy and find a competent replacement to act as CFO, Ben was frustrated by the man's lack of vision. Bill's perception that a woman couldn't function as CFO would hamper Stepley's growth, Ben felt, and damage his own reputation as a higher-thinking executive.

"So he'll get a decent candidate who's a man instead of the best candidate, who was a woman," Ben told Brenda. "Honestly. How Bill keeps his job is a testament to his ability to manage the board and cash in on my hard work. It will be interesting to see how he survives what comes next.

"But that's not my problem. My challenge is how to keep the smartest woman in the world interested in boring old me as we drive for hours on end across the plains of South Dakota, Nebraska and Iowa."

Ever the agreeable negotiator, Ben dutifully advanced the candidacy of a dour man in gray worsted who came with an impressive resume, no family, and no negatives. Pasty-faced, monotonous and boring, the man was perfect for the job, thought Bill, who was thrilled when the man accepted the offer. One month later the new CFO moved into Ben's office. Ben packed his personal effects into seven tightly sealed cardboard boxes and stacked them in the trunk of his black Buick sedan, to be transferred that night to the back of the garage and never again opened.

Frustrated by the hiring process and bored with the lack of actual work, he strode out of the door as though a free man after a long prison sentence. In one swift gesture he tore off his necktie and tossed it in the trash bin next to his designated parking spot. He smirked when he noticed that the name on the parking place had already been changed to the new CFO.

"He can have it. All of it!" he said with a grin.

Exiting the lot, he looked briefly in his rearview mirror at the Stepley façade for the last time as he drove home, enormous smile on his face and contemporary hits blaring on his car radio.

#

Brenda marched through a list of details that needed tending as they prepared for their drive. They talked through them at dinner each night.

"Notified the post office, and they'll hold mail for us till we get back," she said.

"Newspaper?" he inquired.

"Check," came the response, and so on, through the matters that would be put on hold, or canceled, or referred for handling to a friend or a neighbor. They made their way through the elements of their life in one place to free them for a new life in another; two people, two suitcases, a train case full of cosmetics and "women's unmentionables," and two pair of binoculars.

Ben bought the expensive field glasses one Saturday afternoon at a local hobby shop, along with a "Field Guide to American Wildfowl and Other Birdlife." Neophyte ornithologists, they intended to evolve into avid bird watchers as they made their way across the nation, two wandering retirees in search of the elusive Southern Lapwing or the Painted Bunting, said to be the most beautiful bird in North America.

Their friends laughed at Ben and Brenda's choice of hobbies. "They say you become what you've always wished for when you retire," one friend quipped at a cocktail party. "I'm a golfer. Jim over there is a handyman. My wife is a gardener. So what's that make you?"

"A Great Grey Heron," joked Brenda. "Tall and slender, sharp-eyed; the silent, quiet stalker. An efficient hunter."

"You mean Great Blue Heron," challenged the friend.

"Not Ben. Take a look. Pure grey," Brenda retorted.

"That makes Brenda a sand piper," joked a woman, joining the circle. "Darting to and fro, avoiding life's problematic waves and thriving in the sea foam of life."

Brenda and Ben took these jabs in good humor.

"Could've been much worse," Ben quipped as they drove home from the party. "They could have likened me to a buzzard, and you to a road runner..."

"Or a chicken," Brenda added with a laugh. "That'd be me: the dutiful, nesting hen."

Anticipating an unaccountable life of freedom and choice on the road, they eagerly crossed items off their lists as their departure date approached. They were carefree, relaxed and happy, prepared to embrace new freedom with the hope and positivism of newlyweds.

# # #

Ben might have sensed trouble one sunny Tuesday morning as he eased his Pontiac into a parking space at their favorite supermarket. Brenda opened the door to the car and began to exit when Ben stopped her:

"What, no lipstick?"

As long as he had known her, Brenda had always applied a fresh coat of lipstick as they neared their destination. She would lower the passenger-side mirror and squint into her reflection as she painted one lip, then the other, then rolled her lips across one another to ensure a smooth, even texture. An intense scan of the result, sometimes with a deftly-applied swipe of a finger to correct a spot, and they would be on their way.

The ritual was an extension of Brenda's sense of order and propriety, as though the veneer of freshly glossed lips allowed her to face the day in the best possible light, and maintained balance in her world.

Now, though, she seemed shocked at the suggestion.

"Lipstick? Why?" she wondered.

"Why, indeed, my love, and so we're off," Ben replied. Though surprised by his wife's sudden departure from ritual, he dismissed it as of little consequence.

They left Southern California the next Monday morning with a tank full of regular gasoline and sturdy stainless steel rod strung across the Buick's backseat ceiling to protect the sharp creases in his suits and shirts and the gentle folds of her dresses, skirts and blouses. Into the trunk went the matching leather suitcases and train case – retirement gifts from the CEO, emblazoned with Ben's monogrammed initials in ostentatious gold ink. The binoculars went between them on the front seat for easy access and speedy deployment.

They set out on a zigzag route northeast through Nevada and then south to Arizona. They would drive as many hours as they chose each day, always five miles per hour under the speed limit.

"Save gas and money; enjoy the scenery," reasoned Ben.

"Make sure we avoid the local gendarmes," quipped Brenda.

Their plan was to traverse as many states as they could. They rolled down the windows and let the wind blow through their hair while blasting whatever music was available on the car's radio. Country music, classical, rock ("Oh, for God's sake, Ben, can't we do better than that horrid screeching?") and folk music came and went as they took turns twirling the radio dial and the miles sped past.

Freedom felt comfortable, normal, and the open schedule and empty roads brought them depth of peace and happiness they had not felt for years. Traveling absorbed the residue from what tension remained between them, and it was as though they'd left their problems in the shuttered bungalow far behind.

That contentment continued for Brenda but halted for Ben one morning.

They were seated in a diner in Cheyenne, Wyoming, eating a breakfast of poached eggs on English muffins, done with the yolks firm, not hard, but past the point of being runny. Brenda forked a bite into her mouth.

"When do you think we should leave?"

"After breakfast, of course. Why? Do you want to relax at the hotel for awhile?"

"Hotel? What on earth are you talking about? I have to water the garden once more before we leave, and I also want to stop by the post office and ask them to hold our mail while we're gone."

Ben stared at his wife mid-bite, fork in hand. A bit of poached egg fell unnoticed onto the table in front of him. He looked at Brenda, searching for an impish grin that would betray the ruse.

She was joking, certainly.

Nothing.

"I also forgot to cancel the newspaper, so we must call them after breakfast. Honestly, Ben, I don't know why we had to go out to breakfast today. We might have just eaten at home."

Home was 11 days and 1,500 miles behind them, Ben reckoned, as the awful realization struck him that his wife was somewhere other than present. He thought back to the moment, weeks ago, when Brenda's abandonment of her lipstick in the market parking lot gave him pause and sent a warning signal that something was amiss. He had dismissed the incident at the time, as well as the other tiny incidents that when taken together created a concerning pattern: her confusion coming out of the ladies' room at a rest stop in Arizona; the increasing frequency when she would stop in mid sentence, confused; her frustrations over being unable to find the right word. The repeated anecdotes, and questions posed again and again.

Now he was alarmed.

"Sweetheart. We left San Diego a week ago. We're driving across the country. We're in Wyoming. Surely you remember."

He had seen her in a confused state, but nothing like this.

"She's distracted, just muddled," he told himself when, shortly before they left, she had asked him when he planned to officially retire. She furrowed her brow and shrugged when he reminded her that he had retired weeks earlier, and that their cross-country trip lay on the immediate horizon. Brenda dismissed his response.

"Oh, nonsense. You told me nothing of the kind. Honestly, Ben! Do you think I would forget something of that magnitude?"

Worried, Ben had booked an urgent appointment with their general practitioner in San Diego.

"Best that we both get checkups before we take off," he reasoned.

They went to the doctor's office together, as they always did, and one after another trooped into the examination room to shed their clothing and have their pulse, respiration and temperatures taken, their reflexes tested and their eyes checked. Brenda underwent extra tests to measure her short-term memory.

Afterwards, the concerned doctor met privately with Ben.

"Well, Ben, I'm afraid your fears are well founded. Your wife has fairly serious degradation of her short-term recall," he said. "We need further tests so we can determine what's going on." He rested a palm on Ben's forearm. "Your wife is lucid, present and intelligent, but these spells of forgetfulness, as you call them, I fear, are worrisome symptoms. I am sorry, Ben, but I think this is symptomatic of something else…perhaps just memory loss, perhaps something more serious.

"There could be many explanations, and it's best we follow up to rule out the possibilities."

Ben deflected the doctor's request to schedule an immediate appointment with a specialist, promising to pursue the issue when they returned from their trip.

"No point in disappointing her, or me, for that matter; what's to be done? She's just forgetful, like me. Happens to folks our age. I'm sure she'll be fine."

And so she was, for the most part. But in moments like these, arguing with Ben about where they were, sitting in a roadside diner in Wyoming while their eggs grew cold, Brenda was showing signs of serious problems.

"I forget, sometimes," she would say in reflective moments when they would pause to discuss how she was feeling. "It's as if there's a light fog in my head, a mist that blocks my view from what I know to be so. I feel detached from myself, as though I'm not really me at all." She often fretted about the lapses, worrying that the "fog" would become more dominant, more dense, and would eventually consume her.

"No. I don't feel like me. Not like me at all."

Such moments were rare in the early going, and Ben would simply wait for the "spell" to pass. And so it did, once again, as the waitress cleared the plates from the table, the Wyoming morning sun warming them with the promise of another day of perfect weather.

"Oh, silly me. One of my little memory lapses," Brenda said breezily. "You pay the bill. I'm going to powder my nose before we leave. It's a long way to Denver. Such a beautiful city! I am so excited to finally see it!"

He watched her go in stunned sadness that all was indeed not well, and that Brenda's "little memory lapse" was presenting as something deeper, sinister. Brenda had insisted that they visit the Native American reservations of South Dakota, bypassing the southern route Ben had recommended to take them through Denver, a US city she despised with uncharacteristic enmity yet now said she looked forward to visiting.

"It's full of hippies and skiers, and doe-eyed liberals," she had said weeks earlier. "Though I've never been there, I truly loathe the mere idea of Denver. I'd sooner be in Bedford Heights."

20

Ben glanced at the clock on the wall across from his hospital bed: 3:35.

"I fell asleep. And still no doctor to put the permanent cast on!" He stabbed at the nurse's call button strapped to the side of his bed.

Moments later the curtains parted and a nurse poked her head through. Someone new. Again.

"Now see here," Ben scolded. "I simply must see the doctor immediately so she can put the cast on my arm and discharge me. I cannot have this. Please, nurse, my wife is waiting. This is urgent."

The nurse was empathetic, but the doctor's orders were clear: Ben was to be observed a minimum of six hours. They reasoned that delaying the permanent cast would prolong his stay in the ward and give the medical staff time to better evaluate his condition before releasing him.

"Mr. Tremblay. The doctor is busy with more urgent patient needs at the moment. I know you want to leave, and I understand that you're concerned about your wife." She glanced at the chart at the foot of his bed. "I see that we have notified Stonybrook of your accident, so they will have reassured your wife if she is concerned.

"Right now, you are our priority. So please, Mr. Tremblay. Just a bit longer. Try to lie back and relax, maybe get some sleep. The doctor will be with you as soon as possible."

She whirled and tugged the curtains closed, leaving Ben alone. His pulse rate cast a peak-and-valley portrait on the bedside monitor; pulsating white line against black background. The pattern caught his attention, prompting another memory as the minutes ticked by.

# # #

The day had begun in a motel outside Jefferson City. Ben awakened to a chilly room and an empty spot in the bed beside him. Bright light peeked into the room through a slit in the curtains, painting a brilliant swathe across the dark bedspread.

He felt beneath the covers where Brenda had lain. Cold. He leapt from the bed, wrapped himself in a bathrobe and shoved his feet into waiting slippers, rushing from the room into the cold air, and scanning the parking lot for a sign of Brenda. He slipped the room's keycard into his bathrobe pocket as he hurried the length of the sidewalk to the front of the motel complex.

The motel fronted a busy four-lane highway that was already thrumming with a stream of long-haul trucks and early commuters, all exceeding the 55 mph speed limit. There was no sidewalk along the highway, and no guard rail. A walker would be at risk along the narrow road.

Ben strained his eyes left, then right, desperately looking for a sign of Brenda.

Nothing.

He realized the futility of proceeding one way over another, so he rushed back to his room to grab his car keys and widen the search. As he passed the office he spotted a figure slumped in an arm chair by the unmanned front desk.

Brenda.

He rushed to her side, worried and shivering, taking her hands in his. She regarded him with empty, confused eyes.

"We needed milk for our coffee. I looked, and there was none in the refrigerator. I thought I could get some, but the store has gone, I guess. I couldn't find it, and I was getting cold. I think we've been here before, haven't we? Is this close to our home?"

Ben coaxed her back to their room and waited for the episode to pass, as such moments normally did. This time, though, the confusion lingered and then worsened. Brenda became agitated when Ben tried to bring her back to the here and now.

"We're in Missouri, honey bun. San Diego is miles and miles away. This is not our home. It's a motel...."

She waved him off, scolding him for claiming he knew better than she. She threatened to leave the room and show him she could damn well find her way to the corner store and back for a quart of skim milk, angrily wrapping herself in her fluffy blue robe.

Ben reasoned with her, suggesting they go together to buy milk. At last she acquiesced. They drove to a nearby convenience store where they bought milk and instant coffee, two elderly travelers in bathrobes in search of breakfast staples, then returned to the hotel to wrap their chilled fingers around cups of lukewarm brew and let their bodies warm.

"It's like a rip tide," the doctor counseled when Ben reached him an hour later. "It's best to swim with it until you reach calmer waters. Fighting against a rip tide nearly always ends badly. You did well to float with her. But she needs evaluation, and should be seen by a doctor, Ben. See if the problem is progressing."

Ben helped her dress and took her to a nearby emergency room. Hospital staff took Brenda's vital signs and made her comfortable while Ben provided her medical history and answered question after question.

Hours later, a kindly neurologist gave Ben the news.

"She is exhibiting signs of worsening dementia," he said. "Your recitation of her history…increased short-term memory loss, confusion, rapid mood changes, and periodic changes in her ability to communicate…to find the right words to express herself…these are all typical signs of developing dementia, most likely Alzheimer's."

The doctor had placed a call to Ben's physician to gain insight to her medical history.

"From what your doctor tells me about his last visit with her, her condition seems to be deteriorating rapidly. I'm terribly sorry, Mr. Tremblay, but it's possible that constantly changing surroundings are contributing to her condition. She needs to be in a familiar place. I would advise you to return home and seek further diagnosis and care.

"Patients with dementia do much better in stable, familiar settings. Studies have found that the disease advances more slowly, and with less trauma for the patient as well as their families, if the patient is in a place they know, where they feel comfortable."

Three states short of the showdown with his father-in-law - less than an eight-hour drive – unable to confer with his wife and consider her wishes and opinions, Ben made the decision to return to California.

The doctor discharged Brenda from the hospital with a kindly pat on Brenda's shoulder and a handshake with Ben that lasted an extra second or two.

"Go well, Mr. Tremblay," he said. "I hope you can enjoy your time together. No matter what."

Ben drove back to the hotel and left her buckled into the passenger seat while he packed their bags in the trunk and checked out. He guided the car from the motel parking lot, paused for a moment at the exit with a forlorn, extended look to the east, and turned west to begin the long drive home.

# # #

They talked frankly about the episode as the hours and miles sped past.

"I wonder what on earth brought it on?" Brenda mused as they hugged the right lane, talk radio providing low background noise. "I have absolutely no recollection of leaving the room, or walking in the cold air. Then you were at my side at the hospital. It's as though a thick fog suddenly lifted. So many empty hours. So much I simply do not recall. None of it."

As Ben parked the car at a motel for a stopover late that afternoon, he related details of what the doctor had said.

"Stress," the doctor had advised, "can play a significant role in the development of dementia. Is your wife experiencing any particular stress? Perhaps an argument with you, financial problems; a nettlesome family matter?"

"No, no, no," Ben had answered.

Then, "Is she anticipating a potentially stressful event?"

Settling into motel in Kansas for the night several hours later, they talked about the change of plans.

At first Brenda was inconsolable.

"All my life I have avoided the truth with my father, and here I am once again, doing precisely the same thing. I fought and struggled to find the strength to confront him, and when – after all these years! – I finally have the courage to face him, *this* happens. It's not right! This is important! If I don't have my say with my father, I feel like I am a fraud, a failure. If I don't tell him my true feelings, we'll all die knowing that he ran my life to the end."

She turned on Ben, furious.

"And you! All the 'commonality of purpose' nonsense you wrote in our vows, and went on and on and on about, that we would stand together in front of my father and tell him, together! It was all fucking bullshit!"

It was unlike Brenda to use such language, but when angry as her disease had advanced, at times she spoke with a crude edge that made Ben cringe.

He sat for a moment, allowing the moment to pass. Brenda's fury slowly ebbed, and quiet returned to the room.

He found one of Brenda's favorite game shows on the television and turned up the volume so she would be entertained while showered, shaved and regrouped. He veered to the motel door and fit the security chain into place; a calculated move a worried parent might make to keep a child safely confined. Ben left Brenda staring at the screen, fidgeting with her fingers while watching the contestants banter with one another. He retreated to the bathroom and spent the next 30 minutes hastily completing his daily ablutions.

They left the motel an hour later in search of a place for dinner. Brenda resumed voicing her angst over the cancelled trip to Ohio, though with a more measured tone.

Ben listened, hands gripping the steering wheel as he stuck to the speed limit and the bigger issues that governed the state of their marriage.

He reasoned.

"You are right, of course, my love. It's horrible that we won't be able to visit your father. I, too, was looking forward to it. Not to the confrontation, but to putting to rest the power he has had over you - and us - for all these years.

"Earlier, you criticized me for violating our vows, for forgetting my commitment to commonality of purpose. But commonality of purpose can take on many forms. We can choose to define it however we wish. Let's do that together, my dear. Let's not let this challenge divide us. So many other obstacles have failed to drive us apart. Let's not allow this one to do so.

"Here we are, with the circumstances as they present themselves. It is best for you – for us – to take you home. The doctor in Missouri said travel may have made your condition worse. Besides that, we need help, and there are qualified doctors in southern California who know us and can take care of your medical issues while I address your physical needs in our home.

"It's a matter of priorities: I care more about your long-term health and safety than I do about reconciling your relationship with a pathetic little man in Ohio.

"Commonality of purpose now means taking care of you as best I can, following the best advice from medical professionals I can get, and with your best interests in mind. Taking you home and looking after you is of vital importance, my love. To you. To us. Changing plans and going home is the epitome of commonality of purpose, but only if we do it together.

"Besides," he added, smiling softly at her, "They have wonderful oysters in southern California, and I know just where to buy them!"

Over the next two days Brenda came to accept Ben's reasoning as they continued west, listening to music and chatting. As they pulled into their driveway and he began to unpack the car, Brenda turned to her husband and gifted him a moment he would replay over and again in the still of the night for years to come.

"You always do right by me, don't you? You are the one person in my life who genuinely has always had my best interest in mind. My unshakeable rock. My partner. My friend. I do so love you, my dear, and I am grateful for all you do to help me, protect me, and make me comfortable and happy, no matter what challenges I confront you with.

"You will stay by me, won't you? No matter what?"

He held her.

"I am here. And I'll always be here. No matter what."

She hugged him, then held him at arm's length.

"Let's see what state our home is in and then make a shopping list so I can whip up a nice dinner. Fish, maybe. Or shrimp. The shrimp casserole with buttered bread crumbs you love so much.

"No," she said, changing course. "I have it. Let's make baked oysters. With loads of garlic and cheese. We might not be in New York, but there's no reason why we can't celebrate at home. Besides, you promised. Off you go, Mr. Tremblay, to select two dozen of the finest oysters you can find, and pick up a bottle of bubbly on your way home. Champagne and oysters. Finally!"

21

The doctor finished wrapping Ben's arm in a permanent cast just after 5 p.m. Ben supported his injured right arm with his left to scrawl his signature on the release agreement, then made his way out of the emergency room and left the hospital. He piled into a waiting taxi. If he hurried he would arrive at Stonybrook in time for dinner with Brenda.

Best to end the day with a bit of normalcy. For both of them.

Brenda was seated in a wheelchair at her usual table in the brightly lit dining room, wrapped in a soft blue shawl across her shoulders and an all-too-familiar fugue. She stared ahead blankly, alone at a table big enough for four but set for two. Ben slid into the open seat across from her, tucking his injured forearm beneath the table and reaching to cup her hands with his left.

"Brenda," he said. "I'm here."

Nothing.

They were among 50 or so residents and visitors scattered about the room. A clutch of white heads bobbed up and down over plates of institutional food, taking their evening meals in staccato acts of mechanical consumption.

Dinner was a grilled cheese sandwich for Ben and a bowl of vegetable soup for Brenda.

The food arrived, and Ben rose to help Brenda closer to the table.

"Easier to manage, my love," he said, retaking his seat.

Her trembling hand directed a soup spoon into the bowl of steaming liquid, then toward her mouth. A drop of soup spilled from the spoon onto her lap, and Brenda frowned as the drop seeped through the thin paper napkin into her dress. She returned the spoon to the bowl and scrubbed the stain with her napkin.

Unsatisfied, she retrieved another napkin from the stack in the middle of the table, wet it in her glass of water and rubbed at the spot of soup until it disappeared. Content that she had removed the stain, she reached again for the spoon.

Ben watched with combined heartache and yearning as Brenda's eyes darted from the soup bowl to her lap, measuring the distance and calculating a way to eat without soiling her clothes. Her rheumy eyes watered at the corners in frustration over the simple defiant act of consuming what was required to fuel her body.

Brenda's fastidious disdain for soiled clothes, clutter and disorder reminded Ben of what remained of his wife that was hidden from most. He smiled, seeing Brenda not as an unresponsive Alzheimer's patient, but as a woman who had simply removed a spot of soup on her dress before others had noticed.

Ben wanted to help but thought better of it. Instead, he focused on his sandwich and let his thoughts drift.

# # #

Cleanliness next to godliness, Brenda loved to intone in her commitment to keeping their home, clothes and belongings in order. Brenda approached cleaning as a general would armed conflict; with fixed intention, anticipation, and with a clear plan. Ben accepted Brenda's penchant for order as an essential part of their lives.

"People who don't make the effort to keep clean have no self-respect," she believed, a rule pounded into her psyche by her father's demand for a spotless, orderly home. She used the aphorism to power her ritual use of cleaning fluids, polishing waxes, and the industrial-strength vacuum she coveted yet did without until Ben relented and bought one for her.

"Other vacuums remove surface dirt. I'm after all of it. The filth you track in with your shoes, and the mites, and dust – imperceptible bits that infect most homes.

"Not in mine," she concluded with firm-jawed resolve. "I simply won't have it. Not on my watch."

Cleanliness and order: two values enforced by her overbearing father and adhered to by her capitulating mother that ensured predictability in Brenda's childhood home.

"Growing up, I never left the house with so much as a wrinkle on my dress. A spot of dirt or food on my clothes was a disaster. A stain meant the garment would be thrown out or given to charity, and I would earn a stern rebuke from my father for being so careless and wasteful."

" 'Slovenliness leads to unkempt behavior, and a life of disorder, chaos, filth and disreputability,' " she said in a special nasal tone she used when she would mock her father's whiny lectures. " 'This is the sort of personal chaos the people in Bedford Arms embrace. Disorder and filth is the cancer of our society; what threatens our way of life. It may be perfectly fine for Bedford Arms, but not in my home.' "

Bedford Arms was Bedford Heights' low-income housing development, a dense collection of brick row houses that occupied acres of valueless land on the city's outskirts. Bedford Arms was the last stop on the bus route that serviced Bedford Heights' suburbs, guaranteeing its residents the longest possible commute to the city center and back.

More than six thousand underprivileged residents – many of them municipal workers who kept the streets clean, buses running on time, and school corridors polished to a brilliant shine - huddled together in collective irrelevance in the bland clutch of mass housing. A small supermarket provided cheap stores for their refrigerators. A satellite school with rusty playground equipment educated their children. Unlined, pothole-pocked streets were always the last to be attended; afterthoughts of a city content to ignore Bedford Arms, its problems, and its residents.

It was a sequestered sub-society of downtrodden, unfortunate have-nots, many of them minorities.

Brenda's father held Bedford Arms' residents in special contempt. During municipal budget season he always took aim at the meager funds the city's budget earmarked to keep the neighborhood vaguely functional, ignoring pleas from the "spineless do-gooders" who fruitlessly lobbied the City Council for support.

"We have created a community of dependents who, generation after generation, rely on the city to provide housing, education and health care yet contribute disproportionately far less to the tax base. As if the rest of us who have to work for what we earn receive any such benefits," he would rail.

"Now, I am a firm believer in charity, and I regularly and happily give my tithing to my church to help the disenfranchised and indigent. What we have created in Bedford Arms, however, is a culture of freeloading that provides a convenient training ground for the layabouts of our fair city. It's a Petri dish for non-contributing mediocrity."

Black, Hispanic and Asian families had woven a complex cultural quilt in Bedford Arms, joining a small group of undereducated white families for whom social migration was not an option. Many of Bedford Arms' residents were second- or third-generation municipal workers. Family- and community-minded, they left for work early, got home late, paid their taxes, tolerated the regular increases in bus fare into the city, and got along with one another just fine.

They worked hard, complained little, and asked for less; the archetypical American underclass.

They looked upon Bedford Heights residents as wealthy overlords, viewing the middle class majority with silent skepticism that was charitable compared with the contempt with which the mayor and his minions held Bedford Arms folks.

The mayor – like most mean-spirited, selfish conservatives of his ilk – conveniently overlooked the fact that poverty and subpar education gripped Bedford Arms residents in a relentless cycle. That was fine with him: How else to ensure a reliable pool of low-paid, overworked menial employees who would flip the burgers, tend the lawns, and maintain the city's assets in desultory, repetitive acts passed from generation to generation?

Occasionally a promising young student would earn a scholarship to the state university in Columbus, gracing the weekly *Bedford Arms Current* with his or her beaming face in a photo and accompanying article on the front page, as if to inspire others to follow. But such heroes usually dissipated into the better fortunes of a world well away from Bedford Heights, and the *Current* soon forgot their names and returned to the news digest of crime, civic activism, and pot-luck suppers.

Bedford Heights residents – 90% white, a collection of Baptists, Congregationalists and Unitarians, with a smattering of Jews and upwardly mobile African-Americans and Hispanics – overlooked the mayor's elitist, racist sentiments and returned him to office term after term. Bedford Arms residents occasionally offered half-hearted support for challengers yet still voted heavily in the mayor's favor in a "devil you know" act that defied logic and ensured a continuous imbalance of voice and authority.

That the mayor had held office for more than 20 years was a testament both to his staying power as well as the electorate's political myopia. Prosperity had consistently graced Bedford Heights' elite, who lived in comfortable superiority over the struggling middle class and Bedford Arms' overwhelmed working class. There was little appetite for change.

The mayor's rants became more vitriolic as the years passed, but any opponent who decided to challenge him was quickly swept aside by a political machine oiled by years of interwoven municipal government and private business.

Brenda inherited her parents' commitment to cleanliness and order, but she had a different idea of charity. In high school, she volunteered in the Bedford Arms community center, teaching English to the children of first-generation immigrants over her father's objections.

She witnessed first-hand the fierce determination Bedford Arms residents displayed to maintain independent lives. Both parents often worked multiple low-paying jobs. Most didn't own cars, instead trudging to bus stops before dawn to ride public routes for an hour or more, only to repeat the process to return home long after the sun had set. Children spent after-school hours with relatives or friends, though many filled the hours on their own. Teenagers eased into part-time jobs to help make ends meet, or doubled as in-home day care centers for their younger siblings.

"Charity means unconditionally giving to those less fortunate," Brenda firmly believed, and later in life she and Ben wrote generous checks to agencies that provided support to families below the poverty line. "To act charitably without trying to truly understand the plight of people who rely on our help is counterintuitive to the value itself.

"That fact is lost on my father. He thinks everyone has the same opportunity, and that hard work is the simple answer to poverty, hunger and inequality. To him, brown or black skin is a convenient way to judge class and assign societal roles. He believes the inability to speak conversant or fluent English is a symptom of cultural parasitism; someone on welfare is simply lazy, in his world."

Mocking her father, again, 'These people are simply here to take from us whatever they can. Our homes, our jobs, our futures…why, even our children, if they are left to it. Just last week I learned that one of our city councilors' daughters is pregnant by a young Spanish boy from Bedford Arms. Her father is quite reasonably in a state of dishonored shock.

'These people are fortunate to have jobs, a commodity not available in their own countries, or else they wouldn't be here at all.' The mayor's racist logic conveniently overlooked that 100% of Bedford Arms residents were US citizens born with the same rights as the rest of his constituency – and him.

Fueled by their disagreement with most of what the mayor and his wife represented, Brenda and Ben crafted their own set of values – respect for multicultural life, commitment to love, regard for others, openness, tolerance and acceptance, and, importantly, forgiveness – in long talks that spanned years. Their values largely mirrored the guiding principles that shaped Ben's life in his parents' home, and directly conflicted with the rules of life Brenda's father imposed with steely determination.

Ben and Brenda's liberal philosophy irritated the mayor and widened the distance between the young couple and the influences of Brenda's youth.

"They'll either learn the errors of their ways or pay the price," the mayor growled to his wife. "I frankly don't care which, long as they don't come to me for a handout because they've been foolish with their own money."

# # #

Brenda's spoon clattered into her soup bowl, bringing Ben back to the present.

The spoon had slipped from her grasp and now lay mostly submerged in the soup. Brenda contemplated her dilemma with quiet resolve. Using a napkin from the tabletop holder, she cleaned the spillage from around the bowl. She slowly retrieved the spoon from the bowl and wiped it clean with another napkin. Then she folded the napkins into a tight square and placed them to the side; a tiny monument of detritus that bore testament to the travails of a meal gone awry.

Ben barely breathed as he watched.

Brenda assessed the tabletop. With a satisfied, determined smile, she picked up the spoon and dipped it into the soup. She carefully tipped it to allow half the payload back into the bowl - less volume would be easier to transport. With shaking hand and focused stare, Brenda eased the spoon toward her mouth. Despite her careful effort, a bit of soup sloshed onto the table top. She returned the spoon to the bowl and repeated the cleaning process.

Ben resisted the urge to speak, to offer help, or to feed her. His respect for his wife's independence exceeded his interest in solving the problem. It pained him to see his wife struggle. Brenda - so proud, and fastidious, and measured - laboring over the simple act of eating – but refused to dishonor her by intervening.

He swatted at a tear that eased from his left eye, doing his best to hide the swipe from Brenda.

Unwanted pity can exact a toll.

Brenda spotted the dinner roll that rested on the plate to her right. A few moments passed as she formed the plan.

She split the roll, holding half in her left hand. With her right, she spooned a bit of soup toward her mouth. She held the roll beneath the spoon as it traveled the distance, sustenance safely transported over a safety net of white flour and yeast. A drop of soup fell onto the roll as Brenda's trembling hand eased the spoon into her mouth. She swallowed with obvious pleasure and sense of accomplishment.

She smiled at Ben, eyes gleaming.

Problem solved.

"That's my girl," he said, voice cracking. "That's my love, my darling."

22

Dessert was bread pudding – one of Brenda's favorites. She cherished the creamy custard and dense collection of sweetness at its base, and the ice-thin topping with hint of nutmeg, sugar and cinnamon. Ben was a fan of bread pudding, too, though he despised its taste and texture. Ben liked it because Brenda loved it, and it was easy for her to eat.

Presented with glass-footed bowls of pudding topped with a dollop of canned whipped cream, Brenda made short work of the dessert without incident. Ben made a show of picking at his portion, but as usual ate little. He shoved his serving across the table toward his wife. She ignored it.

Brenda rose from the table, gripped her Zimmer walker with both hands, and shuffled her way toward the exit. Ben followed, a hovering, protective shadow.

He eased around her to open the dining room door, then stepped aside as Brenda proceeded through the exit. She cast a grateful glance and nod of her head to acknowledge his thoughtfulness.

"If only you knew," Ben thought. *"If only you could understand how grateful I am simply to be with you. To help you. Look after you. If only you knew that this time with you is more gift to me than it is to you. Perhaps you do know. I certainly hope so."*

This was love.

Not the fawning, doe-eyed wistfulness that kisses a relationship in its early stages. Nor the passionate surges of a developing affair, or the duty-driven commitment that comes with having a family. Or the supportive, earnest encouragement when a partner falters, or fails.

Love in later years means savoring each morsel of whatever is left with unconditional gratitude and peaceful acceptance.

"Rolling with the punches," Ben told acquaintances when they called to see how he was faring. "I give what's necessary; take what's given. I feed on the wonderful memories; cherish the small graces."

Not long after they returned from their aborted trip, love meant selling their home in Southern California and moving to New Mexico to take advantage of the clean air, uncrowded roads, and thinly-populated cities and towns that allowed for a slower, easier pace – and to be close to Stonybrook Acres. It meant leaving their friends and familiar surroundings for a condominium they could inhabit together while Brenda remained able to live independently and close enough to Stonybrook to allow an easier transition when the day arrived that Ben could no longer provide for her – or protect her.

A doctor in San Diego provided Ben with a brochure on Stonybrook, which had developed a well-deserved national reputation for quality care for patients with accelerating forms of dementia. Expensive, exclusive and featuring an attractively low patient/care professional ratio, it was a far better option than what was available in Southern California.

"Besides," the kindly neurologist advised, "at some point it will be difficult for you to maintain your home here, to make your way around San Diego to buy groceries and keep up with your own medical needs. New Mexico – and Stonybrook - are perfectly suited to you and Brenda."

After settling into the condo, Ben hired day nurses to help provide for Brenda's personal care and a cleaner to maintain order. He rarely ventured out alone for his own benefit, limiting solo excursions for necessary errands like food shopping, trips to the bank, and regular visits to the local pharmacy for Brenda's growing list of medications.

When it became clear that Brenda was at risk in the condo, Ben – with the help of Stonybrook staff – silently moved his unobjecting wife out of their home and into the institution where she would remain for the rest of her life. The decision tore at his heart, but he completed the move with the understanding that it was the ultimate act of love.

Brenda's safety first, above all else.

Now, he craved the intimacy of simply being with her.

"She is food for my soul," he told the friendly nurse's aide who was primarily responsible for Brenda's care, and who marveled at Ben's dedication and commitment. "I get more from being here than she does. Of that you may be assured."

The rewards were subtle, yet significant, and motivated Ben to re-dedicate himself to the task of being present. Sometimes there were quiet, intimate moments, or a gracious touch of the hand, a loving hug; often just a glance, a lingering look that conveyed more insight and emotion than a lengthy conversation. Such moments were to Ben as breath to his lungs, a sweater to his shoulders against a night chill, a comfortable chair after an arthritic walk from Stonybrook to his home.

"Cherish the small gifts," Ben reminded himself when Brenda gave him a tiny moment of peace, solidarity, or interpersonal connection that he once took for granted but now yearned for as a starving man wishes for simple meal.

Ben learned to watch for these moments, to gather them hungrily and stow them away. He created a mental catalog of memories and experiences to savor, cherish and, when the day should come that they no longer were available, recall in careful doses to feed the longing.

Ben thought of death every day.

"Death and taxes are the ultimate, unavoidable realities," was one of his favorite sayings, "Except, of course, the predictably poor play of the Cleveland Browns."

For most, aging was a slow spiral toward the end. For Brenda and others like her, the process was a rapid descent to a horrible holding pattern; locked away in a mental jail, with Alzheimer's her warden until the disease robbed her body of its ability to function, and its victim should slip away.

Ben had meticulously researched the disease and its likely progression.

"I cannot be surprised by what will come," he reminded himself, though horrified at the prospect of his wife's slow slide into complete incapacity. "I must have my wits about me, and be prepared."

"I hate who I have become," Brenda told Ben one morning as he appeared bedside with a tray of coffee, weeks before he made the fateful call to their doctor and began the search that placed her in Stonybrook.

"I don't know myself, and I feel like I can't be trusted within my own body. How on earth can you trust me? And, come to think of it, how can you stand to even be around me, when you never know which version of Belinda you'll find before you?"

These days Brenda often referred to herself as Belinda, and Ben was never sure if the mistake revealed a mother's longing for a daughter long lost, or the newest facet of Alzheimer's cruelty. She never acknowledged the misspoken identity, and Ben would have sooner scraped his eyeballs with a potato peeler than point out the error.

"Honestly, Ben. What on earth will become of me? You? Us?" Brenda said one day as they sat next to one another on their living room sofa.

"Why, after all we've been through...our young love, then being apart during the college years, my dreadful parents...the tragedy of losing a child, of finding a way to survive our respective infidelities, to see our marriage fray to the point of fracture only to save it from the brink of failure...why has life dealt me this cruelest of cruel cards? Why must I end my life this way, as less of a woman, less of a human?

"It seems so.....unjust."

A lengthy quiet hung over them.

"Unjust. Yes, I suppose so," Ben at last replied. "And cruel. And wasteful, and soul-eroding, and devastating, and humiliating. All those truths, my love, and many more. Yet this is where we are. We cannot run from this, or force it into submission. We must adapt – adjust and cope, as we always have.

"You and I have been called on to face problems that would crush most relationships, shred them beyond repair and, I'd wager, past the point of recognition to couples unable to resolve life's biggest problems together."

The clock on the mantle ticked away seconds as Ben gathered his thoughts.

"You and I, dear heart, we have proven worthy beyond the pale. We are titanium pillars of marital strength, and we will endure this storm as we have all others. Together.

"Your father once called ours 'a reasonably viable marriage.' It has been my mission to prove him wrong."

He took her hand.

"You remember, my dear: Trust, honesty, fidelity, openness, acceptance, partnership, commonality of purpose and values, and love. Our vows. Our recipe that created something so strong that even two desperately imperfect mortals such as we couldn't erode or weaken it, let alone destroy it.

"We have demonstrated, Brenda, to your father and to the world, the boundless power of love. Our love. And we have reminded one another of our collective strength. Again and again. We have more than survived; we have risen above all of it – your parents, losing Belinda, even each other's foolish, wasteful transgressions - and thrived. We remained, we persevered, and as a result we have given each other time in our marriage that will make it easier to face what comes next.

"Now we must accept. Just as we did when we took our vows and began a life together, we must accept whatever comes our way.

"Age is nature's way of revealing who we are. This is when we learn what we are made of. When we peel away the veneer of the years – the things, the money, the travel, the food, the experiences – we are left with an intellectual and emotional core that is either worth preserving and celebrating, or setting aside and forgetting.

"We are defined by our life together. We are the band of sticks, vulnerable and weak to the point of breaking if alone, but too strong to bend, let alone break, if together.

"You held us together over the years with your strength, while I did my part, I suppose, and provided the means to power our lives.

"In the early going, you found the courage to defy your father, and to survive your mother's bland capitulation to his demands, and her lack of courage to support her only child. You followed your heart, married me, and stood in defiance to your father's ruthless cruelty.

"What a gift. What a monumental compliment. You have to know this: I am in awe of your character, your strength and your courage. Always have been; always will be.

"Then you shaped our life together. You found our first home, and created our life in it even before we were married.

"You managed through the trauma of planning a wedding hosted by parents more interested in its cost and social value to themselves than what it may have meant to you. You found a way to laugh through it, and remain focused on what the day meant to us.

"You even somehow found a way to live with a man whose carelessness robbed you of your only child, causing unthinkable circumstances from which most women would never recover. Far fewer would find room in their hearts to forgive the man who caused such grief.

"But you did, somehow, to my continued surprise and extreme pleasure."

Brenda opened her mouth to speak. Ben silenced her with a finger on her lips.

"Shh, my dear. I am not finished.

"You gave me the strength to move across the country to a new job that opened new doors for us yet created unthinkable challenges to what should have mattered most. Then, after we both committed senseless acts of weakness that threatened everything we had, you found the will to fly across the country, confess your mistake and accept mine.

"You even found the grace to forgive me for losing our dear Belinda. That moment – when you told me of the stalker, and your father's hiring of the detective, and of Belinda's murderer's arrest and his horrible, detailed diary of how he stole our lovely daughter from us – well, it redefined me, Brenda. Your forgiveness restored my soul. It's as though in one generous act you gave me the courage and strength to face the rest of my life – no matter what challenges confront me.

"It was a watershed moment, a transfer of power that gave me everything I will ever need to support you, care for you, and provide for both of us for the rest of our lives.

"You have always been the real power of our relationship, Brenda. The intelligence, wisdom and kindness that molded us. And I have been a witness and the primary beneficiary of your authority, your awesome power, and your measured guidance.

"Without you, I might still be working at the hardware store in Bedford Heights, content to accept whatever life handed me, and blind to the magic and wonders I have experienced because I had you by my side.

"You gave me a life when you married me, Brenda. One I had never imagined, and I am in your debt for all you have done. And then you gave me a second life

– more powerful and stronger than the first – when you brought us back to together and opened the book for the final chapters of our lives.

"Now, my lovely, it is my turn. So fear not, my lovely wife. It is my turn at the helm of the Good Ship Tremblay. Whatever comes, no matter how difficult, or heart breaking, I will be the strength for you that you have been for me. I will be your pillar, your titanium foundation. You can lean on me. Forever.

"I promise.

"Cherish the small gifts, the graces. Two of my favorite sayings, right? Well, caring for you, and ensuring your comfort and happiness as our life enters its final chapter is a gift I shall give to myself."

He planted a lingering kiss on her cheek, then tenderly pressed his fingers to the spot.

"You are my forever honeybunch," he said, then softly began to sing, "and I love you, a bushel and a peck….."

# # #

Ben had a healthy perspective on the idea of his own death. He was both realist and fatalist, and also a staunch believer in a higher power, if not God himself, and the afterlife. His was a quirky blend of philosophies from a working-class Christian upbringing, a career in accountancy, and a lifetime of experiences that caused him to question many of the principles he had been raised to accept.

"When your time's up, it's up no matter what," he believed. "Crossing the street in front of a bus, slipping in the shower, or simply going to sleep and never waking up…it's already in the cards." His commitment to fatalism was tested one day on the golf course when an errant shot sliced by an untalented golfer on an adjacent hole zipped inches past his head and clanged off his golf cart.

"It that'd connected, I'd be a goner," he laughed to his golf partners as he eased a wedge out of his bag and, unfazed by the experience, pitched his ball within a foot of the cup. "But having a near-death experience oughtn't diminish one's skill with a wedge," he added, bolstering his reputation for grace under pressure and homespun realism doused in his understated brand of humor.

His viewpoint on Brenda's mortality was a different matter.

Ben worried constantly about Brenda's health, and feared her death above all. He dreaded the day when she would be gone, and the mere thought brought a clutch to his chest. He often wondered aloud, "What on earth would I do?" Not "will", "would". Use of the subjunctive allowed Ben to detach from the concept, muttering as he washed the dishes and scurrying to be on his way to visit Brenda. Ben's ability to detach and compartmentalize emotional issues kept the notion of Brenda's demise at bay, at odd contrast to his own comfort in the knowledge that his time, one day, would come.

He ignored the idea of Brenda's death as he did his doctor's repeated calls to schedule a follow-up appointment for his own tests. With limited hours and energy to expend each day, his focus was on Brenda, regardless of her mental state.

Tests be damned, he resolved, relegating his promise to return for hospital follow-up well behind his focus on Brenda's declining health. *I've no time for such nonsense. Brenda needs me. Besides, I'm fine.*

She was unusually present tonight, and as she eased into the arm chair in the corner of the room she gestured Ben into the matching chair across from her.

"Come. Sit. Let's have a talk," she said, greeting him as if for the first time that day. Such moments had become increasingly rare, Brenda suddenly emerging from a haze as if from an afternoon nap. How long would she remain?

Ben hurried to absorb as much as he could in what time he had. He stowed the Zimmer walker safely out of the way and sat, drawing to the edge of the seat to be as close to her as possible.

"What would you like to talk about, my love?" he said encouragingly.

"It would be my father's birthday soon, right? I remember we were going to visit them – my parents – and that we came back instead. But we were going to talk to him – confront him – on his 80th birthday. Or was it his 90th? The years have swept by so swiftly; I can scarcely recall how old he was when he died. I so rarely think about him, though when I do it's to reflect on what a horrible human being he was.

"I suppose there's a bit of sadness, too, though that's mostly lament for the fact that he was a terrible father in every sense of the word. Thank goodness I found you, else I would die a woman without a positive male role model in her life."

Many months had passed since Ben decided to abort their cross-country journey and bring Brenda back for treatment. They both paid scant attention when her father died, given Brenda's condition and Ben's singular focus to recalibrate his life to support her. To Ben, it seemed hypocritical – and pointless – for him to attend the services alone, so he sent flowers to his mother-in-law with a terse note of condolence that might have come from a vague acquaintance rather than her only daughter and son-in-law.

Such was the price the woman paid for enabling her husband's selfish, cruel ways.

"Yes, darling. His birthday would be next month. The 13th, I believe, right? I think he would be 92, or maybe 91, or perhaps 94. See? I, too, forget."

Ben liked to encourage Brenda to remember, often goading her into consider questions whose answers he knew all too well; at other times feigning memory loss to suggest that she was no different than he.

"Yes, yes. The 13th. It was our annual dilemma: What to get a man who has had everything? Who finally gave up his iron grip on municipal government after 40 years to spend his days lamenting the inexorable decline of a town he both loved and loathed?

"Oh, how we talked and talked about what to give him, if anything at all. Over the years I bought him all the predictable doo-dads: ties, socks, cufflinks, tea, books. And then we settled upon a gift for his 70th birthday that fit the occasion. Do you remember? We gave him a framed copy of the Monroe Doctrine's famous passages. The ones he loved the most."

Her father's commitment to political sovereignty and isolationism bordered on fanaticism. The delicately framed passages had been the perfect gift for a man who claimed to have all the answers.

"The occasion has been judged proper for asserting, as a principle in which the rights and interests of the United States are involved, that the American continents, by the free and independent condition which they have assumed and maintain, are henceforth not to be considered as subjects for future colonization by any European powers."

And

"We owe it, therefore, to candor and to the amicable relations existing between the United States and those powers to declare that we should consider any attempt on their part to extend their system to any portion of this hemisphere as

dangerous to our peace and safety. With the existing colonies or dependencies of any European power, we have not interfered and shall not interfere. But with the Governments who have declared their independence and maintained it, and whose independence we have, on great consideration and on just principles, acknowledged, we could not view any interposition for the purpose of oppressing them, or controlling in any other manner their destiny, by any European power in any other light than as the manifestation of an unfriendly disposition toward the United States."

Brenda's father believed the doctrine gave him license to reject what he referred to as "external influences," which in his twisted reality included others' opinions and advice, popular music and television, interference from politicians in Columbus, the Ohio state capital, or, heaven forbid, the useless political wasteland of Washington, DC.

It also fueled his misogynist, nativist and racist values which, if assessed honestly, would have qualified him for membership in the Ku Klux Klan. But hizzoner wasn't a joiner, and any Imperial Wizard worth his ceremonial robe would have steered clear of a small-thinking populist zealot with a superiority complex and a home office designed to make him look like an English baron.

Brenda's father had accepted the elegantly framed print with a characteristic grunt. He hung it on the wall behind his desk as a stern reminder to his visitors that the man seated before the historical document was as much an island unto himself as the country he so dearly loved. The gift had scored a direct hit.

Misplaced grandiosity and inflated self-importance were integral components of the mayor's repertoire, and Brenda and Ben celebrated the man's misappropriation of the gift's intent with ironic glee. He referred to the document as if he wrote it himself, pontificating, thumbs in vest pockets, about the importance of sovereignty and independence.

"It always galled me how he viewed his life as a medieval warlord in a castle," Brenda now lamented. "So superior, so elitist." Such contextual comments were unusual for Brenda. This was a special moment; a gift to be savored, cherished.

She laughed. "He truly was one moat short of a land baron. I suspect if there was a way for him to impose a personal tithing on the good citizens of Bedford Heights, he'd have dispatched the tax collector in a heartbeat. A demand from the lord of the manor for his subjects, to subsidize the good fortune they enjoyed under his protection. Oh, the great and powerful Mayor. So benevolent, so wise, so gracious in granting crumbs to the countless impoverished nothings who languished under his rule yet who benefited so much from simply existing within his broad, sweeping shadow.

"What a contemptible, miniscule man.

"He lived with absolute separation from the real matters of life that affect common people. Like the residents of Bedford Arms. Those desperately poor, lovely people he failed to ever know, let alone understand.

"On one birthday – I think his 90th, do you remember? – we gave him a gift that would haunt him and tell him how we felt, even from a distance. Something he could sit with, think about, and bake in the torment of truth as he faced his final days on earth."

Ben smiled. Held her hand.

"It was perfect, my love. The perfect gift for a man who had so very much but understood so little. Oh, yes…I remember. So well."

23

Shortly after Ben retired, his friend the financial adviser counseled him to step up his philanthropic giving.

"You have plenty of money…you'll never spend it all, and estate taxes will take a huge chunk of your holdings when you die," he advised. "Why not do some good with it, rather than send it all to Washington for the politicians to waste? You're childless, with no extended family or designated beneficiaries, other than your chosen charities, who probably can't wait to read your obituary. You are in the unique position of being able to do a lot of good with what you've saved, and I would advise you to get on with it while you can."

Ever the pragmatist – and with financial training that left him skillful at legally avoiding taxes – Ben constructed a generous giving program to support issues dear to him and Brenda while sharing their holdings.

They gave to charities, and social causes and local schools. They donated to the American Cancer Society, disaster relief efforts around the world, and helped finance a school in Peru founded by a friend from their church. When Brenda was first diagnosed, they began giving generously to the Alzheimer's Association.

Any reputable organization that asked received at least a modest donation.

"We can spread a lot of goodwill with little contributions while we look for something to fund with a more substantial gift," Ben reasoned.

Ben beamed when Brenda presented her idea for her father's upcoming birthday over dinner one night.

"Brilliant," he said, and then got to work. He called realtors, contractors and licensing authorities, swearing them all to secrecy in anticipation of "the great man's birthday surprise."

On her father's 90th birthday, Ben and Belinda dispatched their lawyer to cut the ribbon in their behalf on the Bedford Arms Day Center. It was founded in her father's name in a former fire station shuttered by budget cuts years earlier. The building had lain dormant since – a crumbling monument to the mayor's disregard for the neighborhood and its inhabitants. A brass plaque commemorating the day was unveiled near the entrance, forever linking the gathering place for children of Bedford Heights' poorest to the legacy of the long-sitting mayor.

The plaque included an etched image of the mayor in a three-piece suit, thumbs in vest pocket, over an inscription that, while heartfelt in its intent from Ben and Brenda, ironically misstated the mayor's true sentiments.

"Everyone's potential matters," it promised.

The inscription infuriated the mayor, making worse the idea that he would connected to an act of benevolence whose beneficiaries he despised.

In a brief speech on Ben and Brenda's behalf, the lawyer apologized for their absence and announced that they had established a trust to fund the facility in perpetuity in the mayor's name.

Eager to look good on someone else's dime, local, regional and state politicians posed for photos and gave speeches. Bedford Heights' state representative read a proclamation from the governor heralding the facility as a model of civic mindedness that others might replicate. The local newspaper and TV station gave the event prominence in the day's news digest.

Claiming ill health, the mayor stayed home. And seethed. He hung up on a reporter who called to solicit a comment on the event, even after his wife lied to the scribe when she answered the telephone, telling him the elderly solon was too unwell to attend the unveiling but could probably muster the energy to give the reporter a quote.

"They did this to humiliate me!" he shouted at his wife, who as usual kept her distance to shelter from his anger. "How could they lend my good name to a baby-sitting service for social parasites! How dare they! This is an outrage! I'll have it removed, that hateful plaque, and I'll issue a statement that I had absolutely nothing to do with this abomination!"

But he did nothing of the kind. The mayor realized he would do irreparable harm to his legacy by such a spiteful move. Revealing his true sentiments would forever redefine him, and the major recoiled at the idea of such an irreparable fall from grace. Ben and Belinda had outmaneuvered him, boxed him into a corner from which even he, with his oratorical and political skills, could not escape.

As Brenda had anticipated, the mere idea of the center ate at the mayor, causing him agita that led to sleepless nights and intricately woven, angry tirades. Having his name associated with Bedford Heights' low-income housing tormented him. Knowing that "all those people" believed his benevolence made it possible for them to work their menial jobs while their children played safely in a brightly-painted center that bore his name worked him into a frothy lather. The center became the primary target of his whiny rants.

He developed ulcers. Lost his appetite.

He was slept fitfully, if at all, and what rest he got was punctuated by nightmares. In some, brown-skinned children grinned up at him, offering him sugary cupcakes of thanks with their grimy hands. On other occasions, he saw himself holding an infant whose soiled diaper leaked onto his suit.

Piles of cards with heartfelt notes of thanks poured into his home, and that made matters worse.

He took to muttering unintelligibly under his breath, venomous spew laced with audible phrases such as "useless vermin," "the spawn of the unwashed," "and an innocent target of my own ungrateful child's hatred."

His rants about the installation often devolved into erratic ramblings about his daughter's contempt for him, and he railed about the spiteful influence "that untalented, low-life husband of hers" had had over "a spineless child who had forsaken me after giving her all she has in the world."

Brenda's mother stopped taking meals with the intemperate grouch, spending more time at the club over dinners with her friends, many of whom were now widows.

"I do love what the new chef does with a good piece of cod," she breezed, grateful to be in the company of other masters of small talk similarly eager to sidestep the realities of the outside world, and relieved to be away from the toxic atmosphere of her home and husband.

Ben and Brenda took quiet pleasure in the mayor's anxiety, viewing the entire episode as payback for years of torment.

"It's well worth the time and money to get even for the pain he caused us," was Brenda's view. "Not to mention the help it provides to a group of people he holds in such disregard. It feels good to have done something to offset the misery my father imposed on those poor people over the years."

"How better to let him know how we truly feel than to link him to the people he so loathed," Ben agreed. "It's remarkable how much he despises them. Even more than us, and what our marriage represents."

Two years after the unveiling, on a day when Brenda did not recognize Ben as he arrived at Stonybrook, and the Bedford Arms day care center celebrated another year of successful operation, the mayor abruptly sat up while cracking the shell on his hardboiled egg at breakfast. He looked as his wife with a confused, horrified expression, sputtered "Bedford Arms!" clawed at his chest, and then fell face-first onto the dining room table, dead.

# # #

Brenda grasped Ben's arm. Squeezed. Then squeezed harder.

"What are you doing here?" she said with a mixture of confusion and anger that reminded Ben that the unusual moment of lucidity had passed. "What is this place? And why am I here?"

"It's Stonybrook Acres, my love," Ben began. "It's your home. Where you live ....."

She turned her gaze to the window.

Ben slumped back into the arm chair, closed his eyes and sighed.

"You haven't always lived here, my dear," he said as much to the room as his wife. "It wasn't always like this."

24

The day Belinda went missing was the worst day in Ben's life. This was a close second.

Since ending their cross-country drive and moving to New Mexico, Ben had labored to make the condo comfortable and safe for Brenda. He had safety locks installed to make sure she couldn't wander. He replaced the electric stove with a gas version with a locked hob so Brenda couldn't hurt herself – or burn their home down with them in it. He childproofed electrical outlets and bought a large flat screen television and subscribed to an online movie service so Brenda could be entertained for hours watching classic movies, ancient sitcom re-runs, and musicals.

They spent hours driving, Ben chattering at the wheel, Brenda staring out the passenger window as he labored to familiarize her with their new home.

"The more she connects with her surroundings, the more routines, the better, and it makes it more likely she'll be able to remain with you in your home for at least awhile," the neurologist promised.

They became fixtures at several favorite lunch spots, ordering egg salad sandwiches with extra pickles "as a special splurge," Ben cooed. Afterwards, they would sit for hours in a rest stop parking lot high above a vast patch of scrub and sand that stretched to the mountains beyond, field glasses in their laps quickly raised to their eyes when a bird flew into view.

At home, they watched the sun set over the mountains, and Ben kept Brenda updated on the movements of the coyote family that frequented the ridge viewable from their kitchen window.

"Two…no, three! Three cubs, my love…come see!"

He would guide her to his side, and they would grin in quiet appreciation, watching the coyote family frolic as twilight painted the arid landscape with soft, muted tones of brown and grey.

Ben's days became complicated as he assumed the role of carer and primary source of entertainment as well as husband.

He planned frequent outings. One Tuesday morning he decided they would visit Brenda's favorite shopping mall, a sprawling single-story complex that featured a food court where they would have lunch.

He made breakfast, helped Brenda eat, use the toilet and wash and brush her teeth, and then get into her clothes. He chose a beige skirt that fell to her mid-calf, a light green silk blouse and a flowered scarf, with the beige pumps she loved and found most comfortable for walking. Carefully draping the scarf around her neck, he eased a light brown jacket over her shoulders. The outfit presented an understated picture of femininity and beauty, yet his efforts yielded little response from Brenda, who watched sullenly behind a vacant stare into the mirror that reflected a woman neither of them knew.

He drove to the mall and parked in a spot near the elevator to make the journey easier for Brenda. They held hands as they walked through the mall, bought the items Ben sought in the pharmacy, and drank coffee and shared a croissant in the atrium restaurant populated by retirees in search of companionship and a safe walk along the mall's polished corridors.

Returning to their car arm in arm, Ben scowled when the remote control failed to unlock the door. He did so manually, reached across the interior to unlock Brenda's door, and hurried around the car to help her into her seat. He buckled her seatbelt, closed her door and made his way around the back of the car and into the driver's seat. Buckled in, he inserted the key and turned it.

Nothing.

Tried again.

Still nothing.

He removed the key, pressed the lock button on the remote.

Nothing.

Sigh.

"It's a dead battery, my dear, probably in the remote, which triggers the car's security system so it won't start unless you unlock it electronically. We'll have to go back to the mall to have it replaced."

The hardware store in the first floor would have been a short walk from the atrium restaurant. Now, it seemed oceans away. He considered leaving Brenda in the car while he tended to the problem, but dismissed the option as too risky.

He reversed the process, extricating Brenda from the car, into the elevator and to the mall's first floor. When the doors opened and spilled them into the crowded mall, Ben was paralyzed by confusion. Which way was the hardware store? He couldn't recall.

"Excuse me," Ben said, soft of voice and with eager, worried eyes as he halted a middle-aged couple hurrying by, "do you happen to know where the hardware store is?"

They did, and they walked together as a group, men side by side and the women behind, arm in arm, as though four friends taking a casual stroll on a typical morning in their unremarkable lives. Ben shared their story with the man as they made their way. Eager to speak to someone who would listen, nod and perhaps respond, Ben sensed a receptive spirit in the kindly man. Words and emotions streamed forth.

Once he started, he was powerless to stop.

"…so now we're taking it day by day, and I count myself fortunate to have the time and means to care for her. She is my one and only love. It's the least I can do for her, really, to make her comfortable and ensure her safety. After all she's been through, and with all the difficulties I have caused her, all the pain and discomfort. I'm afraid I haven't been precisely the model husband. So much work, and so many mistakes. She deserved better."

The man turned to Ben. Smiled. He nodded at the hardware store feet away and placed his hand on Ben's shoulder.

"Here we are. I wish you well, dear man. Your wife is fortunate to have you by her side, looking out for her, caring for her. Most people delude themselves, propping up their own self images in desperate acts to feel better about themselves. You seem quite the opposite. Humility quite suits you.

"But sometimes we are harder on ourselves than others could pretend to be, or than we deserve.

"I have a few favorite sayings I've collected along the way, and one of them seems appropriate to share with you.

184

"Cherish the small graces, my new friend. It's the little gifts that count, for you, and for your lovely, extremely fortunate wife. As difficult as your circumstances may seem, it looks to me like the two of you have everything you could possibly need. You have each other, and the time to just be. Together.

"You dear man. I hope things go well for you, and I wish you all the very best." He took Ben's hand in his, not shaking it, but holding it. It occurred to Ben that other than periodic cursory contact with Brenda, it was the first physical human contact he had had in months.

Stunned by the reference to one of his own favorite sayings, Ben declined the man's offer for further help. His voice broke as he muttered thanks.

They exchanged parting words, and Ben choked back a tear as he watched the couple walk away. As they turned a corner in the mall, the man turned, smiled at Ben, and saluted.

Ben watched until the couple was out of sight.

"So much goodness, if we can only look for it," he said aloud. Then, "It's just us again, my love," and took Brenda by the hand to enter the hardware store.

He searched the battery display for the correct model while Brenda gazed at seed packets crammed into a rack that ran the length of the aisle. She was contented, amused by the bright colors that promised a summer's bounty.

"You stay here, my love. I'll find help to install this battery and come back in a jiffy."

He returned moments later with remote repaired. Its light flashed red when he pressed the button, a promising sign.

He looked anxiously up and down the aisle.

Brenda was gone.

25

Ben rushed through the store, calling Brenda's name while picking up his pace.

How could I have been so foolish to leave her alone! he chided himself.

Brenda was not to be found in the hardware store, nor in the atrium, or in the crowded corridors that fanned out in each direction like spokes on a wheel. He chose one route and was soon absorbed into a sea of white-haired people, some in wheelchairs, others using walkers and canes, herds of meandering retirees strolling aimlessly in a migration of pointless intent.

He rose to his tiptoes to search for Brenda, for a glimpse of her hair, her brown jacket. He sniffed the air for a whiff of the Shalomar perfume he had dabbed behind her ears before they left the house.

Detecting no sight of her, Ben picked up his pace, breathing rhythmically to remain calm yet beginning to pant from concern, and from the exertion. He pivoted his head, hawk-like and anxious, but saw only strangers, vague shells of humans whose presence conspired to hide her from his longing view. He moved faster, crossing the corridor and peering into shops, spinning and whirling in growing desperation, anxiety and guilt.

"Not again," he said aloud, the fear of loss overwhelming him as it did that summer afternoon so many years before. "Please, not Brenda, too."

He rounded a corner, beads of sweat collecting on his forehead, when he spied her across the hall at a movie theater ticket booth. Even from a distance he could see she was agitated, gesturing and speaking harshly to the baffled clerk. He dabbed at the sweat on his face with a handkerchief, approaching quietly so he could hear Brenda's voice without frightening her. She held a sheaf of documents in her right hand, waving them before the young woman, scolding her. The look on the young woman's face spoke to the depth of the uncomfortable situation.

"Will this help? Can't this suffice? For God's sake, you stupid girl...don't you know how to do your job?" Brenda shouted at the rattled clerk, who clearly was ill prepared to deal with an agitated, confused woman attempting to buy a movie ticket using an expired bus pass and a wad of retail shop receipts.

Ben looked beyond Brenda's shoulder at the poster on the wall behind the counter that promoted the day's feature.

Still Alice.

He approached Brenda from behind, catching her elbow and turning her to face him and away from the clerk. He smiled at Brenda to calm her, and turned his attention to the clerk.

"I'm very sorry, my dear," he said to the woman, "but my wife seems to have forgotten we've already seen this movie," he said with a wan smile. "Fact is, we may be starring in it."

Flushed face, the young woman assessed Ben's comment and recognized its poignancy.

"Of course, sir. No problem. All the best, ma'am, sir. Perhaps another day."

An hour later, Ben settled Brenda in her favorite chair with a cup of milk tea and a lace shawl. He turned the television onto one of her favorite game shows, and then placed a call to her doctor's office. He was immediately put through to their physician.

"Dr. Witherspoon, it's Ben Tremblay. I'm afraid it's time to discuss moving Brenda to Stonybrook. I am no longer capable of taking care of her...."

26

Months earlier, Ben had chosen Stonybrook to provide care for Brenda when the need arose. So he had only to focus on the move itself to complete the transition and ensure Brenda's well-being. His pragmatic side was at peace with the change; his emotional self was a mess. As the hour drew near when they would make the short trip up the hill to her new home, Ben lay awake, dreading the dawn that would start the day, bring the taxi to his door, and pry his wife forever from his side.

Their doctor helped Ben accept the necessity for the move, outlining the care she would receive at Stonybrook. He emphasized the institution's reputation for excellence in treating Alzheimer's patients.

"This situation is not going to improve, Ben," he warned. "Alzheimer's claims its victims incrementally. It will slowly get worse, then she may be lucid and fine for a spell, then decline again. I'm afraid it's a predictable spiral with an unhappy conclusion.

"You've insisted on candor: here it is. This not a disease that goes quietly, nor gently. Alzheimer's is a gradual slide into a series of mental, emotional and physical reactions. I think we both know where this will end."

The doctor spared Ben the details of a conclusion whose horror Ben knew all too well. He had researched the progressive nature of Alzheimer's and foresaw what awaited them.

Ben stared at the floor, defeated yet resolute. Brenda's safety mattered most, and he was convinced that he could no longer protect his wife from herself. Ben had insisted on the truth, and the facts. He had rebuffed the doctor's initial offer of a gentler, rounder assessment of Brenda's situation.

Brenda, under the watch of a home care provider Ben hired so he could meet privately with the doctor, seemed unaware of the proceedings. Her silence worried Ben: *Does she know what I am about to do? Is she aware how serious this is, how permanent?*

"How long?" he breathed, voice empty.

"Hard to say," the doctor replied. "For some, it's years and years; a slow crawl. For others, it's a rapid decline. I have seen the range of conditions and responses, and it's hard for me to judge which is worse: the slow degradation of a patient's mind, or rapid decline.

"One thing is certain: it is always hardest on the loved ones left to care."

Stonybrook's proximity to their condo offered Ben easy, consistent access. *"Fifteen minute walk; 20, tops, even in lousy weather,"* he assessed. He also liked Stonybrook for it soft background music, walls freshly painted in muted tones, for its sloping, verdant lawn, panoramic view of the town and of their home below, and for the facility's well-lit, spacious rooms.

"She'll be able to see where I am from her bedroom window," Ben reasoned. "I'll keep a light on in the kitchen, just so she knows where I am, and that I am close by."

At thousands of dollars per month, Stonybrook was an expense Ben had anticipated and could afford. He was unfazed by the exorbitant fee.

"Not to worry," his financial adviser said reassuringly, "your investments are turning over more than enough to cover the cost. You own your condo outright, and the management fees are a pittance. The trust you set up to fund the day care center in Ohio is performing nicely, so you're in good shape there. Your monthly living expenses are those of a pauper. Fact is, you should probably start thinking of divesting a bit more, unless you've decided to permanently grace humanity with your presence.

"There's enough money, working well enough for you, that Brenda could stay in Stonybrook for years and years and you'd see little erosion of your principal. Spend your energy and time on ways to make her comfortable, and for God's sake spend a little to give yourself a break, too! Leave money management to me."

Ben arranged to have Stonybrook paid directly from his investment accounts, one of the few times he trusted electronic fund transfers to meet his financial obligations.

Ben viewed financial order as Brenda valued cleanliness.

He kept a meticulously balanced checkbook, carefully tracking the debits and credits and verifying all the figures against the monthly statement his bank mailed to his home. He rarely drove his car – which he owned outright – and he prepaid his car insurance to minimize the number of transactions and take advantage of a pre-payment discount.

"One must know where the pennies are if you expect to be in command of the dollars," he opined, tucking a credit card receipt into the back of his wallet after dinner with his friend Jim.

Ben's wallet was a perfect metaphor for his views on money management: orderly, neat, predictable. His friends mercilessly teased him about it.

"Look at the moths flying out of that thing," Jim commented. He stabbed at the black leather billfold worn shiny from years of use. "First that wallet has seen the light of day in months! Do you still have the first dollar you earned in there somewhere? Let me have a look!"

Ben handed it to his friend. Jim thumbed through the wallet's contents.

"Still the same old Ben. Individual tabs for ones, fives, tens and twenties, all the bills facing forward, presidents' heads straight up. Credit card receipts in the back, pending monthly reconciliation. Nice 'n tidy. Shipshape."

He gave the wallet back.

"You are a man of profound order, aren't you? And still a skinflint. No wonder you have such a fat bank account; you've never spent a fraction of what you've earned. Your wife's a lucky woman, particularly now that she's in that expensive mansion on the hill. I could never afford it. When it comes my time, my wife'll drive me into the desert, drop me by the side of the road and leave me for the coyotes."

Ben indeed was frugal, but he viewed Stonybrook as an investment in Brenda's comfort and safety. She had a private room (not that she noticed or cared), fresh and healthful food, and ample friendly and available staff in an unusually low patient/staff ratio.

"The best in the West," was how his doctor described Stonybrook. "You are lucky to have the means to place her there, and that there was an available bed when it came time for Brenda to move."

190

Ben settled Brenda into a corner room far from the facility's lounge and dining room. Three pairs of shoes and her favorite slippers went into the cupboard, along with a selection of her favorite dresses, skirts, cardigans and tops. Three narrow drawers held her personal items. He placed a small collection of cosmetics along the bathroom shelf and rested an atomizer of Shalimar perfume front and center where Brenda could see it and be reminded both of her femininity and of Ben's traditional Christmas gift.

"You should keep valuables at home," Stonybrook's administrator warned him, "to discourage any misplacement or theft, though we have never had any such thing happen here. Casual, costume jewelry she knows and likes is fine…it helps keep patients rooted in their past."

Ben planned to refresh Brenda's wardrobe according to the seasons. Dressing well in clean, pressed clothes was part of Brenda's identity, and Ben re-committed to doing what was necessary to preserve her sartorial dignity. He splurged by arranging with a local dry cleaning company to pick up Brenda's soiled clothes and return them freshly cleaned and pressed.

"You wouldn't appreciate my lack of talent at the ironing board," he joked to Brenda, who didn't respond.

Removed from the noise of visitors and odors from the dining room yet close to a nursing station, Brenda's room was a quiet haven set apart from the facility's activities. Help was steps away and could be summoned by a tug on one of the cords that hung in strategic locations throughout Brenda's room, or by pressing the button on the "life alert" alarm the nurse's aide hung from Brenda's neck each morning. Knowing she was in the best possible situation in the best possible room in one of the nation's top facilities made it possible for Ben to leave her there.

As difficult as it was to see his wife in a perpetual holding pattern, the coming and going was the hardest; the highs and lows of each day filled his heart with the prospect of spending time with Brenda but dashed his hopes with the awful cruelty of her affliction. The facility offered counseling to family members affected by Alzheimer's, and Ben quickly became a front-row regular at the "Alzheimer's and You" weekly sessions.

The Advanced Care Unit – where late-stage Alzheimer's patients were transferred when their mental and physical states posed constant threats to their well being – was located halfway along the corridor that led to Brenda's room. One day soon after she moved in, in a moment of stunning lucidity, Brenda stopped and stared as they approached the crossroads leading to the Advanced Care Unit. She assessed the security door quietly, hand clutched at her throat as if to ward off a chill:

"So that's where I'll wind up," she said unemotionally, "or what's left of me. Huh. Good to know."

She shrugged, spun on her heel and made her way to her room, all straight-backed and independent, as if she could walk away from a demon that was stalking her with every passing moment and was now closing in for the kill.

27

Ben washed the breakfast dishes, periodically glancing out the window. He scanned the mountain ridge, searching for the coyote family. He hadn't seen them for days, and he worried that something had happened to them.

"Everything is so impermanent..." he sighed, and he shifted his gaze to the left, onto the long, sloping whiteness of Stonybrook Acres. He switched off the light over the sink and softly smiled, imagining Brenda starting the day with the help of a nurse's aide. He envisioned Brenda's smiling face, acknowledging her husband's presence as she saw the glow from the kitchen window melt into the light of dawn.

"Good morning, my love. Until soon."

Dressing slowly, Ben remembered his promise to the doctor's repeated requests to schedule a follow-up appointment.

"I guess it's time," he said aloud, made his way to his chair in the living room and dialed the number on the card the doctor had provided. Moments later, he had scheduled a battery of tests at the outpatient clinic adjacent to the hospital.

"Thursday, April 16...day after tax day. How perfect," he joked aloud, noting the appointment in the pocket calendar he carried with him at all times. "Death and taxes. The things we all can count on."

#

Ben was steps away from Brenda's room when he heard her agitated voice.

"You've stolen my jewelry, you bitch! I'll have you arrested! How dare you!"

He quickened his pace and encountered a flustered aide recoiling from Brenda's anger.

"And who the fuck are you?" Brenda demanded of Ben. She was in the worst state he had seen. He rushed to her side.

"Brenda..my love...it's me..Ben. Your husband." She brushed him off.

"You're part of it! All of you! I want to go home. Where's my daughter? My father will have your jobs, all of you! Do you know who I am?"

Brenda's rant continued until a doctor appeared, ushering Ben and the tearful aide out the door into a waiting room down the hall. Ben consoled the sobbing young woman.

"Honest, Mr. Tremblay, I have no idea what happened. She is usually so pleasant, so nice. And today, she just got it in her mind that I'd stolen her jewelry, and that I am holding her here against her will. You know her expensive jewelry isn't here. I showed her the necklaces and earrings you left for her, but she screamed at me, told me I'd stolen her gold jewelry. I have never heard such language from her. Such terrible insults."

"I know, my dear, I know. It's quite unsettling when she is like that, and I've never seen her so agitated, either. Normally I can calm her by speaking quietly to her, or by singing. Today seems worse than usual."

The doctor appeared in the doorway.

"I've had to sedate her, Mr. Tremblay, as she was becoming more and more anxious. These bouts of frustration are becoming increasingly frequent. She had two similar episodes last week, though less dramatic than today's, and I fear we are facing the next phase of the disease."

He sat across from Ben as the aide left the room to give them privacy.

"Mr. Tremblay…Ben..it's time, I am afraid. She needs round-the-clock care, and I think her safety can no longer be guaranteed if she stays in her own room. It is my professional opinion that we need to move her to the Advanced Care Unit – immediately."

Ben stared at the doctor, overwhelmed, paralyzed by the arrival of a moment he had feared most of all.

"I understand how hard this is, Ben, but it's the best for her. We don't want her to be at risk, and I fear that she might injure herself, or worse, without closer monitoring and increased care. The AC unit is where she belongs.

"It's time. I'm sorry."

Ben nodded in acquiescence. Some battles cannot be contemplated, let alone fought, and the advancing army of Alzheimer's was winning the fight for his wife's mind and body.

"She doesn't seem like Brenda anymore," Ben said softly. "Is she gone from me, doctor? Have I lost the love of my life, finally, after everything we have faced together? Have I had the last coherent conversation with my wife I will ever have?

"Am I now, truly and finally and permanently, without her?"

The doctor's taut grimace told Ben all he needed to know. And with a sight nod and a few cryptic notes jotted in the doctor's illegible scrawl, Brenda began the short, irreversible journey that took her less than 100 yards down the hall, but into a world she would never know, and that would hold her for what remained of her life.

Ben sat by Brenda's bed in the fluorescent gloom of Brenda's new room. It was more hospital than care home, lacking the soft lighting, spacious windows and personalized feel of the corner room Ben had so carefully selected months earlier.

The sterile environment had been stripped of all personal items, the furniture cold, the colors bland. It was a holding pen, a place to go to wait to die. Ben felt the finality of it, powerless and lost.

For two hours Ben had sat next to Brenda, speaking softly, stroking her hand, singing her favorite songs. She was unresponsive.

"Oh, my love…are you finally, really lost to me?" He sat for another hour but Brenda – breathing softly as she slept – never stirred. Ben patted her hand: "Until soon, my love. I will leave a light on for you to see," and he left. He knew the light was out of sight from her new room, and that she was beyond being able to see it. The darkness was consuming her, and no light – no matter how strong and bright – could penetrate the final black void.

He made his way home in the dusky glow, into his condo and a new version of solitude that felt more final, more hateful. He sat in the dark in his living room chair, lost in thoughts and memories, and so consumed by sadness that he forgot to turn the light on over the sink.

# # #

Light gray mist fell on the small group gathered graveside as the minister gave a brief eulogy. Several Stonybrook staff, Ben's friend Jim, Brenda's hairdresser Elaine, a few elderly neighbors and Brenda's kindly neurologist bowed their heads in remembrance as dusk settled into the valley.

The service was short, conservative on words and with no flowers. William Foxworthy, Stonybrook's director, rose to speak.

"I've known Ben and Brenda for many years," he began, "first as members of our community, and then, sadly, as Brenda's condition required a change in our relationship that brought her to our door, as patient and her husband. It is impossible to speak of one without referencing the other. Theirs is the most enviable, remarkable relationship I have known. They embodied grace, dignity, kindness and intelligence, and have been valuable members of our community.

"Before Alzheimer's claimed Brenda, this amazing couple formed a foundation that many of us who had the privilege of knowing them admired, respected, and tried our best to emulate..

"Their marriage was based on a series of principles and qualities we should follow in our own lives; principles they articulated at their wedding more than 60 years ago, and in vows that they wrote, together, to create a roadmap for their life as a married couple. Trust, honesty, fidelity, openness, acceptance, partnership, commonality of purpose and values, and love: these are the building blocks of what makes, in Ben's own words, 'much, much more than a reasonably viable marriage. They are the essence of everything good, all that matters.'

"Their words embody love, and commitment, and everything positive about human beings and the potential of creating a partnership that can create a powerful, unbreakable force. These words – and the fact of Ben and Brenda's life together - give promise and hope to those of us left behind to contemplate the meaning of their lives, and of vows written by two people who lived by this credo and valued it above all else.

"Theirs was like all other marriages: full of challenges and flaws, but wonderfully and magically perfect in that it brought two people together who, in union, formed a perfect, powerful bond that all of us benefited from in our everyday lives.

"Life can be wonderful, often filling us with gifts of wonder. And it can leave us despondent, confused and lost in the wake of its cruel irony. Life sometimes takes from us what we cherish most, and we are left to try and make sense of it all. We must not question, but accept, as Ben and Brenda did throughout their life together. We must accept and move forward. Move on.

"And so it is that we say goodbye to one of our community's best….Benjamin Warren Tremblay…and that we extend our love and deepest sympathy to his widow, Brenda, who unfortunately could not be with us today."

Moments later the small group dispersed into the misty gray dusk, leaving the cemetery staff to the task of committing Ben to his final resting place.

# # #

Dusk was beyond view from where Brenda sat as Ben's service concluded. She rested in her armchair, hands in her lap, with the vacant, unblinking stare Stonybrook staff had come to recognize; the light blue shawl she loved so much was draped around her shoulders, warding off the evening chill.

Far up the ridge but visible from the kitchen window in the empty condo, the coyote emerged from her den along the mountain top. Her belly was full of the day's hunt, and with a new generation of pups that would soon emerge. She studied the row of condominiums that rested below, scanning the dark windows for one that usually shone with a bright light. She hungrily sniffed the air, as if detecting a sweet, appealing scent. She growled, low and threatening, then softly whined before turning to make her way back to her den.

Inside Stonybrook Acres, Brenda smiled and took a deep breath.

She began to softly sing in a lilting, girlish tone. "I love you, a bushel and a peck…" She smiled, fixing her stare on a space several feet from where she sat.

"How very, very beautiful. How perfectly wonderful," she said, giggling, then sat upright as though surprised by an unexpected guest, excited, fulfilled: "Oh, it's you! Well, then….

"Until soon, my lovely honeybun…."

DEDICATION

This book is dedicated to Nguyen Thua Nghiep, oil company executive, philosopher, writer, husband, father and grandfather, and my dear friend.

I met Nghiep in a park in Ho Chi Minh City in 2011, and we quickly became fast friends. He was in his 80s; I was in my 50s. I am American; Nghiep was Vietnamese. I had worked in media; Nghiep in oil and gas. Nghiep believed our paths had crossed in past lives. How else to explain the instant closeness between such different people? I felt the same, and I am to this day humbled by the instinctive affection, admiration and trust I had in him.

We wrote to each other often, and I keep the messages among my most cherished. I visited his home with family and friends to share the wisdom and goodness of this extraordinary man who wrote about life, love and family in wistful, eloquent passages. We spent hours discussing philosophy over breakfasts of grilled pork and steamed rice, his favorite and at his home as his wife looked on with quiet admiration.

The idea of Ben and Brenda's vows as a basis for this book came from Nghiep's writing about life, love, and his own remarkable marriage. His fastidiousness – the tabs in Ben's wallet to organize his currencies, for example – came from Nghiep's own commitment to predictability and order.

As his life drew to an end, we exchanged copies of the books we had written, holding in our hands each others' attempt to bring reason, thought and a bit of entertainment to our respective worlds.

One of his emails to me:

Jan, 23.2013

Dear Frank,

I would like to clarify and emphasize my ideas about "FOUR INDOMITABLE AND DANGEROUS HORSES" as follows.

Within each of us, there are four indomitable horses. If we do not keep firmly the reins, they would jump up and run foolishly, regardless of everything and would throw us down on earth, wounded or dead.

They are:

    1. <u>Negative emotion</u> (anger, fretfulness, despair, jaundice, jealous in love, …)

    2. <u>Bad habits</u> (addiction to drinks, smoking, drug …)

    3. <u>Wrongful sexual desire</u> (adultery, rape, … illicit sexual relations …)

    4. <u>Unrighteous ambition</u> (corruption, bribe, illegal actions, encroach, smuggle)

    Many people not vigilant over these four indomitable horses, have fallen into offence, guilt, imprisonment, victim of homicide, suicide, great misery …

    "To be master of oneself" is to be master of these four indomitable horses.

    NGHIỆP

Nghiep died May 14, 2016. He is buried in his family's plot in Tien Giang province, about 90 km from Saigon.

ABOUT THE AUTHOR

Skip (Frank) Yetter is a former newspaper reporter, editor and publisher who also worked in the commercial news business. In 2010, he and his wife, Gabi, sold their home and possessions and moved to Cambodia, where they volunteered and traveled throughout Asia. They co-wrote a book about their experiences (*Just Go! Leave the Treadmill for a World of Adventure*), published in 2015. *A Reasonably Viable Marriage* is his second novel. His first, *Rilertown*, was published in 2016. He and Gabi now live in East Sussex, England.

Made in the USA
Middletown, DE
18 May 2020